Franz Kafka was born in Prague in 1883, the only son of a self-made Jewish businessman. Trained in law, he worked for a Prague insurance company until tuberculosis forced him to retire. He published too little during his lifetime to become known, and intended the unfinished manuscripts of his now famous books to be burnt after his death. These, which have earned him recognition as one of the greatest European writers, were all published after he died and include *The Trial* (1925), *The Castle* (1926) and *Amerika* (1927). He died in 1924.

Franz Kafka

The Trial

A new translation by
Douglas Scott and Chris Waller
with an introduction by J. P. Stern

PICADOR
published by Pan Books

Der Prozess first published 1925
This new translation first published in Picador 1977
by Pan Books Ltd, Cavaye Place, London SW10 9PG
3rd printing 1981
© Pan Books Ltd 1977
Introduction © J. P. Stern 1977
ISBN 0 330 24468 X
Printed and bound in Great Britain by
Richard Clay (The Chaucer Press) Ltd, Bungay, Suffolk

Contents

Introduction

'Kafkaesque' is the only word in common English use which derives from German literature. Its meanings range from 'weird', 'mysterious', 'tortuously bureaucratic' to 'nightmarish' and 'horrible', yet we do not associate it with the horror machines of science fiction or of Edgar Allan Poe. Inseparable from the 'Kafkaesque' effect is its everyday quality. It involves, not outlandish gadgets or inhabitants from Mars, but a process in the course of which the humdrum elements of our experience are estranged from us.

The familiar, in the hands of an artist, becomes representative. If Franz Kafka's reputation is now almost as safe from the ups and downs of fashion as is Dostoyevsky's – if, in the last forty years, he has achieved a strange 'popularity' which is unlikely to be exceeded by any other novelist of his age – then this is because he has creatively heightened, and given expression to, certain moods and problems of that age which survive into ours. 'I have immensely absorbed the negative aspect of my time,' he wrote in a diary in 1918, at the end of the Great War, ' – a time which is very close to me and which I have no right to challenge, but only as it were to represent.'

In this representativeness, as in almost everything else connected with Kafka's work, there is a paradox: the disagreements among interpreters as to *what* these problems and these moods might be seem irreconcilable, and the need for interpretation is almost the only thing they agree on. Yet none of this, not even the fact that usually he has not much of a 'story' to tell, has discouraged his readers. He continues to be read, and his relevance continues to be acknowledged, by many who do not 'understand' him – apart, that is, from sensing that what he has to say is related to their innermost experience. He has become a 'modern classic'.

Franz Kafka was born on 3 July 1883 in Prague, in that part of the Old Town which had once been the Jewish ghetto, and there he spent all but the last few years of his life. His father, whose native tongue was Czech, began life as a pedlar in Southern Bohemia, but by the time Franz was born, Hermann Kafka had become a prosperous businessman, anxious for social advancement among the up-and-coming German-speaking minority of the Bohemian capital. A kindly but weak mother, an overbearing, tyrannical father determined to crush the son's every plan that did not accord with his own materialistic aspirations – this is the characteristic middle-class setting portrayed in the numerous case histories discussed and 'analysed' in Sigmund Freud's early articles, which Kafka knew well. From this setting, which he was incapable of opposing on equal terms, Franz Kafka never entirely freed himself. However, the bondage of mind that tied him to it was shot through with a literary passion.

He studied law at the German University of Prague and in 1908 became an official of a government-sponsored Workers' Accident Insurance Association. He had begun writing in 1904. At about that time he contracted tuberculosis, and though he spent several periods in various sanatoria in Bohemia and Slovakia, he continued in his humdrum but responsible post, working unwillingly but with great conscientiousness, until he was forced to retire through ill health in 1922. His three engagements – two to the same girl – ended unhappily, but in 1923 he finally left Prague ('the little mother has claws' he wrote of the city) and moved to Berlin, where he lived with a woman who was in charge of a Jewish orphanage. The idyll, in great poverty at the end of the German inflation, did not last long. A few months later tuberculosis of the larynx was diagnosed. Franz Kafka was moved back to Prague and then to a nursing home near Vienna, where he died on 3 June 1924, a month before his forty-first birthday. Two years earlier, during one of the many moments when he felt unsure of his poetic gift, he had written to his friend and doctor who was to be with him at the end: 'Anxiety about subject matter is really neither more nor less than life itself coming to a halt. People don't usually suffocate for lack of air, but for lack of lung power.' For him, illness and literature merge into a single syndrome.

Kafka has left behind numerous stories, three novels – *Amerika* (1912–14), *The Trial* (1914–   ) and *The Castle* (1922) – diaries and reflections, as well as several collections of letters. Much of this work is fragmentary, yet there is hardly a sentence (even in those detailed accident reports he wrote as part of his work as an insurance official) which is not recognizably his own; there is hardly a letter, however trivial its content, which is not also a literary rehearsal. He was a writer in spite of himself, with a narrative gift at once so special and so immense that even the most casual of his jottings are coloured by that gift and thus defy the usual distinction between the privacy of letters and diaries and the publicity of literature. In a pencilled note left at the bottom of his drawer and intended, it seems, as a last will, he listed his three unpublished novels and a good many other stories, requesting the writer Max Brod, his friend and first biographer, to destroy them 'unread and in their entirety'. Was this because he was moved by an inward conviction that what he had said in his writings was likely to be injurious and sad, rather than joyful and illuminating? Max Brod disobeyed, and would no doubt have done so had the instructions of the will been less ambiguous, seeing that a number of the stories mentioned had been published already, by Kafka himself. Once more we are faced with a paradox: we can hardly doubt that Kafka's decision to have his works destroyed was genuine, and yet writing was for him not a matter of choice. 'I have no literary interests,' he wrote to one of his hapless fiancées, 'but I consist of literature, it is the only thing I am and can ever be.'

A Jew in the provincial, aggressive society of German Gentiles, a German among Czechs during their era of national revival, a sceptic of uncertain allegiance among orthodox Jewish believers and pew-renters, a bourgeois with a chronic bad conscience about the working classes, a man with an unabating passion for writing in a society of businessmen and petty officials . . . *what was he,* beyond the view others had of him, behind the labels they pinned on him, the 'isms' they ascribed to him? From these tensions – that is, from a consuming, self-destructive urge for the truth about himself and the age to which he belonged – his work is born.

Kafka's search for the truth is in no sense an abstract undertaking. One of its manifestations is his concern with Justice and the Law, visible in the titles of so many of his stories: 'Before the Law', 'The Judgement', 'A Question of the Laws', 'The New Advocate', 'In the Penal Colony', *The Trial* . . . Justice and the Law are, for obvious reasons, age-old concerns of Jews in the Diaspora, but they are in no sense a 'Jewish theme'. On the contrary, this anxious Jewish care is representative of man's reasoned attempts to protect himself against the consequences of arbitrariness and the rule of instinct, to protect the frail and individual by an appeal to the stable and general. The pursuit of Justice under the Law is one of the forms – indeed the chief form – of Kafka's search for the truth: yes, but at the same time it is an intriguing literary problem. For what if the search proved vain, if the Law were to be unknown and remain hidden? If it should turn out to be not the forest of trees that protects men against arbitrariness (as Robert Bolt once described the Law), nor yet simply unjust, 'an ass' (as it is in Dickens), but itself the source of arbitrariness and ambiguity? And – seeing that in Kafka's stories the narrator's perspective is very often (though not always) the same as the central character's – what if the truth of a given situation should turn out to be contingent on the perspective from which it is seen and presented?

The Trial was left unfinished on Kafka's death. It was published by Max Brod in 1925, in a sequence of ten chapters the order of which has been disputed, though it must be added that, apart from the setting of the scene at the beginning and the death of the protagonist at the end, the order hardly matters. It is the story of a young man, a bank official, who wakes up in his lodgings one morning to find himself arrested without knowing what wrong he has done; who throughout the story makes various attempts to 'justify himself' (the words bear a weight of significance) against he knows not what charges, and to influence a number of people (including several women) who, he believes, may affect his acquittal. He is never physically compelled to attend, or prevented from walking out on, the Court that is trying him, and moreover is offered at least one chance of defying its jurisdiction; yet he ends up, on the eve of his thirty-first birthday, being marched off to his execution by two men like 'old ham actors', to die 'like a dog'.

Throughout the story, throughout all those sober and almost flat elaborations of Josef K's predicament, the question is on our lips: Why? What has this unremarkable young man done? What is his guilt? Part of the answer lies in the fact that he never asks the question, though he will subsequently claim that he has asked it. It is an aspect of his guilt that, beyond asserting his innocence, he comes to take a sad, perverse pride in being singled out for judgement.

Josef K. has no friends to protect him, no family or society to which he unambiguously belongs; bacherlordom and isolation are part of his predicament. But we must not exaggerate his alienness, for something like its opposite is also true. Though we never learn very much about him, we gather that Josef K. is a pretty ordinary young man, anxious to do well in his job, treating his superiors at the bank with obsequiousness, ready to put his inferiors in their place, and above all apt to seek in people – especially in women – not what they are but what he can get out of them. And as we read on and get caught up in Josef K's situation – which Kafka describes relentlessly, exhaustively, in that flat, almost colloquial style which is the bane of translators – it comes to us that there *are* answers to the question: What has he done? Not one single answer. But again and again there is a self-assertive movement of Josef K's mind, a certain wantonness in his look, a certain aggressive defensiveness and self-righteousness which suggest that he acknowledges the authority of the sordid Court whose emissaries come to arrest him, that its Law has a foothold in his being.

What Kafka does – and the present translation follows him in this with special faithfulness – is to weave a spider's web of insinuations and admissions between accuser and accused. The most vertiginous aspect of his seemingly humdrum prose consists in intimating in a hundred different ways the insight that some sort of *guilt* accompanies, and gives a terrible meaning to, Josef K's *feeling of guilt*. But how can Kafka do that? Seeing that the Law remains unstated, must not Josef K's guilt remain indeterminate, a mere feeling of guilt – in fact, a neurosis?

The argument so far is likely to have the agreement of most interpreters (at least of those who agree that this is the story of some sort of trial), but beyond this point we face a spectrum of insoluble contradictions. At one end we have all those interpretations which proceed along exclusively psychological lines, placing the entire 'trial' in Josef K's (or Franz Kafka's) mind, presenting it as a mere dream or neurotic delusion. But such interpretations are bound to ignore all that is given as objective fact in the story, independently of Josef K's tortuous interpretations, e.g. his arrest and execution. What is the point of a set of brackets round a complete equation? If it is all a delusion and there is nothing outside, how then do the brackets help one to understand what is inside? Ignoring those less than riveting interpretations which see this 'trial' as a metaphor for the difficulties involved in the writing of *The Trial*, we find at the other end of the spectrum a number of religious interpretations, which present Josef K's entire search for the Law as a parable of all human existence, and the Law as the inaccessible, transcendent decree of the Divine. But if, accordingly, all human beings are guilty, why then is Josef K. singled out from the rest, why is it made clear that several people in the story, though involved in Josef K's fate, are themselves not indicted, are *free*? Kafka poses the question and, quietly but cruelly, withholds the answer: 'But I'm not guilty,' says K. 'It's a mistake. How can a person be guilty at all? Surely we are all human beings here, one like the other.' 'That is right,' he is told, 'but that is the way the guilty are wont to talk.'

In chapter nine, 'In the Cathedral', Josef K. finds himself in the presence of a prison chaplain who tells him a parable illustrating his – Josef K's – own search for the Law. In the course of the telling of this parable, and especially in the exegesis of it that follows, at least this much becomes clear: since the text speaks of a 'radiance coming from the entrance to the Law', both the Law in which Josef K. seeks his justification and the Court from which he seeks his acquittal must stand in some sort of relationship to a divine authority. Whether this authority is good or evil, just or arbitrary, we are not told.

A religious interpretation (so it seems to me) is unavoidable: a transcendent authority is undoubtedly intimated in the novel. But – and this is the point which is not taken sufficiently seriously by critics who have offered such interpretations – the religious meaning is firmly founded in, and overlaps, the social and institutional reality which the story portrays; the religious meaning is embodied in that area of our experience to which Kafka devotes his finest creative attention, the working out of the legal process. There is no evil in another world that is not evil in this world: 'There is only a spiritual world, what we call the physical world is the evil in the spiritual . . .'

Who was Franz Kafka? What matters (I said earlier on) is not that he was a Jew, a German, a bourgeois, but that these were the labels stuck on him, the status qualities ascribed to him by others, and accepted and acted on by him at their behest. This is how we all live in the world today. In this way, too, guilt is ascribed to Josef K. and is accepted and acted on by him. Like the Jew under the rule of Hitler's Germany, he is guilty simply because he is what he is – guilty in the eyes of the world in which he lives, for he fails to repudiate this world and no other world is presented. 'Looking at you,' one of Josef K's relations observes, 'one's tempted to believe the proverb: "To be prosecuted in a case like this means that one has already lost it." ' This is an entirely accurate anticipation of justice under national socialism. 'Why, do you think we would summons anybody unless they have committed some crime?' is not a quotation from *The Trial*, but the remark of a Gestapo official to a Gentile husband who wants to know what his Jewish wife has done that she should be deported to her death.

Unlike the Jews under national socialism, Josef K. has a chance – an uncertain glimpse – of freedom. In his unwillingness to defy the ascription, to step outside the jurisdiction of the Court, his guilt and his feeling of guilt are united. The quiet pathos of this situation is the pathos of one who has had a glimpse of the divine and knows himself for ever separated from it.

The Law Josef K. is seeking is tailor-made for him and for him alone. It is that absurd oxymoron we would have to call 'subjective law', yet it has the validity and the might of objective law.

The purpose of all laws is the pursuit of justice and the protection of men from the rule of arbitrariness – is there, then, any point in speaking of 'the Law' in connection with this novel? What justice is dispensed here, what protection offered? Kafka is aware of our objection. More than that: he builds some of his finest narrative effects from our bewilderment – that is, from the contrast between our ordinary expectations, raised in us by his play with the technicalities of the legal process, and the extraordinary uses to which he puts these technicalities.

Kafka sees the future – and we have constantly to remind ourselves that he died ten years before the first German concentration camps were opened – but, unlike George Orwell, he utters no warning. The age, he feels, is his master, whom 'I have no right to challenge, but only as it were to represent.' He is not a prophet, but the infinitely perceptive novelist of some of Europe's darkest days. While following the intricate lace patterns of his narrative, we forget the cruel ends to which he takes us, and when we take note of the ends, we still challenge, question and admire the way they cohere with the means. In deep darkness, his creative intelligence is still an illumination.

The pioneering work done by Edwin and Willa Muir in translating *The Trial* (1930, revised 1953) is a matter of literary and cultural history. Their great service to English-speaking readers is in no way diminished by the suggestion that there is now need for a new translation. Two factors above all have created this need. Whereas for the Muirs Kafka's work had a fairy-tale quality, which is reflected in their translation, we are able to see the work in the light of recent history and thus to appreciate more fully its seriousness and importance. Moreover, the writings of the postwar period – particularly the works of Samuel Beckett and Jorge Luis Borges – have familiarized us with a new dimension of literature and created a literary climate close to 'the Kafkaesque'.

The great virtue of the present translation is that it dares to do what the Muirs were apparently not prepared to do – to keep close to the syntax and the lustreless informality of the original. The new translators are not afraid to retain the paratactic, hesitant style in which the strange and compelling logic of Kafka's tale – the logic of an endless 'on the one hand, and on the other' – is conveyed. They have avoided the formal and occasionally solemn diction of the previous version. They have had the courage not to break up Kafka's long and exhaustive sentence structures with all their qualifications, admissions and hypotheses, and yet at the same time they have managed not to lose touch with ordinary narrative English. While their predecessors seemed to be, as it were, apologizing for the fitness of Kafka's prose by sometimes arbitrarily varying its structures, the present translators are content to let the text create its effects in its own way.

Kafka's art is a complex thing. He makes transparency opaque, he hides the extraordinary story and enigma of *The Trial* behind very ordinary prose: it is the virtue of the present translation to have conveyed this paradox.

J. P. Stern

Chapter One

The Arrest – Conversation with Frau Grubach –
Then with Fräulein Bürstner

Someone must have been spreading lies about Josef K. for without having done anything wrong he was arrested one morning.
His landlady's cook, who brought him his breakfast every morning at about eight o'clock, did not come on that particular day.
This had never happened before. K. waited a little while, watching
from his pillow the old woman who lived opposite and who was
observing him with a quite uncharacteristic curiosity; but then,
feeling both hungry and disturbed, he rang. At once there was a
knock at the door and a man he had never seen in the flat before
came in. He was slim and yet strongly built; he wore a well-fitting
black suit which was like a travelling outfit in that it had various
pleats, pockets, buckles, buttons and a belt, and as a result (although
one could not quite see what it was for) it seemed eminently
practical.

'Who are you?' K. asked, immediately sitting up a little in bed.
But the man ignored the question, as if the fact of his appearance
simply had to be accepted, and merely said:

'You rang?'

'Anna is supposed to bring me my breakfast,' K. said, endeav-
ouring, silently at first and by careful scrutiny, to work out who
the man actually was. But he did not submit to K's gaze for long,
turning instead to the door which he opened slightly and saying to
someone else who was obviously just on the other side of the door:

'He wants Anna to bring him his breakfast.'

There was a brief burst of laughter from the next room, but it was not clear from the sound whether there might not be more than one person there. Although the unknown visitor could not have learnt anything from the laughter that he did not know before, he now said to K, as if making an announcement:

'It's not possible.'

'This is news indeed,' said K, as he sprang out of bed and hastily pulled on his trousers. 'I'm going to have a look and see who's in the next room and find out what explanation Frau Grubach can give for this intrusion.'

But he immediately realized that he ought not to have said this out loud and that, by doing so, he was to some degree acknowledging the stranger's right to supervise his actions. But it did not seem very important at that moment. Still, that was how the stranger interpreted his words, for he said:

'Hadn't you better stay here?'

'I won't stay here, nor will I allow you to speak to me until you tell me who you are.'

'I meant you no harm,' said the stranger, and now opened the door of his own accord. The next room, which K. entered more slowly than he intended, looked at first sight almost exactly the same as it had the evening before. It was Frau Grubach's sitting-room and perhaps this morning there seemed to be a little more space than usual in this room which was so crowded with furniture, rugs, china and photographs. It was difficult to tell at first, especially as the chief alteration was the presence of a man, who was sitting at the open window with a book from which he now looked up.

'You should have stayed in your room! Didn't Franz tell you?'

'Yes, yes, but what on earth do you want?' said K, glancing from this new acquaintance to the man addressed as Franz (who had remained standing in the doorway) and then back again. Again he caught sight of the old woman through the open window. With a truly senile inquisitiveness she had taken up her stand at the window exactly opposite so that she could continue to see everything that was going on.

'But I want Frau Grubach—' K. said, making as if to break away from the two men (who were, however, still keeping their distance) and leave the room.

'No,' said the man by the window, throwing the book on to a small table and rising to his feet. 'You are not permitted to leave. You've been arrested.'

'So it seems,' K. said. 'But why?' he asked.

'We are not authorized to tell you. Go to your room and wait. Proceedings have been started and you will be told everything in due course. I'm even exceeding my instructions by talking to you so freely. But I hope there is no one else listening except Franz, and he himself has disobeyed all orders by being so nice to you. If you go on being as lucky as you have been with the choice of your warders, then you have reason to be confident.'

K. wanted to sit down, but now he saw that there was nothing to sit on in the entire room apart from the seat by the window.

'You will soon find out how true all this is,' said Franz, and both men came up to him. Franz's companion particularly towered over K. and clapped him on the shoulder a number of times. Both of them examined K's nightshirt and told him that now he would have to wear a much plainer one. They were going, they said, to keep this shirt along with the rest of his underwear and if his case turned out all right, it would all be given back to him.

'It's better to give the things to us rather than leave them in the depot,' they said, 'for things often get stolen at the depot and, besides, they sell everything there after a certain time, whether the proceedings in question are concluded or not. You can't imagine how long some of these cases take, especially lately! Of course, eventually you would recover the proceeds from the depot, but in the first place they would be very small because the price depends more on the bribe than on what's bid. And secondly we know from experience that the proceeds tend to get reduced as they pass from hand to hand, year by year.'

K. paid scarcely any attention to these remarks, for he did not place much value on any rights he might have to dispose of his own property. It was far more important for him to get a clear idea of his position, though in the presence of these men he could not even collect his thoughts, for the second warder – they could not be anything else but warders – kept thrusting his stomach against him in almost friendly fashion. But if K. looked up, he caught sight of a desiccated, bony face quite at odds with the fat body: this face had a prominent nose, which was twisted to one side, and seemed to be conferring over K's head with the first warder. Who on earth *were* these men? What were they talking about? Of which authority were they the representatives? After all, K. lived in a legally constituted state, there was peace in the land, the rule of law was fully established. Who dared seize him in his own flat? He had always tended to take things as easily as possible and only believe the worst when he came face to face with it, and never to worry too much about the future, even when everything looked black. But now this did not seem to him quite right. Of course he could take the whole thing as a joke, a crude joke which was being played on him for some unknown reason – perhaps because today was his thirtieth birthday – by his colleagues at the bank. Yes, that was quite possible. Perhaps he only needed to laugh in the warders' faces in some special way and they would laugh too. Perhaps they were simply porters from the street-corner, in fact they did look rather like that – but nevertheless he was firmly resolved this time, after his very first glimpse of the warder Franz, not to surrender any small advantage he might hold over these people. K. saw a slight danger that he would be accused afterwards of not being able to see a joke, but although he was not in the habit of learning from experience, he remembered certain trifling instances when, unlike his friends, he had deliberately, with no instinct at all for the possible consequences, behaved rashly and had suffered grievously as a result. That was not going to happen again, at least not this time. If it was all an act, he would play along with it.

At any rate he still had his liberty.

'Excuse me,' he said and passed quickly between the warders into his room.

'He seems a sensible fellow,' he heard someone say behind him. In his room he immediately pulled out the drawers of his desk, where everything was in perfect order, but he was so agitated he could not lay his hands right away on the identity papers he wanted. In the end he did find his bicycle licence and was going to take it to the warders, but then the document seemed too trivial and he went on searching till he found his birth certificate. Just as he was going back to the next room, the door opposite was opened by Frau Grubach who was about to come in. He only saw her for an instant, for as soon as she recognized K. she was clearly overcome by embarrassment, made her excuses, and vanished, closing the door again very carefully.

K. would just have had time to say: 'Do come in, won't you?'

But he simply stood in the middle of the room with his papers in his hand gazing at the door which remained closed, and was aroused only by a cry from the warders who, he now realized, were sitting by the open window devouring his breakfast.

'Why didn't she come in?' he asked.

'She's not allowed to,' said the tall warder. 'After all, you're under arrest.'

'How on earth can I be under arrest? And especially like this?'

'Now you're at it again,' said the warder, dipping his slice of bread and butter into the honey-pot. 'We don't answer questions like that.'

'You'll have to answer them,' K. told him. 'Here are my

identity papers. Now show me yours, and first of all show me the warrant for my arrest.'

'Good God!' said the warder. 'Why can't you accept what's happened instead of trying to provoke us pointlessly? Especially as we are now probably the closest friends you've got in the world!'

'That's true enough, you can take our word for it,' said Franz, holding his coffee-cup in front of him and gazing at K. with a long, probably significant, but incomprehensible look. Involuntarily K. found himself lured into exchanging glances with Franz, but then he tapped his papers and said:

'Here are my identity papers.'

'What do we want with those?' the tall warder shouted. 'You're more trouble than a child! What are you trying to do? Do you think you'll get this confounded trial of yours over quicker by arguing with us, the warders, about identity papers and warrants? We're low-ranking employees, we can't make head or tail of a legal document, and we're not concerned with your case except to guard you for ten hours a day and get paid for it. That's all we are, but we're capable of grasping that the high authorities we serve would never have ordered an arrest like this without having an exact idea of the grounds for it and finding out all about the person arrested. There isn't any mistake about that. Our officials (so far as I know, and I only know the lowest grades) never go looking, as it were, for crime among the population, but are – as the Law says – drawn by guilt and then have to send out us warders. That's the Law. How could a mistake occur?'

'I don't know this Law,' K. said.

'So much the worse for you,' said the warder.

'And probably it only exists in your imagination,' said K. He wanted somehow to insinuate his way into the warders' thoughts and either turn them to his advantage or adapt himself to them. But the warder just said brusquely:

'You'll come to feel it.'

Franz butted in and said:

'There you see, Willem, he admits he doesn't know the Law and at the same time he claims he's innocent.'

'You're quite right, but one can't make him understand anything,' said the other.

K. did not reply. Do I have to let myself, he was thinking, become even more confused by the chatter of these minions of the most inferior rank? – they themselves admit that's all they are. Anyway, they're talking about things they don't understand at all. It's only their stupidity that makes them so sure. A few words with someone of my own intellectual class would make everything incomparably clearer than talking for hours to these fellows.

He walked up and down a few times in the uncluttered part of the room and he saw the old woman across the street who had now dragged to the window an even older man, to whom she was clinging. K. felt he must put an end to this performance.

'Take me to your superior,' he said.

'When he tells us to, not before,' said the warder called Willem. 'And now I advise you to go to your room, sit there quietly and see what's decided about you. We advise you not to allow yourself to be distracted by useless ideas. Pull yourself together, for great demands will be made on you. You did not treat us as our obliging attitude deserved, you have forgotten that whoever we may be, we are at least free men compared with you, and that is quite an advantage. Nevertheless, if you have some money we are quite prepared to bring you a little breakfast from the café opposite.'

Without replying to this offer K. stood still for a little while. Perhaps if he opened the door of the next room or even the door leading into the hall, neither of them would dare to stop him, perhaps the simplest solution to the whole thing would be to push matters to extremes. But perhaps they would indeed set on him, and once he had been knocked down he would have lost any advantage that he still, in a way, had over them. So he preferred certainty to the solution which the natural course of events was bound to provide, and he went back to his room without another word being said either by him or by the warders.

He threw himself on his bed and picked up from his washstand a beautiful apple which he had put aside the previous evening for his breakfast. Now it was all he had for breakfast and anyway (as he assured himself when he took his first big bite) it was much better than the breakfast from the filthy café which he might have got as a favour from the warders. He felt at ease and confident. Of course he would miss his morning's work at the bank, but that was easily excused in view of the fairly high position he held there. Ought he to give the real explanation? He intended to. If people did not believe him (which would be quite understandable in the circumstances) he could always call on Frau Grubach to vouch for him, or even the two old people across the way who now most likely were shifting over to the window directly opposite.

It surprised K. (at least when he looked at it from the warders' point of view, it surprised him) that they had urged him to go to his room and had left him alone there, where he had abundant opportunity to take his own life. But at the same time he asked himself, looking at it now from his own point of view, what reason he could possibly have for doing so. Just because those two men were sitting there next door, having grabbed his breakfast? It would have been so senseless to take his own life that, even if he had wanted to, the very senselessness would have prevented him. If the intellectual limitations of the warders had not been so blatant, one might have assumed that they too, for the same reason, would have seen no danger in leaving him on his own. If they wanted to they could now watch him go to a small wall-cupboard where he kept some good brandy and see him take a nip to make up for his breakfast and then a second nip to give himself courage, this second one only as a precaution against the unlikely eventuality that courage would be necessary.

Just then he was startled by a shout from the next room which made his teeth bang against the glass:

'The Inspector wants you!'

It was only the shouting that startled him – that curt, clipped military way of shouting which he would not have thought the warder Franz capable of. The command itself was very welcome.

'At last!' he shouted back, locking the wall-cupboard and hurrying at once into the next room. There he found the two warders, who chased him back into his bedroom as if that were the most natural thing in the world to do.

'What do you think you're doing?' they cried. 'Going to appear before the Inspector in your shirt? He'd have you well and truly thrashed and us as well!'

'Leave me alone, damn you!' cried K. who had already been pushed back to his wardrobe. 'If you burst in when I'm in bed, you can't expect to find me all dressed up.'

'That's no use,' said the warders, who, whenever K. shouted, became quite calm, almost sad, and in this way managed to confuse him or bring him to his senses to some extent.

'Ridiculous palaver!' he grumbled, but by now he was already picking up a coat from the chair and holding it up with both hands for a moment as if submitting it for the warders' approval. They shook their heads.

'It has to be black,' they said. Whereupon K. threw the coat on the ground and said – he did not even know himself what he meant:

'But it's not the official trial yet anyway.' The warders smiled but did not budge from their 'It has to be black.'

'Oh, if it will hurry things up I don't care,' said K, as he opened the wardrobe himself, searched for a long time among his many clothes and selected his best black suit – a lounge suit that had almost caused a sensation among his friends because of its cut – then he took a fresh shirt and began to dress with care. He secretly thought that he had thereby hurried things up, for the warders had forgotten to make him have a bath. He kept an eye on them to see if they might still remember, but naturally it never occurred to them. On the other hand Willem did not forget to send Franz to the Inspector with the message that K. was getting dressed.

When he was fully dressed he had to march, with Willem close behind him, through the empty room next door and into the room beyond, the double doors of which had been left wide open for them. As K. very well knew, this room had been taken a short while ago by a certain Fräulein Bürstner, a typist, who usually went off to work very early, did not come home till late, and with whom he had scarcely exchanged much more than a greeting. Now her little bedside table had been shifted from her bed into the middle of the room to serve as a desk for the interview, and the Inspector was seated behind it. He had his legs crossed and rested one arm along the back of the chair.

In one corner of the room three young men were standing and looking at some of Fräulein Bürstner's photographs, which were stuck into a mat hung up on the wall. A white blouse was hanging on the catch of the open window. In the window opposite the two old people could again be seen, but now they had company, for behind, far taller than either of them, his shirt open on his chest, was a man who was squeezing and twisting his little reddish pointed beard.

'Josef K?' the Inspector asked, perhaps merely in order to attract K's wandering glance. K. nodded.

'You must have been astonished at what happened this morning?' the Inspector asked, rearranging with both hands the few objects that lay on the little bedside table – candle and matches, a book and a pin-cushion – as if they were things he needed for the examination.

'I certainly was,' K. said, overwhelmed by the relief of being confronted at last with a sensible man and of being able to discuss his situation with him. 'Certainly I am surprised, but not really very surprised.'

'Not very surprised?' asked the Inspector, now placing the candle in the middle of the little table and grouping the other things around it.

'Perhaps you misunderstand me,' K. hastened to explain. 'I mean—' and here K. broke off and looked round for a chair. 'I can sit down, I suppose?' he asked.

'It's not usual,' replied the Inspector.

'I mean,' K. now said without any further pause, 'of course I am very surprised, but after all, when one has lived in the world for thirty years and has had to struggle on alone as I have, one gets hardened to surprises and doesn't take them too seriously. Especially not the kind of thing that happened today.'

'Why not that one especially?'

'Well, I am not going to say that I look on the whole thing as a joke. Too many preparations have gone into it for that. All the people in the boarding-house would have to be involved as well as all of you, and that would be going beyond a joke. So I'm not going to say that it's a joke.'

'Quite correct,' said the Inspector and looked to see how many matches there were in the matchbox.

'On the other hand,' K. went on, and now he turned to all of them and he would have liked to include even the three standing by the photographs, 'on the other hand the matter can't be that important. I deduce this from the fact that I am being charged, although I cannot discover the slightest grounds for any accusation. But even this is by the way. The main question is, who is making the accusation? What authority is conducting the proceedings?

Are you people officials? Nobody is in uniform, unless one can call *your* clothes' (and here he turned to Franz) 'a uniform, but they are more like a travelling outfit. I demand clear answers to these questions and I am convinced that once I get them we shall be able to part perfectly amicably.'

The Inspector threw the matchbox down on the table:

'You are making a great mistake,' he said. 'These gentlemen here and I are of no significance at all in your affair, indeed we know almost nothing about it. We might be dressed in the most official-looking uniforms, and your case would not be any more serious. I cannot even tell you positively that you have been charged, or rather I don't know whether you have been or not. You have been arrested, that's true, but I don't know any more than that. Perhaps the warders have hinted at something else, but, if they did, it was only talk. Still, if I don't answer your questions now, at any rate I can advise you not to worry so much about us and about what's going to happen to you. Think more about yourself. And don't make such a fuss about your feelings of innocence. It spoils the quite good impression you make other-wise. Also you ought not to talk so much: almost everything you said just now could very well have been deduced from your behaviour, even if you had said no more than a few words, and anyway it did not do you a great deal of credit.'

K. stared at the Inspector. Was he now going to be ticked off like a schoolboy and by a man perhaps younger than himself? Was he now to be reprimanded for being frank? And was he going to learn nothing at all about the reason for his arrest and those who had ordered it? He became somewhat agitated, paced up and down, no one tried to stop him, he pushed back his cuffs, felt his chest, ran his hands through his hair, walked past the three young men and said, 'But it doesn't make any sense.' The three turned towards him and looked at him sympathetically, but seriously. Finally he came to a halt in front of the Inspector's table.

'The public prosecutor, Hasterer, is a good friend of mine,' he said. 'Can I phone him?'

'Of course,' said the Inspector, 'but I don't know what the point would be, unless you have some private matter to discuss with him.'

'What the point would be?' cried K, more taken aback than annoyed. 'What sort of person are you then? You expect there to be some point in what I do and yet you behave in the most pointless possible way yourself! It's enough to make one weep! First of all these men burst in on me, and now they sit or stand around expecting me to perform for your benefit like some prize exhibit. You ask me what the point of ringing a lawyer would be, when I am supposed to have been arrested? Very well then, I won't ring him.'

'But do,' said the Inspector and pointed to the hall, where the telephone was. 'Please ring him.'

'No, I don't want to now,' K. said and went to the window.

Across the way the group were still at their window, and it was only K's approach to his window that seemed to disturb their silent vigil a little. The old people made an attempt to rise, but the man behind them reassured them.

'You see who's looking on!' K. shouted quite loudly to the Inspector, pointing with his finger. 'Get away from there!' he called across. At once the three of them retreated a few steps, the two old people even going behind the man, who hid them with his broad body and who (judging by the way his lips moved) was saying something that was unintelligible at that distance. They did not, however, disappear altogether, but only seemed to be waiting for a chance to get back to the window again without being noticed.

'What importunate, inconsiderate people!' K. said, turning back to the room. Possibly the Inspector agreed with him, or so K. thought, judging by a hurried glance in the Inspector's direction.

But it was equally possible that the Inspector had not been listening at all, for he had pressed his hand down hard on the table and seemed to be comparing the lengths of his fingers. The two warders were sitting on a chest covered with an ornamental cloth and were rubbing their knees. The three young men had put their hands on their hips and were gazing around aimlessly. It was as silent as in some abandoned office.

'Well, gentlemen,' K. cried, and for a moment it seemed to him that he was carrying the burden for all of them. 'Judging by your appearance this affair of mine must be closed. In my opinion, the best thing would be not to think any more about whether or not your action was justified, but to bring the matter to an amicable conclusion by shaking hands all round. If you agree with me, then please—' and he went up to the Inspector's table and held out his hand. The Inspector raised his eyes, gnawed at his lips and looked at K's outstretched hand. K. still thought the Inspector was going to shake hands. But the man rose to his feet, picked up a hard round hat that lay on Fräulein Bürstner's bed and put it on carefully with both hands, as one does when one is trying on a new hat.

'How simple everything seems to you!' he said to K. as he did so. 'We ought to bring the matter to an amicable conclusion, you think? No, no, that really won't do. But on the other hand that doesn't mean that I'm saying you should give up hope. No, why should you? You're only under arrest, nothing more than that. That was what I had to tell you and now I've done this and I've also seen how you've taken it. That's enough for today and we can take our leave, if only for the moment, of course. I suppose now you will want to go to the bank?'

'To the bank?' K. asked. 'I thought I was under arrest.'

K. said this with a certain amount of defiance, for, although his offer to shake hands had not been accepted, he did feel (particularly since the Inspector had stood up) more and more independent of all these people. He was playing with them. If they went away, he intended to run after them to the gate and offer to be arrested. So he repeated:

'How can I go to the bank, since I'm under arrest?'

'Ah, I see,' said the Inspector, who was already at the door. 'You've misunderstood me. You're under arrest, that's true, but that should not prevent you from doing your job. Nor ought you to be hampered in your ordinary way of life.'

'Then being arrested is not very serious,' K. said and went up to the Inspector.

'I never said it was,' said the latter.

'But then it looks as if you did not have any real need even to tell me about the arrest,' K. said and went still closer. The others had also drawn nearer. Now they were all crowded in a narrow space by the door.

'It was my duty,' said the Inspector.

'Rather an idiotic duty,' K. said intractably.

'Perhaps. But we don't want to waste our time with this sort of talk. I had assumed you would want to go to the bank. Since you are so fussy about words, let me add that I am not compelling you to go. I had only assumed that was what you would want to do. And to make this easier for you and to make your arrival at the bank as inconspicuous as possible, I arranged for these three gentlemen, colleagues of yours, to be here at your disposal.'

'What?' cried K. and stared at the three in astonishment. These anaemic and very ordinary young men, whom he had noticed only as the group beside the photographs, were in fact employees at his bank, not colleagues – that was an exaggeration which indicated a flaw in the Inspector's omniscience – but junior employees of the bank they certainly were. How could K. have overlooked this? How completely preoccupied he must have been with the Inspector and the warders to fail to recognize these three! Formal Rabensteiner, swinging his arms, fair-haired Kullich with his deep-set eyes, and Kaminer with that unbearable smile of his, which was produced by a chronic muscular spasm.

'Good morning,' K. said after a moment and held out his hand to the young men, who bowed politely. 'I didn't recognize you at first. Well, now we can go to work, eh?' They nodded and laughed enthusiastically, as if that was all they had been waiting for the whole time, yet when K. found he had left his hat in his room, they all raced off one after the other to fetch it, which indicated a certain amount of embarrassment. K. stood quietly and watched them through the two open doors: naturally apathetic Rabensteiner came last (he had merely broken into an elegant trot). Kaminer handed over the hat and K, as he had found it necessary to do so often at the bank, had to remind himself expressly that Kaminer's smile was involuntary, indeed that he was quite unable to smile when he wanted to. Then Frau Grubach, looking not in the least guilty, opened the door in the hall for the whole party and, as usual, K. found himself gazing down at her apron-strings which cut into her huge body unnecessarily deeply. Once outside, K, holding his watch in his hand, decided to take a taxi in order to avoid any further delay – he was already half an hour late. Kaminer ran to the corner to fetch a cab, while the other two were obviously trying to distract K's attention; suddenly Kullich pointed to the door of the house opposite where the big man with the reddish pointed beard had just appeared. A little embarrassed for a moment at revealing himself in his full size, he stepped back to the wall and leaned against it. The old people were still presumably on the stairs. K. was annoyed with Kullich for having drawn attention to the man whom he had already noticed himself and had indeed even been expecting to see.

'Don't stare,' he burst out, without realizing how other people would be struck by his way of addressing grown-up men. But there was no need for any explanation, because at that moment the taxi came, they got in and drove off. Then K. remembered that he had not noticed the departure of the Inspector and the warders. Earlier the Inspector had prevented his recognizing the three bank clerks, and they had now diverted his attention from the Inspector. This did not suggest that K. had his wits about him, and K. determined to watch things more closely. Yet he swivelled round involuntarily and peered from the back of the taxi to see if he could still catch a glimpse of the Inspector and the warders. But he turned to face the front again at once and leaned back comfortably in the corner without even having tried to search for anyone. Although it might not have looked like it, he now needed some word of sympathy, but the men seemed tired. Rabensteiner was looking out to the right and Kullich to the left, Kaminer alone was free to help, but he was wearing that grin of his, about which unfortunately it would have been cruel to joke.

That spring K. had got into the habit of spending his evenings in the following way: after work, whenever possible (for he usually stayed in his office till nine o'clock), he went for a short walk alone or with colleagues and then went to a beer-cellar where he joined a group of mostly elderly habitués and usually sat with them till eleven. There were, however, certain exceptions to this arrangement, as when for example K. received an invitation from the manager of the bank, who greatly appreciated K's capacity for work and his reliability, to go for a drive or to dine at his villa. Apart from this, K. went once a week to see a girl called Elsa who worked all night until early in the morning as a waitress in a wine-bar and then during the day received her visitors in bed.

But this evening – the day had passed quickly with plenty of hard work and many flattering and friendly birthday greetings – K. wanted to go straight home. During every brief pause in the day's work he had been thinking about it. Though he did not work it out clearly, it seemed to him that the morning's events had caused complete chaos in Frau Grubach's whole flat and that it was up to him to restore order. Once order had been restored, every trace of these events would vanish and everything would go on as before. In particular there was nothing to be feared from the three clerks, for they had merged once again into the vast bureaucracy of the bank and they did not seem to have changed in any way. Several times K. had summoned them to his office, individually and together, with no other purpose than to observe them. He had always been quite satisfied and let them go.

When he arrived back at half past nine in front of the house where he lived, he was met at the front door by a young fellow who was standing there with his legs apart, smoking a pipe.

'Who are you?' K. immediately asked him and thrust his face close to the fellow's. Not much could be seen in the half-dark of the entrance hall.

'I'm the janitor's son, sir,' replied the lad, taking the pipe from his mouth and stepping aside.

'The janitor's son?' K. said, tapping his stick impatiently on the ground.

'Did you want something, sir? Shall I get my father?'

'No, no,' said K. and there was a note of forgiveness in his voice, as if the young man had done something wrong and yet K. was forgiving him for it.

'It's all right,' he said and went on, but before climbing the stairs he turned round once more and looked back.

He could have gone straight to his room, but as he wanted to speak to Frau Grubach he knocked on her door right away. She was sitting with some darning at the table, on which there lay a pile of old stockings. Absent-mindedly K. asked her to excuse him for coming so late, but Frau Grubach was very affable and waved aside his excuses, saying she was always ready to speak to him and that he knew very well he was her best and favourite lodger. K. looked round the room, everything was back in its place again, the breakfast dishes which had been standing that morning on the little table by the window had been cleared away.

Women's hands get a lot of things done without any fuss, he thought to himself. He might perhaps have smashed the dishes on the spot, but he certainly could not have put them away. He looked at Frau Grubach with a certain gratitude.

'Why are you working so late?' he asked. Now they were both sitting at the table and from time to time K. burrowed his hand into the pile of stockings.

'There's a lot of work,' she said, 'and during the day I give my time to the lodgers. If I want to see to my own things, I only have the evenings.'

'I made a lot of extra work for you today, though, didn't I?'

'How was that?' she asked, showing more interest and dropping the work into her lap.

'I mean with the men who were here this morning.'

'Ah, I see,' she said and relaxed again. 'That didn't give me any work to speak of.' K. looked on silently as she took up the darning once more. She seems to be surprised that I mention it, he thought, in fact she doesn't really think I ought to mention it. So it's all the more important that I do. It's only with an old woman like this that I can talk about it.

'But it did, it certainly made extra work,' he went on, 'only it won't happen again.'

'No, it can't happen again,' she confirmed and smiled almost sadly at K.

'Do you really mean that?' he asked.

'Yes,' she said more gently, 'but above all you mustn't take it too much to heart. These things *do* happen! And as you're talking to me so frankly, Herr K, I can tell you that I did listen a little behind the door and, besides, the two warders told me a few things about it all. It's your happiness that is at stake, and that really concerns me very much, more than it should perhaps, seeing that I'm only your landlady. So I did hear a few things then, but I can't say that it was anything particularly bad. No. Admittedly you are under arrest, but not in the same way as a thief. If one is arrested as a thief then that's bad, but this kind of arrest . . . I get the impression it's something very complex (forgive me if I'm saying something stupid), it seems to me it's something very complex, which it's true I don't understand, but which there is no need to understand.'

'What you're saying is not at all stupid, Frau Grubach. At least I partly agree with you, except that I judge the whole thing more harshly than you and I simply don't believe it is anything complex – I just don't think it matters at all. I was taken by surprise, that's all. If, as soon as I had woken up, instead of being put out when Anna didn't come, I had just got up and come straight in to you without paying any attention to anyone who got in my way, if I had had my breakfast in the kitchen for once, and got you to fetch my clothes from my room – in short, if I had behaved sensibly, nothing else would have happened, everything would have been nipped in the bud. But one is so unprepared for these things. In the bank, for instance, I am prepared, and it would be impossible for anything of that kind to happen to me there. There I have my own personal assistant, the general telephone and the internal telephone are on my desk in front of me, and I am constantly being visited by different individuals and clients and officials. Quite apart from this, and most important of all, I am always immersed in an atmosphere of work and so I have my wits about me, it would be a positive pleasure for me to be faced in the bank with a situation like that. Still it's over now and I really didn't want to say any more about it. It was only that I wanted to hear your opinion, the opinion of a sensible woman, and I'm very glad we agree about it. Now we must shake hands on it, an agreement like this must be confirmed with a handshake.'

Will she give me her hand? The Inspector didn't, he thought, and now he looked at the woman differently, searchingly. She stood up because he himself had stood up, she was a little embarrassed because she had not been able to understand everything that K. had said. As a result of this embarrassment, however, she said something she did not in the least mean to say and which was quite out of place:

'Don't take it so hard, Herr K,' she said, her voice breaking, and, of course, she quite forgot to shake hands.

'I didn't know I was taking it hard,' K. said, suddenly feeling tired and realizing the uselessness of getting this woman to agree to anything.

At the door he asked:

'Is Fräulein Bürstner at home?'

'No,' said Frau Grubach, and as she gave this bald piece of information she smiled with understanding, if belated, sympathy. 'She is at the theatre. Did you want her for something? Shall I give her a message?'

'Oh, I only wanted to say something to her.'

'I'm afraid I don't know when she'll be in. When she goes to the theatre she is usually late.'

'It doesn't matter,' K. said and was already turning towards the door, head bent, 'I only wanted to apologize to her for making use of her room today.'

'It isn't necessary, Herr K. You're too conscientious, in fact the young lady knows nothing at all about it, she's not been at home since first thing this morning and it's all been tidied up as you can see for yourself.' And she opened the door of Fräulein Bürstner's room.

'Thank you, I quite believe it,' K. said, but nevertheless he went to the open door. The moon was shining softly into the dark room. As far as he could see, everything was really where it should be and even the blouse was no longer hanging on the catch

37

of the window. The pillows on the bed seemed surprisingly high and lay partly in the moonlight.

'The young lady often comes home late,' K. said and looked at Frau Grubach as if it were her fault.

'You know how it is with young people!' Frau Grubach said apologetically.

'Of course, of course,' said K, 'but it can be carried too far.'

'Certainly it can,' said Frau Grubach, 'how right you are, Herr K. Perhaps even in this case . . . I certainly don't want to say anything against Fräulein Bürstner. She's a very nice girl, friendly, tidy, punctual, hard-working, and I value all that very much, but there is one thing; she ought to have more pride and keep herself to herself more. I have seen her twice this month already in out-of-the-way streets and each time with a different man. I'm very worried about it and I swear to God I wouldn't tell anybody else but you, Herr K, but I can see I shall have to speak to the young lady herself about it. Besides, it's not the only thing that makes me suspicious about her.'

'You're completely wrong about her,' K. said, getting extremely angry and almost unable to hide it. 'Besides, you have obviously misunderstood my remark about Fräulein Bürstner, I didn't mean it like that. I warn you frankly not to say anything to her. You're completely mistaken, I know the young lady very well and there isn't a grain of truth in what you've been saying. However, perhaps I'm going too far. I won't stop you from saying what you like to her. Goodnight.'

'But Herr K,' Frau Grubach said imploringly and hurried after him to his door, which he had already opened, 'I won't say anything at all to her yet, and of course I was going to carry on watching her first, I haven't told anyone but you what I know. But after all it's bound to be in the interests of all the lodgers that one should try to keep the boarding-house clean, and that is all I was trying to do.'

'Clean!' K. cried out through the crack in the door. 'If you want to keep the boarding-house clean, you'll have to start by giving me notice.' Then he slammed the door shut, ignoring her faint tapping.

He decided, however, that since he did not at all feel like sleeping, he would stay awake and take the opportunity of finding out when Fräulein Bürstner came in. Perhaps then it would even be possible (though it might not be the proper time for it) to have a few words with her. As he reclined at the window and closed his weary eyes, it even occurred to him for a moment to get his own back on Frau Grubach by persuading Fräulein Bürstner to join him in giving notice. But he immediately realized that that would be overdoing things horribly, and he even began to suspect himself of wanting to change his lodgings because of the morning's events. Nothing would have been more senseless and, above all, more pointless and contemptible.

When he had got tired of gazing out on to the empty street he lay down on the couch, after leaving the door to the hall slightly open, so that from the couch he would be able to see straight away anyone who came into the flat. Until about eleven he lay there quietly smoking a cigar. But after that he could not bear it any more and walked about a little in the hall, as if this would hurry Fräulein Bürstner up. He had no special desire to see her, indeed he could not even remember exactly what she looked like, yet he wanted to talk to her now and it annoyed him that her coming home late was further disturbing and disorganizing the end of the day. It was also her fault that he had not had any supper and that he had missed visiting Elsa as he had intended to do that evening. Of course he could still do both these things by going now to the wine-bar where Elsa worked. He would do that later after talking to Fräulein Bürstner.

It was after half past eleven when he heard someone on the stairs. K, who was deep in thought and pacing noisily up and

39

down the hall as if it were his own room, took refuge behind his door. It was Fräulein Bürstner who had arrived. As she locked the front door, she shivered and drew her silk shawl around her narrow shoulders. The next moment she would be in her room where K. could certainly not intrude at midnight. Therefore he had to speak to her at once, but unfortunately he had omitted to put the light on in his room, so that if he stepped out of the dark room it would seem like an attack and at the very least was bound to be frightening. In his helplessness and since there was no time to be lost, he whispered through the crack in the door:

'Fräulein Bürstner.' It sounded more like an entreaty than a summons.

'Is someone there?' Fräulein Bürstner asked and looked round with startled eyes.

'It's me,' K. said and came out.

'Ah, Herr K!' said Fräulein Bürstner, smiling. 'Good evening,' and she held out her hand.

'I wanted to say a few words to you, will you let me do so now?'

'Now?' Fräulein Bürstner asked. 'Has it got to be now? It's a little bit unusual, isn't it?'

'I've been waiting for you since nine.'

'Yes, well, I was at the theatre, I didn't know you were waiting.'

'What I wanted to talk to you about only happened today.'

'Oh, well, I don't have any fundamental objection, except that I'm so tired I'm ready to drop. Come into my room then, for a minute or two. We can't possibly talk here anyway, it would wake everybody up and that would, I think, be even more unpleasant for us than for them. Wait here until I put the light on in my room and then turn the light off here.' K. did so and then waited till Fräulein Bürstner called to him softly from her room.

'Sit down,' she said and pointed to the settee, while she herself remained standing by the end of the bed in spite of the tiredness she had mentioned. She did not even take off her small hat which was adorned with an excessive number of flowers. 'What did you want, then? I am really curious.' She crossed her legs.

'Perhaps you will say,' K. began, 'that the matter is not urgent enough to be discussed now, but—'

'I never listen to introductions like that,' said Fräulein Bürstner.

'That makes it easier for me,' K. said. 'This morning, partly through my fault, your room was disarranged a little. It was done by other people and against my wishes, and yet (as I said) it was my fault: I wanted to apologize for this.'

'My room?' asked Fräulein Bürstner, and instead of examining the room she looked intently at K.

'That's right,' K. said, and now for the first time they looked each other in the eye. 'How it all came to happen is not really worth talking about.'

'Oh, but it is, that's the really interesting part,' said Fräulein Bürstner.

'No,' said K.

'Well I'm not going to pry' said Fräulein Bürstner. 'If you insist that it's not interesting, then there's nothing to be said. I gladly accept your apology, especially as I can't see a sign of anything having been disturbed.' With the palms of her hands laid flat on her hips she made a circuit of the room. She stopped by the mat with the photographs pinned on it. 'No, but look!' she cried out. 'All my photos have been muddled up. That's horrid. So someone has been in my room, then, when they shouldn't have.'

K. nodded and silently cursed the clerk Kaminer who could never control his tedious, pointless habit of fiddling with things.

'It's curious,' said Fräulein Bürstner, 'that I am now forced to forbid you to do something you should forbid yourself to do, that is to enter my room in my absence.'

'But I explained to you, Fräulein,' K. said and went up to the photographs too, 'that it wasn't me who tampered with your photographs. Since you don't believe me, though, I must confess that the Commission of Inquiry brought along three bank clerks and one of them (and I shall get him sacked at the first opportunity) must have picked up your photos. Yes, there was a Comsion of Inquiry here,' K. added because Fräulein Bürstner was looking at him questioningly.

'To see you?' she asked.

'Yes,' replied K.

'No!' the girl exclaimed, and laughed.

'Yes, it was,' K. said. 'D'you believe I'm innocent then?'

'Well, innocent . . .' she said. 'I don't want, right now, to pronounce a verdict which may have grave consequences. And besides, I don't know you very well. But you've got to be a pretty big criminal before they'll set a Commission of Inquiry on you so soon. But since you're at liberty – at least I assume from your calmness that you've not escaped from prison – you can't have committed any crime of that sort.'

'No,' K. said, 'but the Commission of Inquiry may have realized that I am innocent, or at least not as guilty as was at first presumed.'

'Certainly, that could have happened,' Fräulein Bürstner said very carefully.

'Look,' K. said, 'you haven't had much experience in legal matters.'

'No, I haven't,' said Fräulein Bürstner, 'and I have often regretted it because I want to learn everything and I'm particularly interested in law courts. There is a special attraction about a court of law, don't you think? However, I shall certainly be widening my knowledge in that area, for I'm joining the staff of a lawyer's office next month.'

'That's fine,' said K, 'then you'll be able to help me a little with my case.'

'I might,' said Fräulein Bürstner. 'Why shouldn't I? I like to use what I know.'

'But I mean it seriously,' K. said, 'or at least half seriously, as you do. After all, the thing's too petty to drag in a lawyer, but I could well use an adviser.'

'Yes, but if I'm to be an adviser, I must know what it's all about,' said Fräulein Bürstner.

'But that's just the snag. I don't even know myself.'

'Why then, you've just been pulling my leg,' said Fräulein Bürstner, who seemed excessively disappointed. 'It surely wasn't at all necessary to pick this time of night to do that.' And she moved away from the photographs where they had been standing together for so long.

'No, Fräulein,' K. said, 'I'm not pulling your leg at all. I wish you would believe me! I've already told you everything I know. Even more than I know, because it wasn't really a Commission of Inquiry at all. I only call it that because I can't think of a better name for it. There was no interrogation, I was merely placed under arrest, but it was done by a commission.'

Fräulein Bürstner was sitting on the settee and burst out laughing again.

'What was it like, then?' she asked.

'Horrible,' said K, but now he was not thinking about it at all, on the contrary, he was immersed in contemplation of Fräulein Bürstner, who was leaning her face on one hand (her elbow resting on the cushion of the settee) while her other hand was slowly caressing her hip.

'That's too vague,' said Fräulein Bürstner.

'What's too vague?' K. asked. Then he came to and said: 'Shall I show you what it was like?' He wanted to move about and yet he did not want to go away.

'I'm tired now,' said Fräulein Bürstner.

'You came in so late,' K. said.

'Now it ends up with you blaming me, and I deserve it, for I should never have let you in. And it wasn't even necessary, as it's turned out.'

'But it was necessary, and you'll see why right now,' K. said. 'May I bring the little table over from your bed?'

'What's got into you?' said Fräulein Bürstner. 'Of course you can't!'

'Then I can't show you,' K. said, quite flustered, as if some enormous hurt had been inflicted on him.

'Well, if you need it for the demonstration, then go ahead, just move the little table!' said Fräulein Bürstner, and after a while she added in a weaker voice: 'I'm so tired that I'm agreeing to more than I should.' K. placed the little table in the middle of the room and sat down behind it.

'You must get a proper idea of where the people were; that was very interesting. Now, I am the Inspector, the two warders are sitting there on the chest, and over by the photographs are three young men. A white blouse is hanging on the catch of the window (I mention this just in passing). And now it begins. Oh, but I've left myself out. The most important person, that is to say myself, is standing here in front of the little table. The Inspector is sitting here completely at ease, with his legs crossed and one arm hanging down over the back of the chair here, a complete boor of a fellow. And then it really begins. The Inspector shouts at me as if he has got to wake me up, he positively yells at me – and unfortunately, if I am going to give you a proper idea, I must yell too. Anyway, it's only my name that he yells out.'

Fräulein Bürstner, who was laughing as he listened, put her finger to her lips to stop K. from yelling, but it was too late. K. had entered into the part too completely, and he gave a long drawn-out shout: 'Josef K.!' not, after all, as loudly as he had threatened, but in such a way that the shout, after it had suddenly been released, seemed to spread gradually through the room.

Then there came several knocks at the door of the next room, loud, sharp and regular. Fräulein Bürstner turned pale and put her hand on her heart. K. was specially alarmed because for a while he had been quite incapable of thinking of anything except the events of the morning and the girl for whom he was acting them out. Scarcely had he pulled himself together when he sprang towards Fräulein Bürstner and grasped her hand.

'Don't be afraid,' he whispered, 'I'll sort everything out. But who can it be? Next door is only the living-room and there's no one sleeping there.'

'Yes, there is,' Fräulein Bürstner whispered in K's ear. 'Since yesterday there's been a nephew of Frau Grubach sleeping there, a captain. It's the only room vacant. I forgot about it myself. Oh, why did you have to shout so loud? I don't like it.'

'There's nothing to be worried about,' K. said, and now as she sank back on the cushion he kissed her on the brow.

'Oh, go away, go away,' she said, sitting up again hastily. 'Go on, go on, what are you waiting for? He's listening at the door, he can hear everything. How you're tormenting me!'

'I'm not going,' said K, 'until you're a little calmer. Come to the other corner of the room, he can't hear us there.' She let him lead her over there.

'You must remember that though this may be unpleasant for you, there's no danger involved at all. You know very well that Frau Grubach – and she's the one who counts in this business, especially as the Captain is her nephew – positively adores me and absolutely believes everything I say. Besides, she is also under an obligation to me as I've lent her quite a large sum of money. I'll agree to any explanation you suggest of how we came to be here, provided it's at all plausible, and I guarantee to get Frau Grubach to accept it publicly as well as really and truly believe it herself. You mustn't spare me at all in this. If you want it spread around that I assaulted you, then Frau Grubach will be told that, and she will

believe it without losing faith in me, she's so devoted to me.'
Fräulein Bürstner was staring at the ground in front of her without speaking and seemed a little deflated.

'Why shouldn't Frau Grubach believe that I have assaulted you?' K. added. He gazed at her hair, her reddish hair, neatly parted, in a low chignon and firmly fixed. He thought she would glance at him, but without changing her posture she said:

'Forgive me, it was the sudden knocking that frightened me, not so much the possible consequences of the Captain's being there. It was so silent after you shouted and then came the knocking, that's why I was so alarmed. Also I was sitting just near the door, the knocking was right beside me. I'm grateful for what you suggest, but I'm not going to accept it. I can take the responsibility for all that happens in my room, whoever challenges me. I'm surprised you don't see how insulting your suggestions are – although, of course, at the same time I certainly recognize your good intentions. But now do please go, leave me alone, I need to be alone now even more than before. The few minutes you asked for have now stretched out to half an hour or more.'

K. clasped her hand and then her wrist:

'But you're not angry with me?' he said. She brushed his hand away and answered:

'No, no, I'm never angry with anyone.' He tried to grasp her wrist again, this time she permitted it and led him to the door like that. He was firmly determined to leave. But in front of the door he stopped as if he had not expected to find a door there, and Fräulein Bürstner took advantage of that moment to free herself, open the door and slip into the hall, from where she said quietly to K:

'Come on now, please. Look—' and she pointed to the Captain's door under which a light was showing. 'He has switched on his light and is having some fun at our expense.'

'I'm just coming,' K. said. He ran forward, took hold of her, kissed her on the mouth and then all over her face, like a thirsty animal which, after a long search, laps avidly at a fresh spring of water. Finally he kissed her on the neck, just where her throat was, and there he let his lips linger for a long time. A noise from the Captain's room caused him to look up.

'I'm going now,' he said and wanted to call Fräulein Bürstner by her first name, only he did not know what it was. She nodded wearily and, already half turning away, she yielded her hand to him to kiss (as if she did not know what she was doing) and walked with bowed head back into her room.

K. was soon in bed. He fell asleep very quickly, but before he did so he thought for a while about how he had behaved. He was satisfied, and yet was surprised that he was not even more satisfied with what he had done. He was seriously worried about Fräulein Bürstner because of the Captain.

Chapter Two

Initial Interrogation

K. had been informed by telephone that on the following Sunday there would be a brief investigation of his case. He was warned that these investigations would be held regularly, possibly not every week, but more and more frequently as time went by. On the one hand it was to everyone's advantage that the trial should be brought to a swift conclusion, but on the other hand the investigations had got to be thorough from every point of view, and yet must never last too long on account of the stress they involved. Therefore, this compromise of holding brief examinations with small gaps in between had been decided on. And so Sunday had been fixed as the day for the hearing in order not to disturb K's professional work. It was assumed, they said, that he would fall in with this, but if he wanted a different day they would oblige him if it were possible. For instance, hearings could even, they said, be held at night, but then K. might not be fresh enough. At any rate they would leave it at Sunday unless K. had some objection. It was taken for granted that he must definitely appear, there was probably no need to point that out to him. He was told the number of the house where the hearing was to take place: it was a house in an out-of-the-way suburban street where K. had never been before.

When he had been told this, K. replaced the receiver without replying. He immediately decided to go there on Sunday, it was certainly necessary, for the trial was getting under way and he ought to contest it: this first hearing must also be the last. He was still standing pensively by the telephone when behind him he heard the voice of the Deputy Manager, who was wanting to phone but could not get past K.

'Bad news?' the Deputy Manager asked casually, not really wanting information but simply to get K. away from the phone.

'No, no,' K. said, stepping aside, but not going away. The Deputy Manager lifted the receiver and, speaking over the top of the ear-piece as he waited for the operator, said:

'One thing, Herr K: Would you do me the pleasure of joining a party on my yacht on Sunday morning? There will be quite a lot of people, certainly some of your own friends too. Including Hasterer, the public prosecutor. Will you come? Do come!'

K. tried to attend to what the Deputy Manager was saying. It was of some importance to him, for this invitation from the Deputy Manager, with whom he had never got on very well, was an attempt at reconciliation and showed how important K. had become in the bank and how valuable his friendship, or at least his impartiality, was deemed to be by the second highest official in the bank. By giving this invitation the Deputy Manager had demeaned himself, even though he had only flung it out casually, over the top of the ear-piece, while he waited for the operator to connect him. But K. was forced to humble him further by saying:

'Many thanks, but unfortunately I have no time this Sunday as I have another engagement.'

'What a shame,' said the Deputy Manager and turned to speak on the phone, as he had just been connected. It was not a short conversation, but K. was so distracted that he remained standing by the phone the whole time. Not until the Deputy Manager rang off did he start up in alarm and say, by way of an excuse for his needless hovering by the phone:

'Someone just rang me up and asked me to go somewhere, but they forgot to say what time.'

'Well, ring up again and ask,' said the Deputy Manager.

'Oh, it's not that important,' said K, although this weakened still further the already lame excuse he had given before. The Deputy Manager, as he walked away, talked of other things. K. forced himself to reply, but was chiefly thinking that it would be best to go on Sunday at nine o'clock in the morning, since this was the time at which all courts began work on weekdays.

On Sunday the weather was dreary. K. was very tired, he had sat up till all hours the night before at the beer-cellar because of a celebration among the habitués, and he had almost overslept. Hurriedly, and without having time to think things over or to coordinate the different plans he had worked out during the week, he got dressed and dashed off without his breakfast to the suburb which had been specified. By a curious chance, although he had little time to look around, he met the three employees involved in his case, Rabensteiner, Kullich and Kaminer. The first two crossed ahead of him in a tram, while Kaminer was sitting on the terrace of a café, and just as K. went by he leaned inquisitively over the balustrade. They all probably gazed after him, wondering where their boss was hurrying to. A sort of defiance had made K. decide to go on foot. He shrank from accepting the slightest help from others in this case of his, nor did he want to be under an obligation to anyone and thereby give them even the slightest knowledge of his affairs. Apart from all this, however, he did not in the least wish to humble himself before the Commission by being excessively punctual. All the same, he found himself running now to arrive by nine if possible, although he had not even been required to come at any definite time.

He had expected to be able to recognize the house from a distance by some sign or other which he had not exactly pictured to himself, or else by some special coming and going at the entrance. But Juliusstrasse, where it was supposed to be and at the end of which K. halted for a moment, was lined on both sides with almost completely identical houses, tall grey tenements inhabited by poor people. Now, on a Sunday morning, there were people at most of the windows, men in shirt-sleeves were lounging there smoking or were holding small children carefully and tenderly on the window-ledges. Other windows were piled high with bedding, and above this the tousled head of a woman would appear for a moment. People called to each other across the street, and one such shout right above K's head raised a great laugh. Regularly spaced out down the long street and situated below street level so that they could be reached only by going down flights of steps were small shops selling various foodstuffs. Women were passing in and out of the shops or standing gossiping on the steps. A fruit-hawker who was commending his wares to the people in the windows above almost knocked K. down with his handcart since neither was looking where he was going. At that very moment a gramophone which had served its time in better parts of the city set up a murderous caterwaul.

K. went farther down the street, slowly, as if he now had plenty of time or as if the Examining Magistrate were watching him from some window or other and therefore knew that he had arrived. It was shortly after nine. The house lay quite a long way down the street, it was almost exceptionally large and the entrance-gate in particular was high and wide. This was clearly intended for lorries belonging to the different warehouses which, now locked up, surrounded the big yard and bore the names of firms, some of which K. knew from dealings at the bank. Contrary to his usual habit he concentrated on all these external details and he even stood for a while at the entrance to the yard. Near him a barefooted man was sitting on a packing-case reading a newspaper. Two boys were swinging on a handcart. In front of a pump, in a dressing-gown, stood a sickly young girl who looked at K. as the water poured into her can. In one corner of the yard, a line with washing already hanging on it to dry was being stretched between two windows. A man was standing underneath, directing the work with a shout or two.

K. turned to the stairs in order to reach the room where the hearing would take place, but once again he stood still, for in addition to these stairs he saw three other different flights of stairs in the yard, and moreover a small passage at the end of the yard seemed to lead into a second yard. He was annoyed that the whereabouts of the room had not been described to him more exactly, he was certainly being treated with a strange carelessness or indifference and he intended to tell them so, very firmly and clearly. But eventually he climbed the stairs, mentally toying with the memory of a remark made by the warder Willem to the effect that there was a mutual attraction between the court and guilt, from which it followed that the room where the hearing would take place was bound to be up whichever stairs K. happened to choose.

As he went up, he interrupted many children playing on the stairs: they gazed at him angrily as he walked through their ranks. 'Next time if I have to come here again,' he said to himself, 'either I must bring some sweets to win them over, or else a stick to thrash them with.'

Just before reaching the first storey he even had to wait for a moment until a marble stopped rolling, whilst two small boys with the cunning faces of grown-up rogues held on to him by his trousers. If he had tried to shake them off, he would have been bound to hurt them and he was afraid they would yell.

The real search began on the first floor. Since he still could not ask for the Commission of Inquiry itself, he invented a joiner called Lanz – the name occurred to him because that was the name of the Captain, Frau Grubach's nephew – and he now started to inquire at every flat, asking whether a joiner called Lanz lived there, just to get a chance to look into the rooms. It turned out, however, that this was usually possible without any difficulty as almost all the doors stood open and the children were running in and out. They were mostly small single-windowed rooms in which the cooking was also done. Often a woman had a baby on one arm and was working at the stove with her free hand. Half-grown girls, apparently wearing nothing but an apron, ran very busily to and fro. In all the rooms the beds were still in use, occupied by people who were sick or still asleep, or by others stretched out in their clothes. At the flats where the door was shut K. knocked and asked whether a joiner by the name of Lanz lived there. Usually the door was opened by a woman who listened to his question, then turned to ask someone in the room who got up from the bed.

'This gentleman is asking whether a joiner called Lanz lives here.'

'A joiner called Lanz?' asked the man from the bed.

'Yes,' said K, although it was obvious that the Commission was not installed in that room and that consequently his inquiry there was at an end.

Many of them believed it was very important for K. to find the joiner Lanz; they thought for a long time and then remembered a joiner, but he turned out not to be called Lanz at all or to have some name only remotely resembling Lanz, or they asked their neighbours or accompanied K. to a door a long way away where they thought some such man lived, possibly as a sub-tenant, or where there might be someone who might know more about it than they did. In the end K. hardly needed to put any questions himself, but was towed through the various floors in this way. He regretted his plan, which had seemed so practical to him at first. Before he reached the fifth storey, he decided to abandon the search, said goodbye to a friendly young workman who wanted to take him on farther and went back down. But then he became exasperated with the pointlessness of the whole exercise, he went back up again and knocked at the first door on the fifth floor. The first thing he saw in the small room was a large clock on the wall which showed that it was already ten o'clock.

'Is there a joiner named Lanz living here?' he asked.

'Please come in,' said a young woman with flashing black eyes who was in the middle of washing children's clothes in a tub; she pointed with her dripping hand to the open door of the next room.

K. felt he was entering a large gathering. A throng of the most diverse kinds of people – no one took any notice of him as he came in – filled a medium-sized, two-windowed room which, just below the ceiling, had a gallery round it, also completely full so that the people there could not stand upright without hitting their heads and backs on the ceiling. K, who found it was too stuffy in there for him, came out again and said to the young woman who had probably misunderstood him:

'I was asking for a joiner, a man called Lanz . . .'

'That's right,' the woman said. 'Go inside, please.'

Perhaps K. would not have done what she said if she had not gone up to him, grasped the door-handle and said:

'I've got to shut the door after you, no one else is allowed in.'

'Very sensible,' K. said, 'but it's too full already.' However, he went inside again.

Between two men who were talking just by the door – one was stretching both hands out in front of him and making a gesture of counting out money, while the other was looking him sharply in the eye – a hand reached out towards K. It belonged to a small, red-cheeked young lad.

'Come on,' he said, 'come this way.'

K. allowed the young lad to lead him, for it turned out that in the midst of the swarming crowd a narrow path was left free, possibly to divide what seemed to be two parties. This idea was reinforced by the fact that in the first rows to right and left K.

hardly saw one face turned towards him; he could only see the backs of people who were addressing their words and gestures just to the members of their own party. Most of them were dressed in black, in their old Sunday best clothes with long coats hanging down loosely. If it had not been for these clothes K. would have taken the whole gathering for a local political meeting.

At the other end of the hall, to which K. was now conducted, stood a very low dais, also very crowded, and placed diagonally on it was a small table, behind which sat, close to the edge of the dais, a small fat man, breathing hard. Just at that moment he was talking amidst much laughter to another man, who was standing behind him with his legs crossed and leaning one elbow on the back of the chair. Every now and then he threw one arm into the air as if he was caricaturing somebody. The boy who was leading K. had some trouble in announcing his presence. Twice he tried, standing on tiptoe, to say something, without being noticed by the man above. Only when one of the people on the dais drew his attention to the youngster did the man turn to him and bend down to listen to his muttered report. Then he took out his watch and glanced quickly towards K.

'You should have been here an hour and five minutes ago,' he said.

K. tried to make some reply, but he did not have time, for scarcely had the man spoken when a widespread murmuring arose in the right-hand half of the hall.

'You should have been here an hour and five minutes ago,' the man now repeated in a louder tone and again glanced down quickly into the hall. Immediately the murmuring grew louder and, as the man said nothing more, took a long time to die away. It was now much quieter in the hall than when K. had come in. Only the people in the gallery still went on making their remarks. So far as one could make anything out up there in the semi-darkness, in the haze and dust, they seemed to be dressed more shabbily than those down below. Some had brought cushions with them which they put between their heads and the ceiling, so as not to hurt themselves. K. had decided to observe rather than speak, and so he did not bother to defend himself for allegedly being late and simply said:

'I may have come late, but I'm here now.'

There was a burst of applause at this, again from the right-hand half of the hall. These people are easy to win over, K. thought to to himself, and was slightly perturbed only by the silence in the left-hand half of the hall which lay just behind him and from which only quite isolated hand-claps had come. He tried to work out what he might say to win them all over at once or (if that was not possible) at least win the others over temporarily.

'Yes,' the man said, 'but I am no longer obliged to hear you now' – again came the murmur, but this time it was ambiguous, for the man, silencing the people with a wave of his hand, continued – 'however, I'll make an exception today and hear you. But there must be no repetition of this unpunctuality. And now step forward!'

Someone jumped down from the dais so that there was room for K, and he climbed up. He stood pressed close up against the table, and the throng of people behind him was so great that he had to force himself back against them to avoid pushing the Examining Magistrate's table and perhaps even the Examining Magistrate himself off the dais.

The Examining Magistrate, however, paid no attention to this but merely sat quite comfortably on his chair and, after saying a final word to the man behind him, reached for a small notebook, the only object on his table. It was a kind of school exercise-book, old and quite misshapen from much thumbing through.

'Well,' the Examining Magistrate said, looking through the notebook, then turning to K. as if stating a fact, 'you are a house-painter?'

'No,' said K, 'I am senior clerk in a large bank.' The right-hand party down below greeted this reply with a burst of laughter which sounded so genuine that K. could not help joining in as well. The people rested their hands on their knees and shook as if they had a severe attack of coughing. Even a few people in the gallery laughed too. The Examining Magistrate, who seemed to be powerless against the people down below, had become quite angry, he tried to take it out on those in the gallery, jumping up and threatening them, and his eyebrows, which had not been very conspicuous till now, jostled like vast black bushes above his eyes.

But the left-hand half of the room was still quiet, the people were standing there in rows with their faces turned towards the dais and were listening just as calmly to the words exchanged above as they did to the noise of the other party. They even tolerated it when some of their members sided with people from the other party. The left-hand group (who incidentally were fewer in number) might in actual fact have been quite as insignificant as the right-hand group, but their calm behaviour made them appear more important. When K. now began to speak he felt sure he was expressing their viewpoint.

'Your question, Mr Examining Magistrate, as to whether I am a house-painter – although you did not ask a question at all, you made a statement – typifies exactly the kind of proceedings that are being instituted against me. You may argue that they are not legal proceedings at all, and you would be so right, for in fact they are only legal proceedings if I recognize them as such. But for the moment I do recognize them, out of a kind of pity. One cannot adopt any attitude other than one of pity, if one is going to pay them any heed at all. I do not say there is anything disreputable about them, but I should like to offer you this epithet in the interests of your own self-knowledge.'

K. broke off and gazed down into the hall. He had spoken sharply, indeed more sharply than he had meant to, but still it was accurate. What he said might have merited applause here and there, but it was greeted by absolute silence. People were clearly waiting tensely for what was to follow, and perhaps the silence was the prelude to an outburst that would bring everything to an end. It was disconcerting that the door at the end of the hall now opened and the young washerwoman (who had probably finished her work) came in and, in spite of all the care she took, attracted the attention of some of the people. Only the Examining Magistrate's reaction gave K. undiluted pleasure, for the words seemed to have had an immediate effect on him. Until now he had listened standing up, for K's speech had surprised him when he rose to deal with the gallery. Now, during the pause, he sat down slowly as if he hoped it would not be noticed. He took up the notebook again, probably to regain his composure.

'That won't help you,' K. went on. 'Even your little notebook, Mr Examining Magistrate, confirms what I say.'

Satisfied now to hear only his own calm words in the alien assembly, K. even dared to take the notebook brusquely from the Examining Magistrate and hold it up with his fingertips by the middle page, as if in disgust, so that the closely written, smudgy, yellow-edged pages hung down on either side.

'These are the records of the Examining Magistrate,' he said, dropping the notebook on to the table. 'Go on, just carry on reading it if you like, Mr Examining Magistrate, I am really not frightened by your account-book, although I can't read it since I can only touch it with two fingers and would not soil my hands by picking it up.' It could only have been a sign of deep humiliation (or at least it was bound to be taken for this) that the Examining Magistrate reached for the notebook where it had fallen on the table, tried to rearrange it a little and began to read it again.

The faces of the people in the front row were fixed on K. so intently that he gazed down at them for a while. They were all elderly men, some of them with white beards. Were these people perhaps the crucial ones, able to influence the entire assembly, which now, even after the humbling of the Examining Magistrate, would not stir from the apathy into which it had sunk since K. finished speaking?

'What has happened to me—' K. went on, rather more quietly than before, repeatedly searching the faces of the people in the front row (this gave his speech a somewhat disjointed effect), 'What has happened to me is only an isolated instance and therefore not very important in itself, since I do not take it very seriously, but it is an indication of the kind of procedure being adopted towards many people. It is for these I am speaking – not for myself.'

Without meaning to, he had raised his voice. Somewhere somebody clapped with his hands held high and shouted, 'Bravo! Why not? Bravo! And bravo again!' Some of those in the front row were tugging at their beards, but no one turned round in response to the shouting. Even K. attributed no importance to it, but it encouraged him all the same. He now no longer felt it was at all necessary that everyone should applaud: it was enough if most of them began to think seriously about the matter and only one or two were won over by persuasion.

'I have no wish to shine as an orator,' K. said, acting on this idea, 'in fact I'm probably not even capable of it. The Examining Magistrate most likely speaks much better than I do, but then that is part of his job. All I want is the public discussion of a public grievance. Listen, about ten days ago I was arrested. The fact of the arrest I find ludicrous myself, but that's not the point right now. I was taken by surprise in bed early in the morning, perhaps orders had been given – at least this is quite possible according to what the Examining Magistrate has said – to arrest some house-painter or other who is no more guilty than I am, but they picked on me. The room next to mine was taken over by two uncouth warders. If I had been a dangerous gangster, no greater precautions could have been taken. Moreover, these warders were degenerate rascals, they chattered away nineteen to the dozen, they wanted to be bribed, they tried to cheat me out of my clothes and underwear on some pretext or other, and they asked for money supposedly to bring me some breakfast when they had quite unashamedly eaten my own breakfast right in front of my eyes. But this was not all. I was brought before the Inspector in a third room. This was the room belonging to a certain lady whom I very much respect, and I was forced to look on while this room (on my account, but not through any fault of mine) was in a way being contaminated by the presence of the Inspector and the warders. It was not easy to keep calm. But I did manage to do so and I asked the Inspector perfectly calmly – and if he were here, he would have to confirm this himself – to tell me why I had been arrested. But what reply did I receive from this Inspector whom I can still see before me now, sitting on the chair belonging to the aforementioned lady and looking the very personification of dull-witted arrogance? Gentlemen, in actual fact he made no answer at all, perhaps because he really did not know anything – he had simply arrested me and that was all that concerned him. But even that was not all. He also brought into that lady's room three junior clerks from my bank who spent their time handling and disarranging certain photographs that were this lady's property. Of course there was another reason for the presence of these clerks, they, together with my landlady and her maid, were supposed to spread the news of my arrest, damage my public reputation and, above all, undermine my position at the bank. None of this, of course, was the least bit successful and even my landlady, a quite simple person – I should like to mention her name here with the very greatest respect, it is Frau Grubach – well even Frau Grubach was sensible enough to see that an arrest of this kind is no more important than an attack by delinquent youths in the street. I repeat that the whole thing has caused me no more than some unpleasantness and passing irritation, but could it not have had more serious consequences too?'

When K. broke off here and glanced over at the silent Examining Magistrate, he thought he could see the latter giving a signal with his eyes to someone in the crowd. K. smiled and said:

'I see that Mr Examining Magistrate right next to me here has just given one of you a secret sign. So there are some among you who take your instructions from up here. I don't know whether the signal was supposed to produce hisses or applause, and now, by giving the show away prematurely, I know I have lost all chance of ever discovering the real meaning of that signal. But it's a matter of complete indifference to me, and I hereby publicly authorize the Examining Magistrate, instead of making secret signals to his paid agents down there, to issue his orders aloud in so many words, for instance by saying, "Now hiss!" or again, "Now clap!"'

Either from embarrassment or impatience the Examining Magistrate kept shifting his position on his chair. The man behind, with whom he had been talking earlier on, leaned over to him again, either to give him general encouragement or some particular advice. Down below, the people talked quietly but animatedly. The two parties, which before had seemed to hold such contrary opinions, mingled together, a few people pointed at K. and others pointed at the Examining Magistrate. The cloudy haze in the room was extremely oppressive, it even made it impossible to have a clear view of those standing a little distance away. It must have been especially annoying for those in the gallery, and, in order to gain a better idea of what was going on, they were forced, nervously glancing sideways at the Examining Magistrate as they did so, to ask questions in a low voice of those in the body of the meeting, who gave equally quiet answers from behind hands held in front of their mouths.

'I shall soon be finished,' K. said and (in the absence of a bell) struck the table with his fist. Startled by this, the Examining Magistrate and his counsellor instantly jerked their heads apart. 'I am quite detached from the whole business, so I can judge it calmly, and you (if you think this supposed tribunal is of any importance) can learn a lot to your advantage by listening to me. But I beg you to postpone till later any discussion among yourselves of what I'm saying, since I have no time now and I must shortly leave.'

Immediately there was silence, so great already was K's hold over the assembly. There were no longer any shouted interruptions as at the beginning, there was no longer even any applause, people seemed already convinced or well on the way to it.

'There is no doubt,' K. said very quietly, for he was enjoying the rapt attention of the whole assembly, and in this silence there arose a buzzing that was more stimulating than the most enthusiastic applause – 'There is no doubt that behind all the outward manifestations of this tribunal's authority, that is, in my case, behind my arrest and today's investigation, there exists a huge organization. An organization which not only employs corrupt warders, stupid inspectors and examining magistrates of whom the best that can be said is that they recognize their own limitations, but which also makes use of a judicial network of senior and even top-rank officials with a vast and indispensable retinue of servants, clerks, policemen and other auxiliaries – perhaps even hangmen, no, I am not afraid to use the word. And the significance of this great organization, gentlemen? It consists in securing the arrest of innocent persons and in instituting against them senseless proceedings that usually (as in my case) lead to nothing. When the whole organization is so pointless, how can the worst kinds of corruption amongst the officials be avoided? It is impossible – not even the highest judge could do anything about it. That is why the warders try to steal the clothes off the persons of the people they arrest, that is why inspectors burst into strange flats, that is why innocent people, instead of being given a proper hearing, are humiliated in front of whole gatherings. The warders talked of certain depots where the property of the prisoners is kept, but I should just like to have a glance at these depots where the hard-earned property of arrested people is left to rot, if it is not stolen by the thieving depot officials.'

K. was interrupted by a scream from the end of the hall; he shaded his eyes with his hand to be able to see what was going on, for the murky light made the haze whitish and it dazzled him. It was the washerwoman whom K. had spotted as a potential source of disturbance as soon as she came in. Whether or not it was her fault now, it was impossible to discover. All K. could see was that a man had pulled her into a corner by the door and was pressing himself up against her. Yet she was not the one screaming, it was the man who had opened his mouth wide and was staring up at the ceiling. A small circle had formed around them both, and the gallery members nearby seemed to be thrilled that the seriousness which K. had introduced into the proceedings was being dispelled in this way. K's first impulse was to run across at once, as he thought everyone would want to see order restored and at the very least have the couple turned out of the room, but the front rows stayed quite motionless in front of him, no one moved, and no one would let K. through. On the contrary, people tried to stop him, old men held up their arms to bar his way, and a hand (he had no time to turn round) grasped the back of his collar. K. was not really thinking about the couple any longer, for now he felt as if his liberty were being restricted, as if this were a serious attempt to arrest him, and he jumped recklessly down from the dais.

Now he was on an eye-level with the crowd. Had he not judged the people correctly? Had he overestimated the effect of his speech? Had people merely been putting on an act while he was speaking and, now he was coming to his final conclusions, were they getting tired of the charade? What faces the people around him had! Their little black eyes darted to and fro, their cheeks sagged like drunken men's, their long beards were stiff and sparse, and if one were to grasp them it would feel as though one were growing claws on one's hand rather than grasping beards. But under the beards – and this was the real discovery that K. made – badges gleamed on all the coat-collars, badges of various sizes and colours. They were all wearing these badges, as far as he could see. They all belonged together then, these allegedly opposing parties to right and left, and when he turned round suddenly, he saw the same badges on the collar of the Examining Magistrate who, with his hands in his lap, was staring calmly down.

'So I see, then,' shouted K, throwing his arms in the air, for the sudden realization had to be promulgated, 'you are all officials, you are in fact the corrupt group I was attacking, you pushed yourselves in here as spies and snoopers, you formed yourselves into imitation parties and some of you even applauded in order to test me, you wanted to find out how to lead an innocent man astray! Well, your time has not been wasted, I hope, for either you have had some amusement out of seeing that someone was expecting you to defend the innocent, or else – let me go on or I'll hit you,' K. shouted at a trembling old man who had pushed himself particularly close, 'or else you will really have learnt something. And I hope you enjoy your chosen occupation!'

He quickly picked up his hat which was lying on the edge of the table and amidst general silence, the silence of utter astonishment, he pushed his way through to the exit. The Examining Magistrate, however, seemed to have been even quicker than K, for he was already waiting for him by the door.

'One moment,' he said. K. paused, though he was looking not at the Examining Magistrate but at the door, the handle of which he had already grasped. 'I only wanted to point out to you,' the Examining Magistrate said, 'since you may not have realized it yet, that today you have thrown away all the advantage that a hearing affords an arrested man in every case.'

K. laughed, his eyes still fixed on the door. 'You scoundrels!' he shouted. 'You can keep all your hearings!' and he opened the door and hurried down the stairs. Behind him rose the hubbub of the meeting which had become animated again, for the audience seemed to have started discussing what had happened, the way students do.

Chapter Three

In the Empty Interrogation-Room – The Student –
The Offices of the Court

All through the following week K. waited each day for a fresh communication. He could not believe that his repudiation of all hearings had been taken literally and, when the expected communication had not come by Saturday evening, he assumed that he was tacitly expected to re-appear in the same house at the same time. So on Sunday he went there again, and this time he went straight up the stairs and along the passages. Some people who remembered him greeted him at their doors, but now he did not have to ask anyone the way and before long he came to the right door. As soon as he knocked it was opened and, without bothering to glance round at the woman he had already met, who remained standing by the door, he made to go straight into the next room.

'There's no session today,' the woman said.

'What do you mean there is no session?' he asked, disbelievingly. But the woman convinced him by opening the door of the next room. It really was empty and in its emptiness it looked even more wretched than on the previous Sunday. On the table, which still stood just as before on the dais, there lay a few books.

'Can I have a look at the books?' K. asked, not from any special curiosity, but simply in order not to have come all that way for nothing.

'No,' said the woman, shutting the door again, 'that's not allowed. The books belong to the Examining Magistrate.'

'Ah, I see,' K. said and nodded. 'The books must be law books, and this kind of judicial process requires that one should be ignorant as well as innocent when one is condemned.'

'Yes, that must be it,' said the woman, who had not quite understood him.

'Well, in that case I might as well go,' said K.

'Shall I give any message to the Examining Magistrate?' asked the woman.

'Do you know him?' K. asked.

'Of course I do. My husband is a Court usher.'

K. had not realized until now that the room, which a short time before had contained nothing but a wash-tub, was completely furnished as a living-room. The woman noticed his astonishment and said:

'Yes, we have free lodging here, but we have to clear everything out of the room on days when the Court is in session. My husband's job has quite a few disadvantages.'

'It's not the room that surprises me,' K. said and looked at her angrily, 'so much as the fact that you're married.'

'Perhaps you're referring to what happened in the last session when I caused a disturbance in the middle of your speech?' the woman asked.

'Of course I am,' said K. 'It's over now and almost forgotten, but at the time it made me absolutely furious. And now you say yourself that you are a married woman.'

'It wasn't to your disadvantage to have your speech interrupted. People certainly didn't think very much of it afterwards.'

'Perhaps not,' K. said, diverting the conversation from that topic, 'but that's no excuse for you.'

'It counts as an excuse with anyone who knows me. The man you saw embracing me then has been pestering me for ages. Most men may not find me very attractive, but he does. There's nothing I can do to stop it, even my husband has come to accept it now. If he wants to keep his job he's got to put up with it, for that man is a student and is expected to become very powerful eventually. He's always after me, he was here just now before you came.'

'It's all the same pattern,' said K, 'it doesn't surprise me.'

'You want to make things a bit better here, eh?' the woman asked slowly and cautiously, as if she were saying something dangerous both for her and for K. 'I guessed that from your speech, which I liked very much myself. Of course I only heard part of it, I missed the beginning, and during the last bit I was lying on the floor with the student. It's so horrible here,' she said after a pause and took K's hand. 'D'you think you'll manage to make things better?'

K. smiled and twisted his hand round a little in her soft fingers. 'It's not really my job,' he said, 'to "make things better here", as you put it, and if you said as much to the Examining Magistrate, for instance, he would either laugh at you or have you punished. As a matter of fact, I should certainly never have dreamt of interfering of my own free will, and I wouldn't have lost any sleep over the need to improve the legal machinery here. But since I'm supposed to have been arrested – I've actually been arrested, you know – I find myself obliged to intervene, and indeed I have to for my own good. But if at the same time I can also be helpful to you in some way, then I shall naturally be glad to do so. And not just from Christian charity either, but because you can help me too.'

'How could I do that?' the woman asked.

'Well, by showing me the books there on the table, for example.'

'But of course,' the woman cried and dragged him hurriedly after her. They were old, well-thumbed books, the cover on one was almost split down the middle and each half hung together only by threads.

'How dirty everything is in this place,' K. said, shaking his head, and the woman used her apron to wipe off at least the surface dust before K. reached for the books. K. opened the top one and found an obscene picture. A man and a woman were sitting naked on a sofa and the coarse intention of the artist was perfectly clear, but he had so little skill that nothing ultimately emerged from the picture except the all-too-solid figures of a man and a woman who were sitting so rigidly upright that they looked artificial and who, because of the bad perspective, could turn to face each other only with great difficulty. K. did not look at any other pages, but merely opened the second book at its frontispiece; it was a novel entitled *How Grete Was Tormented By Her Husband Hans.*

'So these are the law books that are studied here,' K. said, 'and these are the kind of men who are supposed to be judging me.'

'I'll help you,' said the woman. 'Will you let me?'

'Could you really do that without taking a risk yourself? You said just now that your husband is very much at the mercy of the senior officials.'

'Still, I'll help you all the same,' the woman said. 'Come, we must talk about it. Don't worry about the danger to me. I'm only frightened of danger when I want to be. Come on.' She pointed to the dais and asked him to sit on the step with her.

'You've got lovely dark eyes,' she said when they had sat down, looking up into K's face. 'People tell me I have lovely eyes too, but yours are much lovelier. I noticed them as soon as I saw you, the first time you came in here. It was because of you I came into the assembly-room later on, which is something I don't usually ever do and which in a way I'm not even really allowed to do.'

So that's all it is then, K. thought to himself, she's offering herself to me, she is just as corrupt as everyone else around here, she's had enough of the officials here (which is quite understandable) and so she greets any stranger, no matter who, with a compliment about his eyes. And K. stood up silently, as if he had spoken his thoughts aloud and thus had explained his attitude to the woman.

'I don't believe you can help me,' he said, 'for, to help me properly, you would have to know the senior officials well. But I'm sure you only know the lowest officials who come around here in hordes. You must know them very well and could get quite a lot out of them, I don't doubt that, but the very most that could be got out of them would have no effect at all on the final outcome of the case. But in the process you would have lost some friends. And I don't want that. Just carry on the relationship with these people you've had up till now, for in fact it seems to me that that relationship is essential to you. I say this with some regret, to return your compliment in some way, I must say I like you a lot too, especially when you gaze at me as sadly as you are doing now, though for you, at any rate, there is no reason to be sad. You belong to the group of people I've got to fight against, but in fact you fit into it very well, you even love this student, or at least if you don't love him, you prefer him to your husband. One could easily tell that from what you say.'

'No,' she cried out, remaining where she was and grasping at K's hand, which he did not withdraw quickly enough. 'You can't go away now, you mustn't go away with a wrong opinion of me! Could you really go now? Am I really so worthless that you won't even do me the favour of staying here a little while longer?'

'You misunderstand me,' K. said and he sat down. 'If it's really important to you that I stay, then I'll be glad to stay, I've got the time, after all I came here thinking there was going to be a session today. All I meant by what I said before was to ask you not to try and do anything about my case. But that needn't offend you if you consider that I place no importance at all on the result of the trial and that I shall only laugh at a verdict of guilty.

That's assuming the trial ever does come to any real conclusion, which I doubt very much. I think it's much more likely that proceedings have already been suspended or shortly will be – as a result of laziness or forgetfulness on the part of the officials, or perhaps even because they are frightened. Of course it's possible too that they may make a show of going on with the case, in the hope of getting a bigger bribe, but that will be completely futile for I can tell you now that I shan't bribe anyone. There is one favour you could do me, though, if you could tell the Examining Magistrate or anyone else who likes to pass important bits of information around that nothing, not even any of the numerous tricks they probably have up their sleeves, will ever induce me to offer a bribe under any circumstances. It would be completely pointless, you can tell them that quite plainly. But, in any case, they will perhaps have seen that already for themselves, and even if they haven't, I don't much care whether they find out about it now or not. It's only that it would save them some labour and, of course, spare me some unpleasantness – which I would gladly accept, though, if I knew it meant striking a blow at them. And I shall take care to see that it does. D'you really know the Examining Magistrate?'

'Of course,' said the woman. 'He was the first one I thought of when I offered to help you. I didn't know he was only a minor official, but since you say so, then it's probably true. Still, I believe the reports he passes on to his superiors must have some influence. And he writes so many of them. You say the officials are lazy, but certainly not all of them are, and especially not this Examining Magistrate, he does a great deal of writing. Last Sunday, for example, the session went right on till the evening. Everybody went home, but the Examining Magistrate stayed on in the hall, I had to bring him in a lamp and I only had a small kitchen lamp, but he was satisfied with that and straight away began to write. In the meantime my husband came home, for he was off duty that

Sunday and we went and fetched the furniture back and arranged our room again, and then some neighbours came round and we talked on by the light of a candle, to cut a long story short, we forgot all about the Examining Magistrate and went off to bed. Suddenly during the night – it must have been well on into the small hours – I woke up and found the Examining Magistrate standing by the bed and shading the lamp with his hand so that the light wouldn't fall on my husband. This was a quite unnecessary precaution, for my husband sleeps so soundly that even the light would not have woken him up. I was so frightened that I almost screamed out loud, but the Examining Magistrate was very nice, he told me to be careful and whispered that he had been writing till now, that he had come to return the lamp and that he would never forget the sight of me lying asleep. I'm only telling you all this to show you that the Examining Magistrate really does write a lot of reports, especially about your case, for your interrogation was certainly one of the chief items in that Sunday session. And, after all, such long reports can't really be completely unimportant. Besides, you can see from what happened that the Examining Magistrate fancies me and that, particularly in this first period – he must have only just begun to notice me – I can have a great influence over him. And now I have another proof, too, that he thinks a lot of me. Yesterday he sent along the student, who works with him and who he has a lot of confidence in, with a pair of silk stockings for me, supposedly as a present for cleaning out the hall for the session, but that is only an excuse, because that work is all part of my duty, and my husband gets paid for it anyway. They're beautiful stockings, look,' she said, stretching out her legs and pulling her skirts up to her knees and gazing at the stockings herself. 'Yes, they're lovely stockings, but too fine really and not suitable for me.'

Suddenly she broke off and laid her hand on K's, as if she wanted to reassure him, and whispered:

'Sh-sh . . . Berthold is watching us.'

K. slowly raised his eyes. A young man was standing in the doorway of the interrogation-room. He was short and slightly bow-legged, and had tried to lend himself dignity by growing a short, sparse, reddish beard in which he was constantly poking around with his fingers. K. watched him with interest, for this was the first student in the strange new legal system whom he had met, as it were, on human terms, a man, too, who would probably rise eventually to a high position in the bureaucracy. The student, on the other hand, seemed to be taking scarcely any notice of K. at all, he simply beckoned to the woman with one finger, which he removed from his beard for a moment, and went to the window. The woman bent towards K. and whispered:

'Don't be angry with me, I must specially ask you not to, and please don't think badly of me, I've just got to go to him now, and he's a disgusting man, just look at his bandy legs. But I'll come back straight away and then I'll go with you if you'll take me, I'll go wherever you want, and you can do whatever you like with me, I shall be glad to get away from here for as long as possible, and I only wish it could be for ever.'

She caressed K's hand a little longer, then jumped up and ran to the window. Involuntarily K. was still reaching out for her hand in the void. The woman really attracted him, and even after considering at length, he could think of no real reason why he should not surrender to this attraction. The fleeting objection that the woman would ensnare him for the Court was easily disposed of. In what way could she ensnare him? Wasn't he still free, so free that he could straight away crush the Court completely, at least in so far as it affected him? Could he not have confidence in himself even to that small extent? And her offer of help? It sounded genuine enough, and perhaps it was not entirely without value. And possibly there was no better revenge on the Examining Magistrate and his myrmidons than to entice this woman away from them and take her for himself. It might even happen then that one day the Examining Magistrate, after labouring arduously away at his mendacious reports about K, might come to the woman's bed in the middle of the night and find it empty. And empty precisely because she now belonged to K, because this woman, at the window, this voluptuous, supple, warm body in a dark dress made out of heavy, coarse material, belonged entirely to K, and to no one else.

Having dealt in this way with his scruples about the woman, he began to think that the hushed conversation at the window was lasting too long, so he rapped on the dais with his knuckles and then banged it with his fist. The student glanced briefly over the woman's shoulder towards K, but did not let himself be disturbed, indeed he even pressed up close to her and put his arms around her. She lowered her head right down as if she were listening to him attentively, he kissed her loudly on the throat as she was bending down without breaking off what he was saying. K. saw this as a confirmation of the tyranny which, as she had complained herself, the student exercised over her. K. stood up and walked up and down the room, glancing sideways at the student and pondering how he could get rid of him as quickly as possible, so he was not displeased when the student, clearly disturbed by K's walking around, which at times had even degenerated into a haphazard stamping, remarked:

'If you are impatient, you can go away. Indeed you could have gone away before – no one would have missed you. Yes, and what's more, you should have gone away as soon as I came in, in fact as quickly as you could.'

This remark might well have been an expression of the greatest possible anger, but it also had about it the haughtiness of the future legal official speaking to a defendant he did not like. K. remained standing quite close to him and said with a smile:

'I am impatient, that's quite true, but the easiest way to stop me being impatient is for you to leave us. However, if perhaps you have come here to study – I have heard that you are a student – then I will gladly make room for you and go away with the woman. Anyway, you will have to study a lot more before you become a judge. Of course I am not very familiar yet with your judicial system, but I assume that it by no means consists solely of rude speeches, which you are certainly already able to make with brazen efficiency.'

'He ought not to have been allowed to wander about so much at liberty,' the student said, as if he were trying to give the woman an explanation for K's insulting speech. 'It was a mistake. I said as much to the Examining Magistrate. He ought at least to have been confined to his room in the intervals between the hearings. Sometimes one simply can't understand the Examining Magistrate.'

'It's no use talking,' K. said and held out his hand to the woman. 'Come on.'

'Oh, I see,' said the student. 'No, no, you're not going to get her,' and with a strength one would not have thought him capable of, he lifted her with one arm and ran bent double to the door, gazing up at her tenderly. In doing so he was unmistakably demonstrating that he was somewhat in awe of K, although he was daring enough to irritate him further by caressing and squeezing the woman's arm with his free hand. K. ran along beside him for a step or two, ready to grab him and, if necessary, throttle him, but then the woman said:

'It's no good, the Examining Magistrate has sent for me. I can't go with you. This little monster—' and as she spoke she ran her hand over the student's face, 'this little monster won't let me go.'

'And you don't want to be rescued,' K. yelled out, putting his hand on the shoulder of the student, who snapped at it with his teeth.

'No!' shouted the woman and fended K. off with both hands. 'No, no, anything but that, what on earth are you thinking of! That would be the ruin of me. Leave him alone, please, leave him alone. After all, he is only carrying out the orders of the Examining Magistrate and taking me to him.'

'Then let him clear off, and you, I never want to see you again!' K. said, furious with disappointment, and he gave the student a shove in the back so that he staggered a bit but immediately leapt all the higher with his burden, out of sheer delight that he had not fallen over. K. walked after them slowly, he could see that this was the first indisputable defeat he had suffered at the hands of these people. Naturally this was no reason for anxiety. He had suffered the defeat only because he had sought a fight. As long as he stayed at home and led his usual life, he would be a thousand times superior to any of these people and could clear any of them out of his way with a kick. And he pictured to himself the most laughable scene he could think of, for instance, this pathetic student, this puffed-up infant, this knock-kneed beardie kneeling at Elsa's bedside and begging for mercy with folded hands. This picture pleased K. so much that he decided, if an opportunity ever arose, to take the student with him to Elsa some time.

Out of curiosity K. went to the door, he wanted to see where the woman was being taken, for surely the student would not carry her through the streets on his arm. But it turned out that they did not have nearly so far to go. Right opposite the flat a narrow wooden staircase led upwards, probably to the attic; there was a bend in the staircase so that one could not see where it ended. The student carried the woman up these stairs, though very slowly and with many groans, for he was weakened by the running he had done before. The woman waved down to K. and tried to indicate by shrugging her shoulders up and down that she was an innocent party to the abduction, but there was not much regret about the gesture. K. looked at her unemotionally, as if she

76

were a stranger, he did not want to betray either the fact that he was disappointed or even that the disappointment was one he could easily get over.

The pair had disappeared by now, but K. still stood in the doorway. He was forced to accept not merely that the woman had deceived him, but also that she had been lying when she said she was being taken to the Examining Magistrate, who would surely not be sitting up in the attic waiting for her. The wooden stairs explained nothing at all, however long one looked at them. But then K. saw a small notice near the stairs, and he went over and read what was written there in a childish and inexperienced hand:

'Court offices upstairs.'

Were the Court offices here then, in the attic of this block of flats? This was not an arrangement likely to inspire much respect, and it was reassuring for an accused person to think how little money must be available to this court if it had to establish its offices in a place where the tenants (who were themselves desperately poor) threw all their useless junk. Of course it was possible too that there was enough money but that the officials helped themselves to it first, before it could be used for the purposes of justice. Indeed, going by K's experiences up till now, that seemed very likely; in that case, though, such corruption of the Court was degrading for an accused person, yet basically more reassuring than the Court's outright poverty would have been. Now K. could also understand why at the first hearing they had been ashamed to invite the accused to the attic and had preferred to pester him in his own flat. What a difference there was between K's position and that of the judge, who sat here in this attic whilst K. himself had a big room at the bank with an ante-room and was able to look down through a huge window-pane on to the busy city square! Of course he had no extra income from bribes or embezzlement, and he could not order his assistant to carry a woman into the office in his arms. But K. was willing to forgo that, at least in this life.

K. was still standing in front of the notice when a man came up the stairs, looked through the open door into the living-room, from which the court-room could also be seen, and at length asked K. whether he had seen a woman there a short while before.

'You are the Court usher then, eh?' K. asked him.

'Yes,' said the man. 'Ah yes, you are the defendant K. I recognize you now. Glad to see you,' and he gave K. his hand, which was something K. had not expected at all.

'But there's no session fixed for today,' the usher then remarked, when K. said nothing.

'I know,' K. said and examined the mufti coat of the usher, whose sole official insignia seemed to consist of two gilt buttons, alongside a few ordinary ones, the gilt buttons having apparently been taken off an officer's old overcoat.

'I spoke to your wife a short while ago. She's not here any more. The student has taken her off to the Examining Magistrate.'

'You see?' the usher said. 'She is always being taken away from me. Although today is Sunday and I don't have to do any work, yet, to get me away from here, they send me out with some useless message. And even then they don't send me very far away, so I have some hope that if I really hurry I can perhaps get back in time. So I run as best I can, and when I get to the office I've been sent to, I shout out my message breathlessly through the crack in the door so that they can hardly understand it, then I run back again, but I find the student has been even quicker than me, of course he has a shorter way to go, he only has to run down the stairs from the attic. If I didn't depend on them so much I would have squashed that student on the wall ages ago. Here, next to the notice. I'm always dreaming of doing it. Here he is, just here, a little above the floor, firmly stuck on with his arms outstretched, his fingers spread out, his bandy legs writhing round and round, and splashes of blood all over the place. But so far it's only been a dream.'

'Isn't there any other way?' K. asked with a smile.

'I couldn't think of any,' said the usher. 'And now it's getting even worse. Before, he only took her to his own place, but now he has started taking her to the Examining Magistrate, and that's something, of course, I've been expecting for a long time.'

'But isn't it your wife's fault at all?' K. asked, and he was forced to control himself in asking this question, so strongly did he now feel pangs of jealousy.

'But of course,' the usher said. 'In fact she is actually the one that is mostly to blame. She's attached herself to him. As for him, he runs after all the women. In this place alone he has already been thrown out of five flats where he has sneaked in. My wife is certainly the best-looking in the whole building and I just seem to be the one who isn't allowed to defend himself.'

'Well if that's really how it is, there definitely isn't anything to be done,' K. said.

'But why not?' asked the usher. 'All you'd have to do one day when he's trying to touch my wife is give that student – he's a coward – a real thrashing and he wouldn't ever dare try it again. But I can't do it myself, and nobody else will do me the favour, for they are all frightened of his power. Only a man like you could do it.'

'How could I do it?' K. asked in astonishment.

'You're an accused man,' said the usher.

'Yes,' K. said. 'But then I have all the more reason to fear that, even if perhaps he can't influence the outcome of the trial, he can probably still influence the preliminary investigation.'

'Yes, of course,' said the usher, as if K's opinion were just as correct as his own. 'But generally we don't institute proceedings unless they look promising.'

'I don't agree with you,' K. said, 'but that won't prevent me from dealing with the student if the opportunity arises.'

'I would be very grateful to you,' the usher said with a certain formality, but he did not really seem to believe it possible that his supreme wish could be fulfilled.

'Perhaps other officials of yours, indeed perhaps all of them even, deserve the same treatment.'

'Yes, yes,' said the usher, as if they were discussing something self-evident. Then he looked at K. with a trusting glance, something which in spite of all his friendliness he had not done before, and added:

'People are always rebelling.' But the conversation seemed to be making him feel a little uncomfortable, for he broke it off by saying, 'Now I must report to the Court offices. Would you like to come with me?'

'But I've no business there,' K. said.

'You can have a look at the offices. No one will pay any attention to you.'

'Are they worth seeing then?' K. asked with some hesitation, although he had a great wish to go along there.

'Well, I thought it would interest you,' the usher said.

'Right,' K. said finally, 'I'll go with you,' and he ran up the stairs faster than the usher.

As he went in he almost fell over, for on the other side of the door there was another step. 'They don't have much thought for the public,' he said.

'They don't have much thought for anybody,' the usher said. 'Just look at the waiting-room here.'

It was a long passage, off which crudely carpentered doors led to the separate compartments of the attic. Although there was no direct access for daylight it was not completely dark, for at the side of the corridor, instead of uniform walls of planks, a number of the compartments had stark wooden lattice-work reaching up to the ceiling, through which some light penetrated and individual officials could be seen working at tables or even standing at the lattice-work and watching the people in the corridor through the holes. Probably because it was Sunday there were not many people in the corridor. Those who were there made a very unspectacular impression. They sat at almost regular distances from one another on the two rows of long wooden benches that were arranged on both sides of the corridor. Their clothes, without exception, looked shoddy, although most of the people there belonged to the upper classes, judging by the expression on their faces, by their manner, by the way their beards were trimmed and by many small details that were hard to define exactly. Since no clothes-hooks had been provided, they had placed their hats under the benches – probably they had followed one another's example. When the ones who were nearest the door saw K. and the usher, they got up to say hello, and when the others saw this they believed that they too should rise, so that as the two went by, all the people on both sides rose to their feet. They never stood completely erect, their backs were bent, their knees were buckled, in fact they stood like street beggars. K. waited for the usher, who was walking a little way behind him, and said:

'How humbled they must be.'

'Yes,' said the usher, 'they are all defendants, in fact all the people you see here are defendants.'

'Really!' K. said. 'Then they are all colleagues of mine.' And he turned to the nearest one, a tall, slim man whose hair was almost grey.

'What are you waiting here for?' K. asked him politely.

But the man was confused by being addressed unexpectedly, and his confusion was all the more painful to watch since he was clearly a man with some experience of the world who anywhere else was certainly master of his emotions and did not surrender lightly the superiority he had gained over others. But here he was unable to answer even such a simple question, and he looked at the others as if they ought to help him and as if he could not be expected to answer if he got no help from them. Then the usher came up and in order to reassure the man and cheer him up, said:

'This gentleman here is only asking you what you are waiting for. Come on, answer him.' The usher's voice which was probably familiar to him, had more effect.

'I'm waiting—' he began, and then stopped. Obviously he had chosen to begin this way with the intention of giving a quite precise answer to the question as it had been asked, but then he could not think how to go on. Some of those waiting had come nearer and surrounded the three of them, so the usher said to these:

'Move along now, move along. Don't block up the corridor.' They moved back a little, but did not return to where they had been sitting before. In the meantime the man who had been asked the question had pulled himself together and even gave a little smile as he answered:

'A month ago I offered some evidence concerning my case and I am now waiting for the result.'

'You seem to be taking a lot of trouble,' K. said.

'Yes,' said the man, 'it is my case, after all.'

'Not everyone thinks as you do,' K. said. 'For example, I am also a defendant, but as sure as I'm alive I swear that I have offered no evidence, nor have I done anything else of the kind. Do you believe it is necessary?'

'I don't really know,' said the man, once again completely undecided. He clearly believed that K. was pulling his leg, and so now he would probably have liked most of all – for fear of making another mistake – to repeat his previous answer in its entirety, but under K.'s impatient eye he merely said:

'I for my part have offered evidence.'

'Possibly you don't believe that I am an accused person?' K. asked him.

'Oh, but I do, certainly,' the man said and stepped a little to one side, although his answer betrayed not that he believed K. but that he was frightened.

'So you don't believe me?' K. asked and, provoked unconsciously by the man's humble manner, he grasped hold of him by the arm as if he intended to force him to believe. But he did not mean to cause the man any pain and only held him quite lightly, nevertheless the man screamed out loud, just as if K. had grasped him, not with two fingers but with a pair of red-hot tongs. This absurd shrieking eventually made K. lose patience with him. If they didn't believe him when he said he was a defendant, so much the better. Perhaps the man even took him for a judge. And now, as a parting gesture, he really took a firmer grip on the man, thrust him back on to the bench and walked on.

'Most of the defendants are sensitive like that,' the usher said. Behind them, almost all those who were waiting had now gathered round the man, who had already stopped screaming, and they seemed to be questioning him closely about the incident. Now K. was approached by a warder who was recognizable as such chiefly by the sabre he wore, the scabbard of which (at least judging by its colour) was made of aluminium. K. was astonished at this and even reached out to touch it. The warder, who had come because of the screaming, asked what had happened. The usher tried to reassure him with a few words, but the warder explained that he still had to check for himself, so he saluted and went on with rapid, but very short steps that were probably dictated by gout.

K. did not give much thought to him or to the people in the corridor, especially as about halfway up the corridor he saw a chance to turn right into an opening without a door. He asked the usher whether this was the right way in and the usher nodded, so K. did in fact turn in there. It annoyed him that he always had to walk one or two paces in front of the usher, since it might give the impression (at least here in this place) that he was being led away under arrest. Therefore, he would frequently stop to wait for the usher, but the latter immediately dropped back again. Finally, in order to put an end to his discomfort, K. said:

'Well, now that I have seen what it looks like here, I think I'll go.'

'But you haven't seen everything yet,' the usher said with absolute ingenuousness.

'I don't want to see everything,' said K, who was, moreover, feeling really tired by now. 'I want to go. How does one find the way out?'

'Surely you haven't got lost already?' the usher asked in astonishment. 'You go along here as far as the corner and turn right, then straight down the corridor until you reach the door.'

'Come with me,' K. said, 'and show me the way. I shall miss it, there are so many turnings here.'

'It's the only way you can go,' said the usher reproachfully. 'I can't go back again with you, I've got to deliver my message and I've already wasted a lot of time because of you.'

'Come with me!' K. repeated, more sharply now, as if he had at last caught the usher out in a lie.

'Don't yell like that,' the usher whispered, 'there are offices all round here. If you don't want to go back alone, then walk on a little bit with me or wait here until I've delivered my message and then I will gladly walk back with you again.'

'No, no,' K. said. 'I shan't wait. You've got to come with me now.'

K. had not as yet paid the slightest attention to the place where he now found himself, and it was only when one of the numerous wooden doors that were to be seen on all sides opened that he looked that way. A girl, who must have been summoned by K's loud voice, appeared and asked:

'What did you want, sir?' A long way behind her in the semi-darkness K. could also see a man approaching. K. looked at the usher. The latter had, after all, said that no one would bother K. and yet now there were already two of them there. It wouldn't take much before the officials began to pay attention to him and would demand some explanation of his presence. The only intelligible and acceptable explanation was that he was a defendant and that he wanted to find out the date of the next hearing, but this explanation was the very one that he did not wish to give, particularly as it was not even the truth, since his motive for coming there had merely been curiosity or (and this was even more impossible as an explanation) a desire to establish that the interior of this legal system was as repugnant as its exterior. And it now seemed that his assumption was right, so he did not wish to pry any further; what he had already seen was quite enough to put him off, and he was not in the right frame of mind just now to come face to face with a senior official, who might emerge from behind any door. He simply wanted to go away, either with the usher or by himself if he had to.

But his attitude of standing there dumbly was bound to attract notice, and in fact the girl and the usher were both looking at him as if some great transformation were likely to take place in him the very next minute and they did not want to miss seeing it. The man whom K. had noticed earlier in the distance was standing in the doorway. He was holding firmly on to the beam above the low door and was rocking lightly on his toes, like an impatient onlooker. But the girl was the first to realize that K's behaviour was due to a slight feeling of discomfort; she brought a chair and said:

'Would you like to sit down?'

K. sat down at once and, as if to get even better support, leaned his elbows on the arms of the chair.

'You feel a little giddy, don't you?' she asked him. He now saw her face close in front of him, it had that severe expression which the faces of many women have in the very flower of their youth.

'Don't worry about it,' she said. 'It's not at all unusual here, nearly everybody has an attack like that when they come here for the first time. It's the first time you've been here, isn't it? Well, then, it's nothing unusual, the sun burns down on to the roof timbers here, and the hot wood makes the air very close and heavy. So the place is not very suitable for offices, whatever other big advantages it may have. But as far as the air is concerned, on days when there is a great mass of clients coming and going (and that means practically every day) you can scarcely breathe. And when you further consider that lots of washing is hung out to dry here – one can't altogether forbid the tenants to do that – then it's not surprising that you feel a little sick. Though in the end one gets quite accustomed to the air. When you come back here for the second or third time, you will scarcely notice the oppressiveness of it. Do you feel better now?'

K. did not answer, he was too distressed at being put at the mercy of these people by his sudden weakness, and besides, now that he realized why he felt ill, he felt no better for it, on the contrary he felt a little worse. The girl noticed this at once and, to provide a bit of fresh air for K, she took a pole with a hook on it from where it was leaning against the wall and pushed open a dormer window which was situated just above K's head and led to the open air. But so much soot fell in that the girl had to close the window again at once and clean the soot from K's hands with her handkerchief, for K. was too weary to see to it himself. He would have liked to sit there quietly until he was strong enough to leave, yet the more they kept fussing him, the longer that was bound to take. But now the girl said:

'You can't stay here, we are getting in the way of people passing . . .' With his eyes K. asked whose way he was getting in. 'If you like, I'll take you to the sickroom. Help me, please,' she said to the man in the doorway who at once came closer. But

K. did not want to go to the sickroom, to be taken any further was precisely what he wanted to avoid, for the further he went the worse it was bound to become.

So he said, 'I can walk now,' but because he had been spoilt by sitting so comfortably, he found himself trembling when he stood up. And then he felt he could not stay on his feet.

'I can't do it,' he said, shaking his head, and he sat down again with a sigh. Then he thought of the usher, who could so easily lead him out in spite of everything, but he seemed to have disappeared long ago. K. peered between the girl and the man, who were both standing in front of him, but he could see no sign of the usher.

'I believe,' said the man, who incidentally was smartly dressed and was wearing a particularly impressive grey waistcoat which ended in two long, sharp points, 'that the gentleman's indisposition is due to the atmosphere in here, and, therefore, the best thing for him, in fact what he would like best, is for us to take him out of the Court offices altogether rather than take him to the sickroom.'

'That's right,' K. cried, so overjoyed that he almost interrupted what the man was saying. 'I shall certainly feel better straight away then, I am not really so weak at all, I only need a little support under my arms, I won't be much trouble to you, I haven't even got far to go either, just take me to the door, then I shall sit down for a little while on the stairs and I'll be well in no time, you see I'm not at all subject to attacks like this, I'm really quite surprised at myself. I'm an official too, myself, and I'm used to the air in offices, but here it seems really too bad, you say so yourselves. So would you mind going with me a little way? I feel giddy, you know, and it comes over me when I stand up by myself.' And he raised his shoulders to make it easier for the pair of them to grasp him under the arms.

The man did not take up the suggestion, but instead calmly kept his hands in his trouser pockets and laughed out loud.

'You see,' he said to the girl, 'I was dead right then. It's only in here that the gentleman doesn't feel well – not anywhere else.'

The girl smiled too, but she tapped the man lightly on the arm with her fingertips, as if he had indulged in too rude a joke at K's expense.

'But what can you be thinking?' the man said, still laughing. 'I really will take the gentleman out.'

'That's all right then,' the girl said, lowering her graceful head for a moment. 'Don't pay too much attention to that laugh of his,' she said to K. who was now staring dejectedly in front of him again and did not seem to be in need of any explanation. 'This gentleman— you don't mind if I introduce you, do you?' (the gentleman gave permission with a wave of his hand) 'Well, this gentleman is the Information Officer. He provides the clients who are waiting for their cases to come up with any information they need, and since our judicial system is not very well known to the public there are a large number of inquiries. He has an answer to every question. Some time, if you like, you can test him out. But that is not his only outstanding talent, he has another one, and that is for dressing smartly. We, that is the officials, reckoned that the Information Officer, who is always dealing with clients – indeed he has to see them first – ought to be smartly dressed in order to create a good impression right away. I am afraid the rest of us, as you can see at once by looking at me, all dress very badly and unfashionably. There is not much point, you see, in spending a lot on clothes, since we are almost always in the Court offices, indeed we even sleep here. But, as I say, we did think that the Information Officer should be beautifully dressed. But since the administration, who are rather peculiar in this respect, would not provide anything, we took a collection – even the clients contributed – and we bought him this beautiful suit and other ones as well. So now everything is set for him to make a good impression, but he goes and spoils it all again with this laugh of his and scares people off.'

'Yes, that's right,' the man said scornfully. 'But I don't understand, my dear girl, why you are telling this gentleman all our little secrets, or rather why you are foisting them on him, because he doesn't want to hear them at all. Just look at him sitting there, obviously wrapped up in his own affairs.'

K. did not feel like contradicting him – the girl's intentions might well have been good, perhaps she meant to take his mind off things or give him a chance to pull himself together, but she had chosen the wrong way to go about it.

'I had to explain to him why you were laughing,' the girl said, 'it was quite insulting, you know.'

'I think he would forgive even worse insults than that if I were to take him out of here eventually.'

K. said nothing, he did not even look up, he simply endured their discussing him as if he were an object, for in fact that was just what he wanted. But suddenly he felt the Information Officer's hand on one arm and the girl's on the other.

'Up you get then, you feeble man,' said the Information Officer.

'I am very grateful to you both,' K. said, pleasantly surprised. He got up slowly and himself guided their hands to the places where their support would be most useful to him.

'It must look,' the girl said softly in K's ear as they approached the corridor, 'as if I was especially anxious to show the Information Officer in a good light, but believe me, I only want to say what's true. He's not really hard-hearted. It's not his duty to take clients out when they feel ill, and yet he does it, as you can see. Perhaps we're not any of us hard-hearted, perhaps we would all like to help, but as officials of the Court we easily take on the appearance of being hard-hearted and of not wanting to help anybody. In fact it's a particular regret of mine.'

'Wouldn't you like to sit down here for a little while?' asked the Information Officer. They had already reached the passage and in fact were standing just in front of the defendant whom K. had spoken to earlier. K. felt almost ashamed now in the presence of this man, before whom he had previously stood so erect, while now he needed two people to hold him up; the Information Officer was balancing K's hat on the tips of his widely splayed fingers, K's hair was all untidy and straggling down on his perspiring brow. But the defendant did not seem to notice any of this, he just stood humbly before the Information Officer, who gazed away over his head, and simply tried to excuse his presence.

'I know,' he said, 'that the answer to my affidavits cannot be given today. But I came just the same, I thought I could wait here, it's Sunday today, I've got plenty of time and I'm not in anybody's way here.'

'There's no need for you to offer so many excuses,' said the Information Officer. 'You deserve credit for taking so much trouble, it's true you are taking up a little space unnecessarily, but all the same, provided I don't find it a nuisance, I shan't stop you from following closely the course of your affairs. When one has seen people shamefully neglecting their duty, one learns to have patience with people like you. Sit down.'

'How well he knows how to talk to the clients,' whispered the girl. K. nodded, but immediately started up in alarm when the Information Officer repeated his question, 'Don't you want to sit down here?'

'No,' K. said, 'I don't want to have a rest.'

He had said that with the utmost determination, but in reality he would have liked very much to sit down. It was like being seasick. He felt he was on a ship in a rough sea. It seemed to him as if the water were dashing against the wooden walls, as if a roar were sounding from the end of the passage just like breaking waves, as if the passage were rocking at a steep angle, and the clients waiting on either side were being raised and lowered. That made the calmness of the girl and the man who were guiding him all the more difficult to understand. He was at their mercy, if they let go of him he would fall like a log. Sharp glances flashed to and fro between their little eyes, K. could feel their regular paces, but did not fall in with them, for he was almost being carried along step by step.

At last he realized that they were speaking to him, but he could not understand them, he could only hear the noise which filled everything and through which an insistent high note like a siren seemed to sound.

'Louder,' he whispered with his head bent, and he felt ashamed for he knew that they had spoken quite loud enough, even if he could understand nothing. Then at last, as if the wall in front of him had been split asunder, a draught of fresh air blew towards him and he heard someone say nearby:

'First he wants to go, and then when you tell him a hundred times that this is the exit here, he won't move.'

K. now realized that he was standing in front of the door which led outside and which the girl had opened for him. He felt as if suddenly all his strength had come back, and in order to get a foretaste of freedom he at once set foot on a step of the staircase, and from there he said goodbye to his guides, who bent down towards him.

'Many thanks,' he repeated and pressed their hands over and over again, breaking off only when he thought he noticed that they were feeling very ill in the comparatively fresh air that blew from the stairway, so used were they to the atmosphere of the Court offices. They were almost incapable of answering him, and the girl would perhaps have fallen if K. had not shut the door again extremely quickly. Then K. stood still for a moment, with the help of a pocket mirror he straightened his hair, he picked up his hat which was lying on the landing (the Information Officer must have thrown it there) and then ran down the stairs so energetically and with such long leaps that he was almost frightened by his sudden change of mood. His normally quite robust constitution had left him totally unprepared for such surprises. Was his body perhaps planning a rebellion and preparing a new trial for him, now that he had endured the old one with so little trouble? He did not altogether reject the idea of going to a doctor at the first opportunity, but at any rate – and here he was able to counsel himself – he would make better use of his Sunday mornings in future.

Chapter Four

Fräulein Bürstner's Friend

During the next few days K. did not get a chance to exchange even a few words with Fräulein Bürstner. He tried in every possible way to approach her, but she always managed to avoid him. He came straight home from the office, stayed in his room without turning on the light, sat on his sofa and did nothing else except watch the hall. If, for instance, the servant-girl went past and shut the door, because his room seemed to be empty, he would get up after a while and open it again. In the mornings he arose an hour earlier than usual so that perhaps he might meet Fräulein Bürstner alone when she was going to the office.

But none of these attempts met with any success. Then he wrote to her, both at her office and at her flat, and tried once again in the letters to justify his behaviour. He offered to make any kind of reparation he could, promising never to overstep the limits she might set him, and only asked her to give him the opportunity of speaking to her on some occasion. In particular, he said he could not arrange anything with Frau Grubach until he had first talked it over with her, and finally he told her that on the following Sunday he would stay in his room the entire day, waiting for some sign from her which would hold out a prospect of his request being answered, or which would at least explain why the request could not be met, even though he had promised to bow to her wishes in everything. The letters were not returned, but neither did he receive any answer to them.

However, Sunday did bring a sign which was sufficiently clear in its meaning. Very early in the morning K. noticed through the keyhole that in the hallway there was an unusual amount of movement, which was soon explained. A teacher of French – she was in fact a German girl by the name of Montag, a frail, pallid girl who limped a little – who had had her own room up to now, was moving into Fräulein Bürstner's room. For hours she could be seen shuffling to and fro through the hallway. Repeatedly some piece of underwear or a cloth or a book was forgotten and a special journey had to be made to fetch it and carry it across to the new room.

When Frau Grubach brought K. his breakfast – since the time when she had made K. so angry, she did not allow the maid to perform even the smallest service – K. could not help addressing her for the first time in five days.

'What's all that noise in the hall today, then?' he asked as he poured out his coffee. 'Can't it be stopped? Do the rooms have to be tidied up on a Sunday?'

Although K. did not look up at Frau Grubach, he noticed that she breathed out deeply as if with relief. Even these severe questions of K's she took as a sign of his forgiveness or of his readiness to forgive.

'There's no tidying up going on, Herr K,' she said. 'It's only that Fräulein Montag is moving in with Fräulein Bürstner, and she is shifting her things over.' She said nothing more, but waited to see how K. would take it and whether he would permit her to go on speaking. But K. decided to test her, he thoughtfully stirred his coffee with the spoon and said nothing. Then he looked up at her and said:

'Have you abandoned your previous suspicions of Fräulein Bürstner?'

'Herr K!' cried Frau Grubach, who had been waiting for just this question, and she held out her folded hands towards K. 'The other day you took a casual remark of mine too seriously. Nothing could have been further from my mind than wanting to hurt you or anyone else. I mean you've known me long enough, Herr K, to be quite certain of that. You've no idea how I've suffered during the last few days! Me, slander my lodgers! And you, Herr K, you believed it! You said I should give you notice! Give you notice!' Her last outburst was already stifled by her tears, she lifted her apron to her face and sobbed out loud.

'Don't cry, Frau Grubach,' K. said and gazed out of the window; he was thinking only about Fräulein Bürstner and about the fact that she had taken a strange girl into her room. 'Don't cry now,' he said again, turning back into the room and finding Frau Grubach still crying. 'I didn't mean anything very serious myself at the time. There was just a little bit of misunderstanding on both sides. Even with old friends that can sometimes happen.'

Frau Grubach moved the apron away from her eyes to see whether K. was really appeased.

'Come on, that's what happened,' K. said, and since the Captain – to judge from Frau Grubach's manner – had not revealed anything, he then ventured to add, 'Do you really think that I could fall out with you on account of a strange girl?'

'Yes, that's just the thing, Herr K,' Frau Grubach said. It was her misfortune that, as soon as she felt a little more relaxed, she went on at once to say something maladroit. 'I kept on asking myself: Why should Herr K. be so keen to defend Fräulein Bürstner? Why does he quarrel with me on her account, even though he knows that a single angry word from him will stop me sleeping? After all, I never said anything about the Fräulein except what I've seen with my own eyes.'

K. made no reply to this, he ought to have driven her out of the room as soon as he heard the first word, but he didn't want to do that. He contented himself with drinking his coffee and making Frau Grubach feel that her presence was superfluous. Outside the dragging step of Fräulein Montag could be heard once more passing diagonally across the hall.

'Do you hear that?' K. asked and pointed towards the door.

'Yes,' Frau Grubach said with a sigh. 'I tried to help her and even suggested the maid might help her, but she has her own ideas, she wants to move everything herself. I'm quite surprised at Fräulein Bürstner. It's often been a nuisance to me to have Fräulein Montag as a lodger, but now Fräulein Bürstner actually goes and takes her into her room.'

'You needn't worry about that at all,' K. said, crushing the last of the sugar in his cup. 'Does it do you any harm in any way?'

'No,' Frau Grubach said. 'In actual fact, I quite welcome it, it means that I get an extra room free and can put my nephew, the Captain, in there. I've been worried for a long time that you might be disturbed by him, especially the last few days when I had to let him occupy the living-room next door. He is not very considerate.'

'What an idea!' K. said and rose to his feet. 'There's no question of that. You certainly seem to think me over-sensitive, just because I can't put up with these trips Fräulein Montag is making – there, now she's coming back again.'

Frau Grubach was feeling completely helpless:

'Shall I tell her, Herr K, to put off the rest of the moving? If you want me to, I'll do it straight away.'

'But she's got to move in with Fräulein Bürstner!'

'Yes,' Frau Grubach said, not quite understanding what K. meant.

'Well then,' K. said, 'in that case she's got to carry her things over.'

Frau Grubach just nodded. This dumb helplessness, which had all the appearance of defiance, irritated K. even more. He began to walk about the room between the window and the door, pacing to and fro, thus making it impossible for Frau Grubach to leave, which otherwise she probably would have done.

K. just happened to have got as far as the door once again, when there was a knock. It was the maid; she told him that Fräulein Montag would be glad to have a few words with him, and so asked him to come to the dining-room where she was waiting for him. K. listened thoughtfully to the maid, then he turned with an almost scornful look to the startled Frau Grubach. This look seemed to say that K. had long been expecting this invitation from Fräulein Montag and that, moreover, it was thoroughly consistent with the general disturbance that he was having to put up with, this Sunday morning, from Frau Grubach's lodgers. He sent the maid back to say that he would come at once and then went to his wardrobe to change his coat, and when Frau Grubach began moaning quietly about the troublesome lodger, he made no reply except to ask her to take away the breakfast things.

'But you've hardly touched a thing,' said Frau Grubach.

'Oh, do take it away!' K. shouted. It seemed to him as if, in some way, there was the taste of Fräulein Montag mixed up with the food, making it repugnant.

As he passed through the hall, he looked towards the closed door of Fräulein Bürstner's room. But he had not been invited to go in there, only to the dining-room, the door of which he snatched open without knocking.

It was a very long, narrow room with a single window. There was only enough room in it to place two cabinets diagonally in the corners on the side where the door was, and the rest of the space was completely taken up by the long dining-table which began near the door and reached almost as far as the big window, which as a result was almost inaccessible. The table was already laid, with many places in fact, for on a Sunday almost all the lodgers had their lunch there.

When K. went in, Fräulein Montag came over from the window along one side of the table towards K. They greeted each other in silence. Then Fräulein Montag said, as usual holding her head extremely erect:

'I don't know whether you know me.'

K. looked at her with narrowed eyes. 'Certainly I do,' he said. 'You've been living here at Frau Grubach's for quite a long time.'

'But you're not very interested, I think, in what goes on in the boarding-house,' said Fräulein Montag.

'No,' said K.

'Wouldn't you like to sit down?' she said.

In silence they each brought forward a chair at the extreme end of the table and sat down opposite one another. But Fräulein Montag immediately stood up again, as she had left her handbag lying on the window-sill and now went to fetch it. She shuffled across the length of the room. When she came back, lightly swinging the handbag, she said:

'I only wanted to have a few words with you, on behalf of my friend. She wanted to come herself, but she does not feel very well today. Perhaps, she says, you would be kind enough to excuse her and listen to me instead. She couldn't have told you anything different from what I shall tell you. On the contrary, I think I shall be able to tell you even more since I am comparatively un-involved. Don't you think so too?'

'What is there to say?' replied K, who was getting tired of seeing Fräulein Montag's eyes permanently fixed on his lips. It was her way of arrogating to herself power over anything he might want to say.

'Fräulein Bürstner obviously does not want to grant me the personal interview I asked her for.'

'That is so,' Fräulein Montag said. 'Or rather it is not so at all, you are putting it surprisingly strongly. Generally speaking, surely, one neither grants interviews nor does one do the opposite. But it may happen that one considers interviews superfluous, and that is the case here. Now, in view of your remark, I see I am at liberty to speak openly. You have asked my friend, either in writing or by word of mouth, for a talk. But now my friend knows, at least so I must assume, what this talk will be about, and consequently she is convinced, for reasons I am unaware of, that it would not be of any use to anyone if this talk did in fact take place. Besides, she didn't tell me about it until yesterday, and then only just in passing, and she said too that even you yourself cannot in any case be placing very much importance on the interview, since, she said, you could only have hit upon such an idea by accident and, she said, you yourself would soon see, without any specific explanation, the pointlessness of the whole thing, if not now, then before very long. I replied that this might be so, but thought that, to clarify the matter completely, it would be advisable to give you a definite answer. I volunteered to per- form this task, and after some hesitation my friend gave in and agreed. I hope that I have also acted in your interest, however, for even the slightest uncertainty in the most insignificant matter is always upsetting, and if, as in this case, that uncertainty can easily be removed, the sooner it's done the better.'

'I'm grateful to you,' K. said at once; he got to his feet slowly and looked at Fräulein Montag, then across the table, then out of the window – the house opposite was bathed in sunlight – and finally he went to the door. Fräulein Montag followed him for a few steps, as if she did not altogether trust him. But in front of the door they were both obliged to move back, for it opened, and Captain Lanz came in. It was the first time that K. had seen him close to. He was a tall man of about forty with a sunburnt, fleshy face. He made a slight bow which was also meant for K, then went up to Fräulein Montag and kissed her hand respectfully. His movements were very deft. His politeness towards Fräulein Montag made a striking contrast with the treatment she had received from K. Still, Fräulein Montag did not seem to be angry with K, she would even have liked, or so K. thought he observed, to introduce him to the Captain. But K. did not wish to be introduced, he would not have been able to be at all friendly either to the Captain or to Fräulein Montag, the hand-kissing had, in his eyes, united them in a conspiracy which, whilst feigning complete innocuousness and disinterestedness, was trying to keep him from Fräulein Bürstner. But K. thought he detected more than this, he realized too that Fräulein Montag had chosen an effective, if admittedly a double-edged, method. She was exaggerating the importance of the relationship between Fräulein Bürstner and K, and above all she was exaggerating the importance of the interview he had requested, and at the same time she was trying to make it look as if it was K. who was exaggerating everything. She was deluding herself, K. had no wish to exaggerate anything, he knew that Fräulein Bürstner was only a little typist who would not be able to resist him for long. Here he was deliberately and completely leaving out of account what he had heard from Frau Grubach about Fräulein Bürstner. He was considering all this as he left the room, hardly bothering to acknowledge the others as he did so. He meant to go straight to his own room, but a snigger from Fräulein Montag which he heard coming from the dining-room behind him gave him the idea that he could perhaps spring a surprise on the pair of them – the Captain and Fräulein Montag. He looked around and listened to see if he was likely to be interrupted by anyone coming from one of the nearby rooms, but it was quiet everywhere – only the conversation in the dining-room could be hard and the voice of Frau Grubach from the passage leading to the kitchen. It seemed a good opportunity, so K. went to the door of Fräulein Bürstner's room and knocked softly. When nothing stirred he knocked again, but there was still no reply. Was she asleep? Or was she really not well? Or was she only pretending not to be in because she suspected that it would only be K. who was knocking so quietly? K. assumed that she was pretending not to be there and he knocked louder and, eventually, as the knocking produced no result, he cautiously opened the door – not without feeling he was doing something which was wrong and futile into the bargain.

There was no one in the room. Moreover, it bore hardly any resemblance to the room K. had seen before. Now there were two beds placed one behind the other by the wall, three chairs near the door were piled high with dresses and underwear, and a cupboard was standing open. Fräulein Bürstner had probably gone out whilst Fräulein Montag had been haranguing K. in the dining-room. K. was not very much put out by this, he had scarcely expected that Fräulein Bürstner would be caught so easily, he had made the attempt almost solely out of spite against Fräulein Montag. But it was all the more distressing for him that, as he closed the door again, he saw Fräulein Montag and the Captain talking in the doorway of the dining-room. Perhaps they had been standing there ever since K. had opened the door. They gave no sign that they might have been watching, they were talking quietly and only following K's movements with the absent-minded air of people who look around while immersed in a conversation. But their glances weighed heavily on K, and, keeping close to the wall, he hastened to his room.

Chapter Five

The Flogger

An evening or two later, K. was passing along the corridor that lay between his office and the main stairway – on this particular occasion he was almost the last to leave for home, only two assistants in the dispatch department were still working in the small patch of light thrown by an incandescent lamp – when he heard moaning coming from behind a door which (though he had never seen the room himself) he had always supposed led to a lumber-room. He stopped in astonishment and listened a moment to make sure he had not been mistaken. It was quiet for a while, then the sound of moaning began again. At first he wanted to call one of the assistants, perhaps he might need a witness, but then he was seized by such invincible curiosity that he virtually wrenched the door open. As he had rightly supposed, it was a lumber-room. All kinds of useless old printed matter lay about inside, as well as empty earthenware ink-bottles thrown on the floor. In the room itself three men were standing, bent over in the low, confined space. A candle fixed on a shelf gave them some light.

'What are you doing here?' K. asked, the words tumbling out of him in his excitement, but he did not speak loudly. One of the men, who clearly dominated the other two and first caught K's attention, was encased in a kind of dark leather garment, which left his throat naked down to his breast and the whole length of his arms bare. He did not answer. But the other two shouted:

'Sir! We're going to be flogged because you complained about us to the Examining Magistrate!'

It was only now that K. realized these were actually the two warders Franz and Willem, and that the third man was holding a birch with which to flog them.

'Now,' K. said, staring at them, 'I did not make any complaint, I only said what happened in my rooms. And, anyway, you certainly did not behave impeccably.'

'But, sir,' said Willem, while Franz was clearly trying to hide behind him for protection from the third man, 'if you only knew how badly we're paid, you wouldn't judge us so harshly. I have a family to feed, and Franz here wants to get married, we try to earn more, as best we can, but it can't be done simply by working, even if one works one's hardest. I was tempted by your fine underwear – of course the warders are forbidden to do things like that, it was wrong, but by tradition the underwear belongs to the warders, it's always been that way, you can take my word for it. It's understandable, too, for what use can things like that be to someone who is unlucky enough to be arrested? But then if he should talk about it openly, punishment's sure to follow.'

'I had no idea of all this, and I never asked for you to be punished. I was only concerned about the principle of the thing.'

'Franz,' said Willem, turning to the other warder, 'didn't I tell you that this gentleman never asked for us to be punished? Now you see he did not even know that we were going to be punished.'

'Don't be taken in by such talk,' the third man said to K. 'The punishment is as just as it is unavoidable.'

'Don't listen to him,' Willem said, and broke off only to raise his hand, which had received a sharp stroke from the birch, quickly to his mouth. 'The only reason we are being punished is because you made an accusation against us. Otherwise nothing would have happened to us, even if they had found out what we had done. Can that be called justice? The two of us, especially me, have done our job well as warders over a long period of time –

you yourself must admit that, from the point of view of the authorities, we kept a good watch on you. We had every prospect of promotion in our job and we were certain soon to be made floggers like this bloke, who has simply had the good luck not to be denounced by anyone, for a denunciation like that is really very unusual. But now, sir, everything is lost, our whole career is finished, we'll have to do much more menial tasks than keeping watch, and what's more we'll be given this terribly painful flogging.'

'Can the birch really be as painful as all that?' K. asked, and felt the birch which the Flogger was waving in front of him.

'We shall have to strip completely naked,' said Willem.

'Ah, I see,' K. said and looked closely at the Flogger, who was burnt quite brown like a sailor and had a savage, healthy face. 'Is there no chance of saving these two a flogging?' he asked him.

'No,' said the Flogger and, smiling, shook his head. 'Get undressed!' he ordered the warders. And to K. he said:

'You mustn't believe everything they say. Being afraid of the flogging has made them a little weak-minded. What this one here, for example,' he pointed at Willem, 'was telling you about his possible future career is completely ridiculous. Look how fat he is – the first few strokes of the birch will simply be lost in that fat. Do you know how he got so fat? He's in the habit of eating the breakfasts of all those he arrests. Didn't he eat your breakfast too? I told you. But no man with a belly like that can possibly ever become a flogger, it's completely out of the question.'

'There are floggers just like me,' Willem maintained, as he loosened the belt of his trousers.

'No,' said the Flogger and gave him a stroke across the neck with the birch, so that he gave a convulsive jerk. 'You shouldn't be listening, you ought to be undressing.'

'I would reward you well if you let them go,' K. said and, without looking at the Flogger again – such transactions are best conducted on both sides with averted gaze – took out his wallet.

'You obviously want to denounce me too, then,' said the Flogger, 'and even get me a flogging as well. No, no.'

'Be reasonable,' K. said. 'If I had wanted these two to be punished, would I be trying to buy them off now? I could simply close the door again. I could refuse to see or hear anything else and just go home. But I'm not doing that; on the contrary, it's my sincere wish to get them set free. If I had imagined that they would be punished or even that they could be punished, I would never have mentioned their names. In fact I consider them to be absolutely blameless. It is the organization that's to blame. It is the high officials who are to blame.'

'That's right,' shouted the warders and immediately got a stroke across their backs, which were already bare.

'If you were birching one of the senior judges,' K. said, and as he spoke he pushed down the birch which was already being raised again, 'I assure you I would not hinder you from laying on, on the contrary, I would give you money so that you could build yourself up for the good work.'

'I can quite believe what you say,' the Flogger said, 'but I'm not going to allow myself to be bribed. It's my job to flog people, and that is what I am going to do.'

The warder Franz, who perhaps expecting that K's intervention would lead to a favourable outcome, had been fairly taciturn until then, came to the door dressed only in his trousers, fell to his knees and, hanging on to K's arm, whispered:

'If you can't manage to get us both off, then try at least to get me freed. Willem is older than me and less sensitive in every way, and besides he's already had a light flogging, a few years ago, but I am not disgraced yet, and it was only through Willem that I've been brought to this kind of thing, for he's my teacher for better or worse. Downstairs, outside the bank, my poor fiancée is waiting to see how it's all going to end. I feel so miserable and ashamed.'

He used K's coat to dry his face, which was streaming with tears.

'I'm not waiting any longer,' said the Flogger, grasping the birch with both hands and hitting out at Franz, while Willem cowered in a corner and secretly watched without daring to turn his head. Then came the scream from Franz, continuous and unchanging, it did not sound like the scream of a human being, but seemed to come from a tormented instrument, the whole corridor echoed with it, the whole building must have heard it.

'Don't scream,' K. shouted, he could not stop himself, and as he gazed tensely in the direction from which the assistants were sure to come, he gave Franz a push, not hard, but hard enough to make the unconscious man fall over and scrabble convulsively with his hands on the floor. But he did not escape the blows, the birch found him even on the ground. As he writhed about beneath it, its tip swung regularly up and down. And already one of the assistants appeared in the distance, followed by the other a few steps behind. K. had quickly flung the door to, had then gone to one of the windows which looked out on to the courtyard and opened it. The screaming had completely stopped. To prevent the assistants from coming nearer, he shouted:

'It's me!'

'Good evening, sir,' they shouted back. 'Has anything happened?'

'No, no,' K. replied. 'It was only a dog howling in the yard.' When the assistants still did not move, he added:

'You can get on with your work.'

In order not to have to get drawn into conversation with them, he leant out of the window. When he looked into the corridor a few moments later, they had already gone away. But K. remained at the window, he did not dare go into the lumber-room and he didn't want to go home either. The courtyard which he was looking down into was a small square one with office rooms all round it, where all the windows were already dark and only the top ones were catching the reflection of the moon. K. strained his eyes desperately in an attempt to peer into one dark corner of the courtyard where some handcarts stood all jumbled together. It distressed him that he had not succeeded in stopping the flogging, but it was not his fault that he had failed. If only Franz had not screamed – certainly it must have hurt terribly, but at a crucial moment like that one has to control oneself – if Franz had not screamed, K. would have found, or at least he most likely would have found some other means of persuading the Flogger.

If all the most subordinate officials were riff-raff, why should, of all people, the Flogger, who had the most inhuman job, be any different? Moreover, K. had noted very clearly how his eyes had lit up at the sight of the banknote, it was obvious he had only gone on seriously with the flogging to raise the amount of the bribe a little. And K. would not have been parsimonious, it really was a matter of importance to him to free the warders. Now that he had begun to fight against this corrupt legal system, it was self-evident that he should intervene in this matter too. But from the moment when Franz began to scream, it was naturally all over. K. could not allow the assistants, and perhaps all sorts of other people too, to come and surprise him negotiating with that particular gang in the lumber-room. Nobody could really expect K. to make such a sacrifice. If he had thought of doing so, it would almost have been easier for him to strip off his clothes and offer himself to the Flogger as a substitute for the warders. But the Flogger would certainly not have accepted him as a replacement, since by doing so he would have gained no advantage, and yet he would have failed seriously in his duty and, in all probability, have failed in it doubly, since K, as long as he was engaged in legal proceedings, must surely be secure against violation by employees of the Court. Admittedly, it was possible that particular regulations might apply here. In any case, K. had

had no alternative but to slam the door, although by doing this he had not, even now, eliminated all danger to himself. The fact that at the end he had given Franz a push was regrettable and only to be excused by his flustered state.

In the distance he could hear the steps of the assistants. In order not to attract their attention he closed the window and went towards the main staircase. At the door of the lumber-room he stopped for a moment to listen. All was quiet. The man might have flogged the warders to death, they had been delivered up completely into his power. K. had already stretched out his hand towards the door-handle, but then he drew it back again. He could be of no further help to anyone, and the assistants would be sure to come at once. He vowed to himself, however, that he would bring the matter up for discussion again and do every-thing in his power to see that the ones really to blame, the senior officials (not even one of whom had as yet dared to reveal himself to K.), were suitably punished. As he went down the steps outside the bank he carefully observed all the passers-by, but even in the distance there was no young woman to be seen who could have been waiting for anyone. So Franz's remark that his fiancée was waiting for him turned out to be a lie, which was certainly excusable, intended, as it was, merely to arouse greater sympathy.

Even the next day K. could not get the warders out of his mind. He could not concentrate on his work, and in order to finish it had to stay on a little longer in the office than he had done the day before. On his way home, as he came past the lumber-room again, he opened the door as if out of habit. What he saw, instead of the darkness he had been expecting, destroyed his self-possession completely. Everything was exactly the same, just as he had found it the evening before when he opened the door. The old files and ink-bottles just inside the door, the Flogger with his birch, the warders still completely undressed, the candle on the shelf, and the warders immediately began to complain and shout:

'Sir, sir!'

K. at once slammed the door and beat on it with his fists, as if that would make it shut more tightly. Almost in tears he ran to the assistants, who were working quietly at the copying-machines and, in astonishment, paused in their work.

'It's time you cleared out that lumber-room!' he shouted. 'We're absolutely smothered in filth.'

The assistants said they would do it the next day and K. nodded. At this late hour in the evening he could not force them to do it immediately, as he had originally intended. He sat down a moment to keep the assistants near at hand for a while, he fumbled around with some of the copies hoping to give the impression that he was checking them, and then, realizing that the assistants would not dare to leave at the same time as he did, he went home, weary, his mind a complete void.

Chapter Six

K's Uncle – Leni

One afternoon – K. was very busy signing the mail – his uncle Karl, a small landowner from the country, came pushing into the room between two members of the staff who were bringing in documents. K. was less horrified at the actual sight of his uncle walking in than he had been for some considerable time at the prospect that his uncle might come. His uncle was sure to come, K. had known this for about a month. He had pictured him as long ago as that, just as he looked now, stooping a little, his squashed panama hat in his left hand, his right hand thrust out towards K. from afar and then stretching with reckless haste over the desk, pushing out of the way everything that lay in his path. His uncle was always in a hurry, for he was pursued by the unfortunate idea that during the time he was in the capital (where he never stayed more than a day) he must accomplish everything he had planned to do and yet could not allow himself to forgo any conversation or business or pleasure that might offer itself. In the process K, who, because his uncle used to be his guardian, was under a special obligation to him, had to give him as much help as possible and, in addition, put him up for the night. He used to call him 'the spectre from the country'.

Immediately they had shaken hands – he had no time to sit down in the armchair which K. offered him – he begged K. to grant him a short conversation in private.

'It's necessary,' he said, swallowing painfully. 'It's necessary for my peace of mind.'

K. at once sent the clerks out of the room with instructions not to let anyone in.

'What's this I hear, Josef?' cried his uncle, when they were alone. He sat down on the desk and, without looking at them, stuffed various papers under himself so that he could sit more comfortably. K. said nothing, he knew what was coming, but suddenly released as he was from the strain of exhausting work, he surrendered for the moment to a pleasant lassitude and looked out of the window at the opposite side of the street, of which he could see, from where he was sitting, only a small triangular section, a patch of empty house-wall between two shop windows.

'You're looking out of the window!' his uncle shouted, raising his arms. 'In God's name, Josef, answer me! Is this true, can it really be true?'

'My dear Uncle,' K. said, wrenching himself out of his vacant mood, 'I don't even know what you're talking about.'

'Josef,' his uncle said in a warning tone, 'you have always told me the truth, as far as I know. Am I to take your last words as a bad omen?'

'I do have some idea what you are after,' K. said obediently. 'You've probably been hearing something about my trial.'

'That's it,' his uncle replied, nodding slowly. 'I've heard about your trial.'

'Who did you hear it from, then?'

'Erna wrote to me about it. She doesn't see much of you, unfortunately you don't pay much attention to her, I know, but still she did hear about it. Today I got a letter from her and naturally I came straight here. I had no other reason for coming, but this seems enough in itself. I can read you the bit of the letter that concerns you.' He took the letter out of his wallet. 'Here it is. She writes:

I have not seen Josef for a long time. Last week I did go to the bank, but Josef was so busy that I couldn't get in to see him. I waited for nearly an hour, but then I had to go home as I had a piano lesson. I would like to have had a chance of speaking to him, perhaps I shall have a chance to before long. He sent me a big box of chocolates for my birthday, it was very nice and thoughtful of him. I forgot to write to you about it at the time, and I only remembered about it now that you asked me about him. Believe me, chocolates tend to disappear straight away in the boarding-school; you no sooner realize you've been given a present of chocolates than they're all gone. But about Josef – there was one thing I wanted to tell you. As I mentioned, I didn't get to see him at the bank because at the time he was dealing with a gentleman. After I'd been waiting quietly for a bit, I asked a clerk whether the interview would go on much longer. He said that it might well because it was probably connected with the legal proceedings that are being taken against the Senior Clerk. So I asked what sort of proceedings these were, and whether he was not making a mistake. But he said he wasn't making a mistake, that there really was a trial and a serious one at that, but he said he didn't know any more than this. He said he himself would be glad to help the Senior Clerk, for Herr K. was a nice gentleman and very fair, but he had no idea how to set about doing it, and he only hoped that some influential people would take Herr K's side. He said this was sure to happen and it was certain to be all right in the end, but for the moment it didn't look at all good, judging from the mood the Senior Clerk was in. Naturally I didn't attach much importance to these remarks, but I tried to reassure this naïve clerk, and I told him not to speak to other people about it. I consider the whole thing to be idle gossip. But still it might perhaps be a good thing if you, my dear Father, could follow the matter up on your next visit, it would be easy for you to find out more details about it, and if it should really be necessary you could get some of your big influential friends to intervene. If, however, it shouldn't be necessary, which is really the most likely, then it would at least give your daughter a chance to hug you soon, which would please her very much.

'She's a good girl,' his uncle said, as he finished reading, and wiped a few tears from his eyes.

K. nodded. As a result of the various distractions of the last few days he had completely forgotten Erna and had even forgotten her birthday – the story about the chocolates had obviously been invented simply to protect him from what his uncle and aunt might think. It was very touching, and the theatre tickets which he planned to send her regularly from now on would certainly not be sufficient recompense, but at the moment he did not feel up to visits to the boarding-school and conversations with a little eighteen-year-old grammar-school girl.

'Well, what do you say to that?' asked his uncle, who, thanks to the letter, which he now seemed to be reading through again, had forgotten all his urgency and excitement.

'Yes, Uncle,' K. said, 'it's true.'

'True?' his uncle cried. 'What's true? How on earth can it be true? What sort of a law case is this? Surely not a criminal case?'

'Yes, a criminal case,' K. answered.

'And you can sit there calmly with a criminal case hanging over you?' shouted K's uncle, getting louder and louder.

'The calmer I am, the more chance there is of a successful out-come,' K. said wearily. 'Don't be alarmed.'

'That won't reassure me!' cried his uncle. 'Josef, my dear Josef, just think of yourself, think of your relations, think of our good name! Up to now you have been a credit to us, you can't let yourself be a disgrace to us now. I don't like your attitude,' he said, looking at K. with his head inclined to one side. 'That's not the attitude of an innocent person, if he's still in his senses. Just tell me quickly what it's all about, so that I can help you. It's something to do with the bank, of course, isn't it?'

'No, it isn't,' K. said and got to his feet. 'But you're talking too loud, my dear Uncle, the clerk is probably standing on the other side of the door, listening. I don't like that at all. We'd better go out. Then I can answer all your questions as best I can. I know very well that I owe the family an explanation.'

'You're right, you're absolutely right!' his uncle yelled. 'Hurry up, Josef, hurry up!'

'I must just give a few instructions,' K. said, and he telephoned for his deputy, who came in a few moments. K's uncle, so agitated was he, indicated with a gesture of his hand that K. had sent for the man, which was in any case obvious enough. K, standing in front of his desk, pointed to various documents and quietly explained to the young man, who listened coolly but attentively, what still remained to be done that day in his absence. His uncle disconcerted him, first of all, by standing around wide-eyed and then by nervously biting his lips, without actually listening, but the fact that he seemed to be was disconcerting enough. Then he started to walk up and down the room, stopping every now and then in front of the window or in front of a picture, where he would continually erupt into various exclamations, such as:

'I find it completely incomprehensible!' or 'Heaven knows what all this will lead to!'

The young man behaved as if he noticed nothing of all this, he listened quietly until K. had finished his instructions, noted down one or two things, and went out after bowing to K. and to his uncle, who just turned his back on him, stared out of the window and reached out his hands to crumple the curtains.

Scarcely had the door closed when K's uncle exclaimed:

'Well, at last that spineless idiot has gone, now we can go too! About time!'

Unfortunately, when they reached the main hall, which at that very moment the Deputy Director happened to be crossing, and where, also, a few clerks and officials were standing around, K. could find no way of getting his uncle to stop asking questions about the trial.

'Well, Josef,' his uncle began, answering the bows of those standing around with a slight nod of the head, 'now tell me frankly what kind of a trial this is.'

K. made a few meaningless remarks and laughed a little, and it was not till they got to the steps that he explained to his uncle that he had not wanted to talk openly in front of these people.

'Quite right,' his uncle said. 'But now tell me.'

With his head bent and smoking a cigar in short, hasty puffs, he listened to his nephew.

'First of all, Uncle, there's no question at all of this being a trial before an ordinary kind of court.'

'That's bad,' said his uncle.

'What do you mean?' K. said, looking at his uncle.

'That it's bad,' his uncle repeated. They were standing on the outside steps that led down to the street. Since the door-keeper seemed to be listening, K. drew his uncle down the steps. Here they were swallowed up by the busy traffic. K's uncle, who had taken his nephew's arm, did not go on pressing him so urgently with questions about the trial and they even walked along in silence for a while.

'But how did it come to happen?' his uncle finally asked, coming to a stop so abruptly that people walking behind recoiled in alarm. 'Things like this don't just happen suddenly, they take a long time to develop, there must have been some advance warning of this. Why didn't you write to me? You know I would do anything for you, and I am in a way still your guardian and up to now I have always been proud of that. Even now I will naturally do what I can to help you, the only thing is that if proceedings have already started it's very difficult now. In any case it would be best if you took a short holiday and came to us in the country. Besides, you have got a bit thinner, I can see that now. In the country you would get your strength back, and that would be a good thing, for you've certainly got some difficult times ahead. But in addition, it would take you out of the reach of the Court to some extent. Here they've got every possible resource available which, if necessary, they will automatically make use of against you. But in the country they would first have to delegate agents, or else they would only have letters or telegrams or the telephone as a means of getting at you. This would naturally weaken the effect, and though it wouldn't set you free, of course, it would at least give you a breathing-space.'

'Still, they might forbid me to leave the city,' said K, who had been prompted by his uncle's speech to try to enter, to some degree, the minds of the authorities.

'I don't believe they'll do that,' his uncle said reflectively, 'the power they would lose over you by your going away would not be that great.'

'I thought,' K. said, grasping his uncle under the arm to stop him from standing still, 'that you would attach even less importance to the whole thing than I do, and now I find you taking it so seriously.'

'Josef!' cried his uncle, trying to wrestle himself free in order to be able to stand still, but K. would not let go, 'you've changed! You always had such a very good grasp of things. You haven't lost it now of all times, have you? Do you want the case to go against you then? Do you know what that will mean? It will mean that you will simply be wiped out. And that all your relations will be ruined too or at least dragged in the dust. Josef, pull yourself together. Your indifference is driving me mad. Looking at you, one's tempted to believe the proverb: "To be prosecuted in a case like this means that one has already lost it." '

'My dear Uncle,' K. said, 'it's no good getting excited, there's no point in your getting worked up, and it wouldn't make any sense if I did. One doesn't win cases by getting worked up, let my practical experience count for something too, in the same way as I have always deeply respected your experience – even when I find what you say surprising – and I respect it even now. You say the case would involve the family too – which is something that for the life of me I simply cannot understand, but that's beside the point – I will gladly do anything you say. The only thing is that I don't think it would be a good idea, even from your point of view, for me to come and stay in the country, as that would look like running away and bad conscience. Besides, although it's true that they persecute me more here, I can press my case better myself.'

'Quite right,' said his uncle, in a tone which suggested that they were at last beginning to find common ground. 'I only suggested it because I thought that, if you stayed here, your in-difference would endanger the case, and so I thought it would be better if I worked on your behalf instead. But if you intend to press it yourself as forcibly as you can, then that, of course, is far better.'

'We're agreed on that then,' K. said. 'And have you any suggestion now about what I should do first?'

'I'll have to put a bit more thought in on that, of course,' said his uncle. 'You must realize that I have been living in the country almost continuously now for twenty years and that makes one lose a little of one's flair for this kind of thing. Various important contacts with people who perhaps know their way round here better have faded of their own accord. In the country I'm a little bit isolated, you know that already. One only realizes it oneself when something like this crops up. To some extent, too, this affair of yours took me by surprise, even though after Erna's letter I did have a remarkable premonition of something of this kind, and today I knew it almost for certain at the first sight I had of you. Still, that does not matter, the most important thing now is that we mustn't lose any time.'

Even while he had been speaking he was standing on tiptoe, signalling a taxi, and now, simultaneously shouting out an address to the driver, he dragged K. into the car after him.

'We're going now to Huld, the lawyer,' he said. 'He was at school with me. You know his name, of course? You don't? But that's extraordinary. He has a great reputation as a defence counsel and as an advocate representing those in need of legal aid.

But I have special confidence in him as a human being.'

'I'm quite satisfied with anything you decide to do,' said K,
although the hasty and urgent fashion in which his uncle was
treating the business caused him some misgivings. It was not very
encouraging for an accused person to consult a poor man's
lawyer. 'I didn't know,' he said, 'that one could consult a lawyer
in a case like this.'

'Of course one can,' his uncle said, 'that goes without saying.
Why ever not? And now tell me, so that I am properly informed
about the case, everything that has happened up to now.'

K. at once began to tell him without keeping anything back,
for complete frankness on his part was the only way in which he
could allow himself to protest against his uncle's view that the
case was a great disgrace. Fräulein Bürstner's name he mentioned
only once and in passing, but this did not make his account any
the less frank, since Fräulein Bürstner was not connected at all
with the case. While he was telling his story, he looked out of the
window and saw that they were now getting near the very
suburb where the Court offices were situated. He pointed this
out to his uncle, who was not, however, particularly struck by
the coincidence. The car stopped in front of a dark house. His
uncle at once rang the bell of the first door on the ground floor.
While they were waiting, his uncle bared his big teeth in a smile
and whispered:

'Eight o'clock. A strange time for clients to go visiting. Still,
Huld won't hold it against me.'

At the peep-hole in the door there appeared two large black
eyes, which examined the two guests for a while and then disappeared. But the door did not open. K. and his uncle assured
each other of the fact that they really had seen two eyes.

'A new parlour-maid who's frightened of strangers,' said K's
uncle and knocked again. Once more the eyes appeared, and now
they looked almost sad, but perhaps that was only an illusion

created by the naked gas-jet which was burning just above their heads, hissing loudly but not giving off much light.

'Open up!' called K's uncle and banged his fist on the door. 'We're friends of the lawyer's!'

'Herr Huld is ill,' came a whisper behind them. In a doorway at the other end of the small passage stood a man in a dressing-gown who relayed this information in an extremely quiet voice. The uncle, who was already furious after waiting so long, jerked round and shouted:

'Ill? You say he is ill?' and went up to the man almost threateningly, as if the man himself were the illness.

'The door's already open,' the man said, and, pointing to the lawyer's door, gathered his dressing-gown around him and disappeared.

The door had in fact been opened. A young girl – K. recognized the black, slightly protruding eyes – was standing in the hallway in a long white apron, holding a candle in her hand.

'Next time open the door sooner!' K's uncle said by way of a greeting whilst the girl gave a little curtsey. 'Come, Josef,' he then said to K, who slowly pushed his way past the girl.

'Herr Huld is ill,' the girl said as K's uncle, without stopping, hurried up to a door. K. was still gaping at the girl, who had meanwhile turned round to fasten the door of the flat again. She had a round, doll-like face. Not only were the pale cheeks and chin rather round, but so were the temples and the edges of her brow.

'Josef!' his uncle shouted again, and he asked the girl: 'Is it his heart?'

'I think so,' the girl said. She had found time to go on ahead with the candle and open the door of the room. In one corner, which the light from the candle did not manage to reach, a face with a long beard rose up in the bed.

'Who is it then, Leni?' asked the lawyer who, dazzled by the light of the candle, failed to recognize his guests.

'It's your old friend Albert,' K's uncle said.

'Ah, Albert,' the lawyer said, slumping back on the pillows, as if he didn't need to keep up any pretences with this visitor.

'Is it really as bad as that?' K's uncle asked and sat down on the edge of the bed. 'I don't believe it. It's a touch of your old heart trouble and it'll go away just like it did before.'

'Perhaps,' the lawyer said quietly, 'but it's worse than it's ever been before. I can hardly breathe, I don't sleep at all and I'm weaker every day.'

'I see,' K's uncle said, pressing his panama hat firmly down on to his knee with his big hand. 'That's bad news. But are you being looked after properly? And it's so dismal in here, too, so dark. It's a long time since I was here last, but it seemed nicer then. And your little servant-girl here doesn't seem very cheerful, or else she's putting on an act.'

The girl was still standing near the door with the candle. As far as one could tell from her indecisive glance, she was looking at K. rather than at his uncle, even when the latter was talking about her. K. was leaning against a chair which he had pushed near the girl.

'When one is as ill as I am,' the lawyer said, 'one must have peace and quiet. I don't find it dismal.' After a short pause he added: 'And Leni looks after me well, she is a good girl.'

But K's uncle was not convinced by this, he was clearly prejudiced against the nurse, and even though he did not answer the sick man, he now followed her with a sharp look as she went up to the bed, put the candle on the bedside table, bent over the sick man and whispered to him as she arranged his pillows. K's uncle almost forgot all consideration for the sick man, he stood up and paced to and fro behind the nurse, and K. would not have been surprised if he had taken hold of her skirts from behind and pulled her away from the bed. K. himself watched everything calmly, indeed the fact that the lawyer was ill was not entirely unwelcome, he had not been able to counter the enthusiasm which his uncle had shown for his case, and he willingly accepted the fact that this enthusiasm was now being diverted without any help from him.

Then his uncle, perhaps only with the idea of insulting the nurse, said:

'Fräulein, please leave us alone for a while, I have some personal business to discuss with my friend.'

The nurse, who was still leaning right over the sick man and smoothing the sheet by the wall, merely turned her head and said very calmly, in a way that made a striking contrast with the faltering and then eruptive fury of K's uncle's words:

'But you can see Herr Huld is so ill he isn't able to discuss any business.'

It was probably only out of idleness that she repeated K's uncle's words, yet even somebody quite uninvolved might have thought her remark scornful. K's uncle, of course, leapt up as if he had been stung.

'Damn you!' he said, and in the first gurgle of emotion his voice was not really intelligible. K. was alarmed, although he had been expecting something like this, and he ran up to his uncle, determined to clap both hands over his mouth. Fortunately, however, the sick man raised himself in bed behind the girl, and K's uncle glowered as if he were swallowing something disgusting, then said more calmly:

'I assure you we have not lost our senses altogether. If what I was asking were impossible, I would not ask it. Please, go now!'

The nurse was standing erect by the bed, facing K's uncle, and with one hand she was stroking (or so K. thought he had noticed) the lawyer's hand.

'You can say anything in front of Leni,' the sick man said, obviously making an urgent request.

'This matter doesn't concern me,' K's uncle said, 'it's not my secret.' And he turned round, as if he had no further intention of discussing the matter, but was giving them a moment or two to think it over.

'Who does it concern then?' the lawyer asked in a failing voice and slumped back again.

'My nephew,' said K's uncle, 'I've brought him along with me.' And he introduced K: 'Josef K, Senior Clerk.'

'Oh,' the sick man said with much more animation and stretched his hand out towards K, 'forgive me, I quite failed to notice you. Go now, Leni,' he then said to the nurse, who offered no further resistance, and he gave her his hand as if they were parting for a long time.

'So you haven't come,' he said at last to K's uncle who, also placated now, had drawn a little closer, 'to visit me because I'm ill, you've come on business.'

It was as if the idea of a sick-visit had been paralysing the lawyer up to now, for at this moment he seemed quite invigorated, propping himself up all the time on one elbow, which must have been quite a strain for him, and continually pulling at one strand of hair in the middle of his beard.

'You look much better already,' said K's uncle, 'now that that witch has gone.' K's uncle broke off and whispered: 'I'll bet she's listening!' and he leapt to the door.

Yet there was no one behind the door, K's uncle came back, not disappointed – for the fact that she had not been listening seemed to him even more malicious – but he was embittered.

'You're misjudging her,' said the lawyer, without adding anything else in her defence. Perhaps he thereby wanted to show that she did not need to be defended. But in a much more sympathetic tone he went on: 'As far as your nephew's business is concerned, I should deem myself very fortunate if my strength proved sufficient for this extremely difficult task. I very much fear that it won't be sufficient, but at any rate I will do all I can.

If I can't manage it, then one could, of course, call in somebody else. To be candid, the case interests me too much for me to bear the thought of forgoing any participation in it. If my heart doesn't last out, this will at least be a worthy occasion for it to break down totally.'

K. did not think he had understood a word of this entire speech, he glanced at his uncle for some explanation, but his uncle, holding the candle in his hand, was sitting on the bedside table, from which a medicine bottle had already rolled on to the carpet, and was nodding at everything the lawyer said, agreeing with every word, and every now and then looking at K. as if inviting the same measure of agreement from him. Had his uncle perhaps told the lawyer something about the case already? But that was impossible, everything that had happened so far made it unlikely.

So he said: 'I don't understand . . .'

'Have I misunderstood you, perhaps?' asked the lawyer, just as astonished and embarrassed as K. himself. 'Perhaps I was being too hasty? What were you wanting to talk to me about, then? I thought it was in connection with your trial.'

'Yes, of course,' K's uncle said and went on to ask K: 'What's the matter?'

'Yes, but how on earth do you know anything about me and my trial?' K. asked.

'Ah, I see,' the lawyer said, smiling. 'After all, I am a lawyer and I move in legal circles, people often talk about different cases, and one remembers the more striking ones, especially if the nephew of a friend is involved. There's nothing remarkable in that, surely.'

'What's the matter, then?' K's uncle asked him once more. 'You're so on edge.'

'You move in those legal circles?' K. asked.

'Yes,' said the lawyer.

'You're asking questions like a child,' K's uncle said.

'Whom should I associate with, if not the members of my own profession?' the lawyer added.

It sounded so irrefutable that K. made no reply at all. He had wanted to say: 'But surely you work in the Law Courts in the Palace of Justice, and not in that one in the attic?' but he could not bring himself actually to say it.

'You must remember,' the lawyer went on in a tone that suggested he was unnecessarily and casually explaining something self-evident, 'you must remember that my moving in these circles is of great advantage to my clients in many ways, one's not always even allowed to talk about it. Naturally at the moment, as a result of my illness, I am at a bit of a disadvantage, but I still receive visits from good friends of mine from the Courts, and so I get to hear things. Perhaps I get to hear more than some people who are in the best of health and who spend their whole day at the Courts. For example, at this very moment a dear friend is visiting me,' and he pointed into a dark corner of the room.

'Where then?' K. asked, speaking almost rudely in his initial astonishment. He looked around uncertainly; the light from the small candle fell a long way short of the opposite wall. But something did indeed begin to stir in the corner there. By the light of the candle, which his uncle now held up high, an elderly man could be seen sitting there at a little table. He must have been scarcely breathing to have managed to remain unnoticed for so long. Now he got ceremoniously to his feet, manifestly put out by having attention drawn to him. It seemed as if he were trying, with little movements of his hands which he fluttered like small wings, to ward off any introductions or greetings, as if he did not wish to disturb the others in any way by his presence, and as if he were urgently begging to be consigned to the darkness again and to have his presence entirely forgotten. But this could now no longer be granted him.

'You surprised us, you see,' the lawyer said by way of explanation, and he waved encouragingly to the gentleman to get him to come nearer, which the latter slowly did, looking round hesitantly and yet with a certain dignity. 'The Director of the Court offices – ah, but excuse me, I haven't introduced you yet – this is my friend, Albert K, and this is his nephew, Josef K, Senior Clerk, and this is the Director of the Court offices . . . The Director was kind enough to pay me a visit. The value of such a visit can really only be properly appreciated by someone in a position to know how overworked the Director is. But, in spite of that, he did come and we have had a gentle chat, in so far as my weakness allowed it. It's true we didn't actually tell Leni not to admit visitors, for we didn't expect any, but we did think we would be left alone, but then you came banging on the door, Albert, and so the Director moved back into the corner with his table and chair, and now it seems we have the chance – that is, if we all want to – to discuss a certain matter together, and so it might be a very good idea to move our chairs close together again. Please, sir,' he said, with a bow of his head and an obsequious smile, pointing to an armchair near the bed.

'Unfortunately I can only stay a few minutes longer,' the Director said amicably, seating himself comfortably in the armchair and looking at his watch. 'Business calls. But anyway I don't want to miss the opportunity of getting to know a friend of my friend.' He tilted his head slightly to Josef's uncle, who seemed very pleased to make this new acquaintance but was prevented by his very nature from expressing feelings of obeisance, and he greeted the Director's words with a loud, embarrassed laugh. An ugly sight! K. found himself able to watch everything calmly, for no one was bothering about him at all. The Director of the Court offices, now that he had emerged into the limelight, proceeded to take charge of the conversation, as he was apparently in the habit of doing; the lawyer, whose initial weakness had perhaps only been intended to drive away his new visitors, listened attentively with his hand cupped to his ear; Josef's uncle, acting as candle-bearer – he was balancing the candle on his thigh and the lawyer more than once looked at him anxiously – was soon over his embarrassment and was now completely entranced both by the Director's manner of speaking and by the delicate, undulating movements of the hand with which he accompanied his words. K, who was leaning against the bedpost, was entirely ignored (perhaps on purpose) by the Director and served only as an audience for the old gentlemen. Moreover, he scarcely knew what they were talking about and soon found himself thinking about the nurse and the disgraceful way his uncle had treated her. Then he wondered whether he had not seen the Director before at some time or other, perhaps even in the meeting at his initial examination. He might be mistaken, but the Director would have fitted perfectly into the front row of those present at the meeting, among the old men with sparse beards.

Then there came a noise from the hallway, like the sound of smashing china, and everybody stopped to listen.

'I'll go and see what's happened,' K. said and went out slowly as if he wanted to give the others a chance to stop him from going. He had scarcely reached the hall and was trying to get his bearings in the dark when his hand, still grasping the door-handle, was suddenly held by another hand, which was much smaller than K's and which quietly closed the door. It was the nurse, who had been waiting for him there.

'Nothing's happened,' she whispered. 'I just threw a plate against the wall to bring you out.'

In his embarrassment K. said: 'I was thinking about you, too.'

'All the better,' said the nurse. 'Come on.'

After a few steps they came to a door of frosted glass, which the nurse opened to let K. through.

'Go in, then,' she said.

This turned out to be the lawyer's study. As far as one could see by the light of the moon, which was now illuminating only a small square patch of floor in front of each of the three large windows, it was fitted out with heavy, old pieces of furniture.

'Over here,' the nurse said and pointed to a dark chest with a carved wooden back. Even when he had sat down, K. looked round the room. It was big and high, and the pauper clients of the lawyer must have felt lost in it. K. imagined he could see the little steps with which the visitors approached the huge desk. But then he forgot about this and had eyes only for the nurse, who was now sitting quite near him and was almost pressing him up against the side of the chest.

'I thought,' she said, 'you would come out to me of your own accord, without me having to call you first. That was curious. To begin with, you were looking at me continuously, right from the moment you came in, and then you kept me waiting. But anyway, call me Leni,' she added quickly and unexpectedly, as if they could not afford to waste a single second of this conversation.

'I'd like to. But as for its being curious, Leni, that's easy to explain. In the first place, I had to listen to the old men rambling on, and I couldn't just run off without any excuse, and, secondly, I am not very courageous, I'm rather timid in fact, and even you Leni, didn't really look as if you would leap into my arms.'

'That wasn't it,' Leni said, resting her arm on the back of the seat and gazing at K. 'The fact is you didn't like me, and you probably still don't like me even now.'

'Liking somebody doesn't mean very much,' K. said, dodging the point.

'Oh, oh!' she said with a smile; and K's remark and this little exclamation of hers won for her a certain ascendancy. So K. remained silent for a while. As he had already grown used to the darkness of the room, he was able to distinguish various items of furniture. He was particularly struck by a large painting that hung on the right-hand side of the door, and he bent forward to see it better. It showed a man in a judge's robes; he was sitting on a high throne, the gilding of which stood out from the picture in many places.

The unusual thing about it was that this judge was not sitting there in tranquillity and dignity, but was pressing his left arm firmly against the back and arm-rest of the chair, while he had his right arm completely free and was grasping the chair only with his hand, as if he were just on the point of leaping up with a violent and perhaps furious gesture in order to say something decisive or even pronounce sentence. The accused could be imagined at the foot of the flight of steps, the top ones of which were covered with a yellow carpet and could just be seen in the painting.

'Perhaps that is my judge,' K. said and pointed to the picture.

'I know him,' Leni said and looked up at the picture, too. 'He often comes here. The picture was done when he was young, but he can never have looked remotely like that, for he is very small, almost tiny. Still, he had himself drawn out to that length in the picture, for he is absurdly vain, like all of them here. But I'm vain, too, and I'm very disappointed that you don't like me at all.'

K's only reply to this last remark was to take Leni in his arms and pull her close: without saying anything, she leant her head against his shoulder. But to the rest of what she had said he answered:

'What's his rank?'

'He is an Examining Magistrate,' she said, seizing the hand with which K. was embracing her, and playing with his fingers.

'Only an Examining Magistrate again,' said K, disappointed. 'The highest officials certainly hide away. But he's sitting on a throne.'

'That's all just made up,' said Leni with her face bent over K's hand. 'Actually he's sitting on a kitchen chair which has got an old horse-blanket draped over it. But have you got to keep thinking about your trial?' she added slowly.

'No, not at all. Probably I don't think about it enough.'

'That's not the real mistake you make,' Leni said. 'You are too inflexible, from what I've heard.'

'Who's said that?' K. asked. He was aware of her body against his breast and looked down at her rich, dark, firmly plaited hair.

'It would be giving away too much if I told you that,' Leni answered. 'Please don't ask me for names, but do something about that weakness of yours, don't be so inflexible from now on. There's no way at all that you can defend yourself against this Court, you have to admit your guilt. Make a full confession as soon as you can. Only then will you be able to escape from them, and not until then. Even then, however, you won't manage it without help from somebody else, but you needn't worry about that, I'll help you myself.'

'You know a lot about this Court and about all the trickery that one needs to use here,' K. said and, as she was pressing too violently against him, he drew her on to his lap.

'That's nice,' she said and made herself comfortable there, smoothing her dress and putting her blouse straight. Then she clasped her hands round his neck, leaned back and gazed at him for a long time.

'And if I don't confess my guilt, then you won't be able to help me?' K. asked experimentally. I'm always recruiting women to help me, he thought to himself, almost with amazement, first Fräulein Bürstner, then the usher's wife, and now this little nurse who seems to have an incomprehensible desire for me. Look how she's sitting on my lap as if that's the only proper place for her!

'No,' Leni answered and shook her head slowly, 'then I shan't be able to help you. But you don't really want my help at all, it's

129

not important to you, you are obstinate and won't listen to reason. Have you got a girlfriend?' she asked after a moment.

'No,' K. said.

'Oh, I bet you have,' she said.

'Yes, I have really,' K. said. 'And just imagine, here I am disowning her, and yet all the time I've got her photo in my pocket.'

When she begged him to, he showed her Elsa's photograph, and, curled up on his lap, she studied the picture. It was a snapshot, taken as Elsa finished a whirling dance, the kind of dance she liked to do in the wine-bar, her skirt still swirling around her in a flurry of folds, and she had her hands on her firm hips and was laughing to one side with her chin jutting out. It was impossible to tell from the picture whom she was laughing at.

'She's very tightly laced,' Leni said, and pointed to the place where she thought this tightness could be seen. 'I don't like her, she's clumsy and coarse. But perhaps with you she's soft and kind, one might imagine that from the photograph. Big strong girls like that often can't help being soft and kind. But could she sacrifice herself for you?'

'No,' said K. 'She isn't soft and kind, and she wouldn't sacrifice herself for me. And so far I haven't demanded either softness or sacrifice from her. In fact I haven't even examined the photograph as carefully as you have.'

'So you don't really care about her very much at all,' said Leni. 'So she's not your girlfriend at all.'

'Yes, she is,' said K. 'I'm not going to retract my words.'

'She may be your girlfriend at the moment,' said Leni, 'but you wouldn't miss her very much if you lost her or if you swapped her for somebody else – me, for instance.'

'Certainly,' K. said with a smile, 'that's conceivable, but she has one great advantage over you, she doesn't know anything about my trial, and even if she did know something about it, she wouldn't give it a thought. She wouldn't try to argue me into being flexible.'

'That's no advantage,' said Leni. 'If that's the only advantage she has over me, I needn't lose heart. Has she any particular physical defect?'

'Any physical defect?' K. asked.

'Yes,' said Leni, 'like I have. Look.'

She spread wide the middle and ring fingers of her right hand, and the web of skin joining them reached up almost as far as the top joints of the short fingers. In the darkness K. did not realize at once what she was trying to show him, so she pulled his hand near for him to feel.

'What a freakish phenomenon,' K. said, and having examined the whole hand he added: 'What a pretty little claw!'

With a kind of pride Leni watched while K. in astonishment went on separating the fingers and putting them together again, until finally he gave them a fleeting kiss and let them go.

'Oh!' she cried out at once. 'You've kissed me!'

Hastily, with her mouth open, she clambered on her knees all over his lap. K. looked up at her almost in dismay. Now she was so close to him, a sharp, provocative fragrance like pepper came from her, she pressed his head against her, bent over it and kissed his neck, biting even into his hair.

'You've got me in exchange for her!' she cried out from time to time. 'Look, now you've got me instead!' Then her knee slipped, and with a little cry she almost fell on to the carpet. K. put his arm round her to stop her falling and was dragged down to her. 'Now you belong to me,' she said.

'Now you've got the key of the house, come whenever you want to,' were her last words, and a badly aimed kiss landed on his back as he went away. When he stepped out of the main door of the house, it was raining a little. He intended to walk over to the middle of the street so that perhaps he would be able to glimpse Leni still at the window, but then suddenly his uncle leapt from a car which was waiting in front of the house and which K. had been too preoccupied to notice at all, seized him by the arms and shoved him against the main door of the house as if he wanted to nail him there.

'Boy, oh boy!' he shouted. 'How could you go and do that! You've done the most terrible damage to your case, which was going along quite nicely. You sneak off with that dirty little minx, who is obviously the lawyer's mistress anyway, and then you stay away for hours. You didn't even make any pretence about it, you don't conceal it at all! No, you're quite open about it, you go running off to her and stay with her. And in the meantime we're all left sitting together – your uncle who is really putting himself out for you, the lawyer who has to be won over to your side, and above all the Director of the Court, that great man who has complete authority over your case as it stands at present. We are trying to discuss the best way of helping you, and I have to treat the lawyer very discreetly, and he has to do the same with the Director, and you might be expected to have every reason at least to back me up. Instead of that, you just stay away. In the end it can't be concealed any longer; well, they are polite and diplomatic men, they don't talk about it, they spare my feelings, but finally even they can't do anything about it and since they can't talk about it, they fall silent. We sat there for minutes on end without saying anything and just listened to see if you would eventually come. All in vain. Finally the Director stood up – he had stayed much longer than he originally meant to – said goodbye, obviously pitying me but unable to do anything to help me, waited a little while longer at the door out of sheer kindness, which was really surprising, and then went. I was naturally glad when he had gone, it was getting so that I couldn't breathe. The effect on the sick lawyer was even more serious, the poor man couldn't talk at all when I left him. You've probably helped to give him a complete breakdown and thus hastened the death of a man on whom you are entirely dependent. And as for me, your own uncle, you keep me here waiting for hours in the rain – just feel, I'm soaked through – letting me worry myself sick about your troubles.'

Chapter Seven

Lawyer – Manufacturer – Painter

One winter morning – it was dull outside and snow was falling – K. was sitting in his office; although it was early, he was already extremely tired. To protect himself at least from the junior employees, he had given instructions to the clerk not to let any of them in, as he was engaged on some fairly important work. But instead of working, he was swivelling in his chair and slowly moving several things about on his desk. Then, without realizing it, he let his whole arm lie outstretched on the top of the desk and he sat there motionless with his head lowered.

The thought of the trial never left him now. Often, already, he had wondered whether it might not be a good thing to prepare a written defence and hand it in to the Court. In this defence he wanted to present a short account of his life and, when he came to any event which somehow was more important than others, to explain what reasons had led him to act in such and such a way, and to say whether his course of action was, in his present estimation, to be approved or repudiated, and what grounds he could adduce for his present approval or repudiation. The advantages of such a written defence, as against merely being defended by a lawyer (who would not, in any case, be impeccable), were indisputable. K. had no idea at all what Huld was doing about the case. Anyway, it could not be anything much, for it was a month since the lawyer had asked to see him and none of the earlier consultations had given K. the impression that the man could do much for him.

Above all, Huld had almost entirely omitted to interrogate

him. And yet there were so many questions that ought to be asked. Asking questions was the most important thing. K. had the feeling that he himself was capable of asking all the necessary questions. But the lawyer, instead of asking questions, would either do all the talking himself or sit opposite K. in silence, leaning forward across the desk (probably because of his bad hearing), pulling at a strand of hair in his beard and looking down at the carpet, perhaps at the very place where K. had lain with Leni. Now and then he gave K. a few vacuous admonitions, such as children are given. These speeches were as boring as they were useless, and K. had no intention of paying a penny for them when the time came to reckon up their accounts.

When the lawyer thought he had humbled K. sufficiently, he usually began to try to cheer him up a little. He now told how he had often had cases like this which he had gone on to win, either completely or partially. Cases, he said, which, even if they were, in reality, perhaps not quite as difficult as this one, had all the appearance of being even more hopeless. In fact he had a list of such cases in the drawer – at which point he tapped some drawer in the desk – unfortunately, though, he could not show the records of the cases, since these involved official secrets. But nevertheless all the wide experience he had acquired through these cases would, of course, benefit K. now. Naturally, he said, he had set to work on the case immediately, and the first plea was almost ready for presentation. This plea was very important, because the initial impression made by the defence often decided the whole course of the proceedings.

Unfortunately, he had to warn K, it sometimes happened though, that the first pleas were never read at all by the Court officials, who simply placed them with the documents and added the rider that, for the time being, interrogation and observation of the accused were more important than any written plea. If the petitioner pressed the point, it was stated that, before the final decision, as soon as all the material connected with the case had been assembled, all the documents, including this first plea, would be examined. But unfortunately this was often not true, the first plea was usually mislaid or went completely astray, and even if it was preserved until the very end, it would scarcely ever be read – judging by what the lawyer had heard, though of course this was only a rumour. That was all very regrettable, but not entirely without justification.

K. might care to remember that the proceedings were not public, they could be opened to the public if the Court thought this was necessary, but the Law did not insist on publicity. As a result of this, the Court records, above all the record of the charge, were not accessible to the accused or to his defence. Hence, generally speaking, one did not know, or knew only very imprecisely, what it was that the initial plea had to contest, and so it was really only pure chance if this plea contained something that was of any importance to the case. It was only later on that really pertinent and closely reasoned pleas could be prepared, when the separate charges and the evidence on which these were based emerged more clearly or could be divined during the course of the hearings. Naturally, in such circumstances, the defence was placed in a very disadvantageous and difficult situation. But this, too, was deliberate. For defence counsels were not really provided for under the Law, they were only there on sufferance, and even whether the relevant passage of the Law could be interpreted to mean that their presence should at least be tolerated was in dispute. Strictly speaking, therefore, no lawyers were in fact recognized by the Court at all, and all those who appeared before this Court as counsels were in actual fact merely hole-and-corner lawyers. This was naturally very humiliating for the whole profession, and the next time K. returned to the Court offices he ought to have a look at the lawyers' room, just for the sake of having seen it. He would probably be horrified at the collection of people he found assembled there.

The very room assigned to them, cramped and low, showed the contempt the Court had for these people. The only light in the room came from a small skylight, placed so high that, if you wanted to look out, you first had to get some colleague to hoist you on his back, and even then the smoke from a nearby chimney would go up your nose and blacken your face. In the floor of this room – just to give one more example of the conditions – for more than a year there had been a hole, not big enough for a man to fall into, but large enough to put your leg right through. The lawyers' room was in the upper attic, so if you slipped through, your leg would hang down into the lower attic, in fact, right into the passage where the petitioners were waiting. It would be no exaggeration if lawyers described these conditions as disgraceful. Complaints to the authorities produced not the slightest result, but the lawyers were absolutely forbidden to have anything in the room altered at their own expense.

But there was a reason, too, for treating the lawyers like this. It was desired, as far as possible, to eliminate the defence counsel altogether, so that the whole onus would be placed on the accused man himself. This was, in actual fact, not a bad principle, but it would be quite wrong to infer from this that the defendant was not in any need of a lawyer before this Court. On the contrary, in no other Court was a lawyer so necessary. The proceedings were generally kept secret not merely from the public, but also from the defendant himself – kept secret, naturally, only as far as this was possible, but it had turned out to be possible to a large extent. Even the defendant, in fact, had no access to the Court documents, and it was very hard to tell from the hearings the nature of the documents on which the hearings were based, particularly for a defendant who was self-conscious and distracted by every possible kind of anxiety. This was where the defence counsels came in. Generally speaking, defence counsels were not permitted to be present at the hearings, and so they had to question the accused about the hearing after the hearings, if possible even at the very door of the interrogation-room, and from these reports, which were often very incomplete, the counsel had to extract anything that was useful for the defence.

But that was not the most important thing, for not much could be learnt in this way, although of course, here, as everywhere, an experienced man could learn more than others. The really important thing was, however, the personal contacts which the lawyer could make with the officials, and this was the chief value of the defence counsel. From his own experience, K. had probably learnt by now that the lowest rank of the Court organization was by no means perfect, containing disloyal and corrupt employees, so that to some extent there were lacunae in the strict administration of the Court. It was here that most of the lawyers forced their way in and most of the bribery and pumping for information went on. Indeed, in the past at any rate, there had even been instances of documents being stolen. It could not be denied that in this way it was possible to achieve, temporarily at least, some surprisingly favourable results for the defendants, thus enabling the petty lawyers to swagger around and tout for new clients, but, as far as the subsequent course of the lawsuit was concerned, this meant nothing, or at any rate nothing beneficial. Nothing was of any real value except respectable personal contacts, and then only with senior officials, which meant, of course, only senior officials of the lower grades. It was only by this means that the progress of the lawsuit could be affected, only imperceptibly at first, but, as time passed, more and more obviously.

Of course only a few lawyers were capable of achieving this, and that was where K's choice had been so fortunate. There were perhaps only one or two lawyers who had contacts as good as

Dr Huld's. Of course, these men did not bother about the crowd in the lawyers' room and had nothing at all to do with them. But their links with the Court officials were all the closer. It was not even always necessary for Dr Huld to attend the Court, to wait in the antechambers of the Examining Magistrates in case they happened to appear, and to achieve, depending on their mood, a success which was usually only apparent or not even that.

No, K. had surely seen for himself how the officials, including even quite high ones, would come by themselves and volunteer information which was unequivocal or at least could be easily interpreted, or discuss the next stage in the cases; indeed they would even allow themselves to be persuaded in individual cases and accept gladly the opinion of others. Of course, in this respect, they were not altogether to be trusted, for however definitely they might express a new point of view in favour of the defence, they might then perhaps go straight back to their offices and the next day issue a statement which contained the precise opposite of what they had said and might well bear much more harshly on the accused than their original intention, which they claimed they had completely abandoned. Naturally there was no redress against this, since what they said in private was simply said in private and could not be pursued in public, even if the defence was not in any case bound to try to keep in with these gentlemen. On the other hand, it was also certainly true that it was not mere benevolence or friendliness that caused these gentlemen to establish contact with defence counsel, and then only, of course, with competent counsel, for they were to a certain extent dependent on defence counsel. At this point the disadvantage of a judiciary system which, from the very beginning, sanctioned secrecy made itself felt. The officials were out of touch with the public, they were well enough equipped to deal with the ordinary run-of-the-mill type of case, for this kind of case would proceed almost under its own momentum and only needed an occasional push. But when faced with quite simple cases or especially difficult ones, they were often at a total loss, because they were continuously, day and night, hamstrung by their legal system and lacked a proper feeling for human relations. And in such cases that feeling was all but indispensable.

Then they would approach the lawyers for advice, followed by a clerk carrying the documents that were usually kept so secret. At that window many a gentleman whom one would never have expected to see might be found gazing out in a state of absolute despair into the street, while the lawyer would be sitting at his desk studying the documents in order to be able to give him good advice. Moreover, from this kind of thing one could see just how exceptionally seriously these gentlemen took their work and how they were thrown into deep despair by obstacles which they, by their very nature, were prevented from overcoming. There were other ways in which their position was not an easy one, and it would be an injustice to them to regard that position as easy. The hierarchical structure of the Court was unending, parts of it were invisible even to the initiated. Proceedings in the Court were generally kept secret from the lower officials, so that they could hardly ever follow up completely the subsequent course of the cases they were working on. A legal question might, therefore, enter their circle of jurisdiction and then move on, often without their knowing whence it derived or what happened to it later. So nothing of what could be learnt from studying the different stages of the case, the final verdict and the reasons for it, was available to the officials. They could concern themselves only with the part of the case demarcated for them by the Law, and usually knew less about the rest, that is about the results of their own work, than the defence counsel, who, after all, was generally in touch with the defendant almost to the end of the trial. So, in that respect too, the officials could learn much of value from the defence counsel. Was K. surprised then, in view of all this, that the officials should be irritable or that they should sometimes say insulting things to the clients? Everyone found this. All the officials were irritable, even if they seemed to be quite calm outwardly. Of course the petty lawyers in particular had to put up with a lot.

For example, the following story, which had all the appearance of truth, was told. One old official, a well-disposed and quiet man, was faced with a difficult case, which had been complicated above all by the lawyer's pleas, and he had studied this case continuously for a whole day and night – these officials were actually very hardworking, more so than anyone else. Well, towards morning, after twenty-four hours' work and probably not much to show for it, he went to the entrance door, stationed himself there in ambush, and when any lawyer tried to get in he threw him down the stairs. The lawyers gathered on the bottom landing and discussed what to do. On the one hand, they had no real claim to be admitted, so they could hardly get legal redress against the official, and, as already mentioned, they also had to be careful not to set the authorities against them. On the other hand, every day they were not in Court was a day lost to them, so it was very important for them to force their way in. Finally they agreed that they would try to tire the old man out. One lawyer after another was dispatched up the stairs and there, with the greatest possible show of passive resistance, he would let himself be thrown down, whereupon he was picked up by his colleagues. This lasted for about an hour, and then the old man, who was already exhausted after working through the night, became really tired and went back into his office. At first those below could not believe it at all and sent one of their number out to look behind the door and see whether he had really gone. Only then did they move in, and probably they did not even dare to complain. For the lawyers – although the most insignificant among them could, at least to some extent, see how things lay – never dreamt of wanting to initiate or accomplish any improvements in the Court, whereas – and this was very typical – practically all defendants, even quite simple people, were no sooner involved in a case than they began to think out ways of improving matters, and would often spend time and energy on this which could be much better employed in other ways. The only correct thing to do was to reconcile oneself to things as they were. Even if it had been possible to make tiny improvements – but that was superstitious nonsense – at best one would have achieved thereby something of benefit to future clients, but at the same time would have done untold damage to oneself by the very fact that the particular attention of the ever-vengeful officials had been aroused. The vital thing was not to arouse their attention! Keep quiet, however much it went against the grain! Try to understand that this great legal system was always to some extent in a state of delicate balance, and that, if one took it upon oneself to make any independent alteration in it, one was liable to cut away the ground from under one's feet and bring oneself toppling down, whilst the vast system itself could easily compensate elsewhere for the little disturbance, since everything was connected, and would remain unchanged – that is if it didn't, as it probably would, become still more rigid, more alert, more severe and more evil. The lawyers must surely be left to do their work without being disturbed. Reproaches were of little use, especially if it was impossible to make intelligible the complete significance of the grounds for them, but all the same it must be stated that K. had done himself a lot of harm by the way he had behaved to the Director of the Court offices. This influential man could already almost be crossed off the list of those who would support K. He now quite blatantly and deliberately ignored the slightest mention of the case. In many ways the officials were like children. It often happened that they became so offended by the most trivial things – and, unfortunately, K's behaviour was not a trivial thing – that they stopped talking even to good friends of theirs, would turn their backs on them when they met and work against them in every possible way. But then, surprisingly enough, for no special reason, they could be made to laugh by some small joke that one only dared to make because things seemed hopeless, and then they would be friends again.

In short, dealing with them was difficult and easy at the same time. It was impossible to lay down any hard and fast rules. It was sometimes astonishing to think that in the course of an average lifetime anyone could acquire all the knowledge required for some degree of success in such a profession. There were gloomy times, certainly, such as anyone had, when one believed one had achieved nothing at all, times when it seemed that only the lawsuits which were destined to succeed from the very beginning – and would have succeeded without any assistance – did in fact have a happy ending, whereas all others failed in spite of all the running around, all the trouble and all the small apparent successes that had brought so much pleasure. Then, of course, nothing seemed certain any more, and it was no longer possible to deny with certainty, if one were questioned, that one's very efforts had merely served to misdirect some cases which, left to themselves, would have stayed on the right track. Of course, even this brought some kind of reassurance, but it was the only kind that one was left with. Lawyers were especially prone to these moods – for naturally they were only moods, and nothing more – when a case which they had been conducting urgently and satisfactorily enough was suddenly taken out of their hands. This was certainly the worst thing that could happen to a lawyer. It was not that the defendant would take the case away from him, for that certainly never happened: once a defendant had taken on a particular lawyer he was obliged to stick to him, whatever happened. For, once he had availed himself of someone's help, how could he manage by himself? So that did not happen, but it certainly did sometimes happen that the case took a turn where the lawyer was no longer permitted to pursue it. Then the case and the defendant and everything were simply taken away from the lawyer. Once that happened, it was no use being on the very best possible terms with the officials, for they themselves knew nothing about it. The case had in fact reached a stage where no more help could be given, where it was being dealt with by courts that could not be reached, and where even the defendant was no longer accessible to the lawyer. One day you would come home and find on your table all the countless pleas which you had worked so hard to make in connection with the case and in which you had placed the highest hopes. They had all been returned, for at this new stage of the trial it was no longer permissible to hand them in, they were just so much waste paper. Of course this did not mean that the case was lost, not by any means, at least there were no decisive grounds for this assumption, it was simply that one heard no more about the case and could not find out anything.

Of course, luckily, these were exceptional cases, and even if K's turned out to be one, it was still a long way from reaching that stage. In his case there was still plenty of opportunity for a lawyer to get to work, and K. could be quite sure that good use would be made of that opportunity. As had already been mentioned, the plea had not yet been handed in, but there was no hurry for that. It was much more important to have introductory discussions with the officials concerned, and these had already been held. With varying success, as must be frankly conceded. It would be better for the time being not to divulge any details, for they might have a bad effect on K. by making him over-optimistic or much too anxious. Yet this much could be said: some officials had expressed very favourable opinions and had also shown themselves very ready to help, while others had expressed less favourable opinions but had by no means absolutely refused their cooperation. On the whole, therefore, the result was very cheering, but no special conclusions ought to be drawn from it since all preliminary negotiations began like that and it was only in the light of further developments that one could judge the real value of these negotiations. At any rate nothing had been lost so far, and if, despite everything, they could still succeed in winning over the Director of the Court offices – various things had already been set in motion towards this end – the whole affair could be described as 'a clean wound' (as the surgeons called it) and one could await subsequent developments without any qualms.

The lawyer had an inexhaustible supply of speeches like this. They were rehearsed at every visit. It always turned out that progress had been made, but it was never possible to say exactly what this progress was. More work was always being done on the first plea, but it was never finished, and at the next visit this was usually shown to have been a great advantage, since, for reasons which could not have been foreseen, the last few days would have been a very unfavourable time for submitting the plea. If, sometimes, K, worn out by all these speeches, pointed out that, even allowing for all the difficulties, progress seemed to be very slow, he was met with the retort that progress was by no means slow, but that things would probably have got much further by now if K. had come to the lawyer when he should have done. But unfortunately he had failed to do this, and that meant there would be other disadvantages, and not merely to do with time either.

The only pleasant interruption to these visits was Leni, who always contrived to bring the lawyer his tea while K. was there. Then she would stand behind K, apparently looking on as the lawyer bent down low to his cup with a kind of greed, poured out the tea and drank it, and yet all the time she was surreptitiously allowing K. to hold her hand. There was complete silence. The lawyer was drinking his tea, K. squeezed Leni's hand, and Leni sometimes dared to stroke K.'s hair softly.

'Are you still here, then?' the lawyer asked, when he had finished.

'I wanted to take away the crockery,' Leni said. They had one last squeeze of the hand, then the lawyer wiped his mouth and started to harangue K. again with fresh energy.

K. had no idea whether the lawyer was trying to comfort him or reduce him to despair, but he certainly felt sure of one thing: his defence was not being handled properly. Everything the lawyer told him might be true, though it was also obvious that he wanted to occupy the limelight himself as much as possible and had probably never before been in charge of such an important case as he thought K.'s was. But his continual emphasis on his personal connections with the officials was suspicious. Was it certain that these connections were being exploited exclusively for K.'s benefit? The lawyer never omitted to point out that he was dealing only with the lower class of official, that is, only with officials in a very subordinate position whose promotion might probably be affected by certain turns in these cases. Were they perhaps making use of the lawyer in order to achieve those turns in the case which would, of course, always be unfavourable to the defendant? Perhaps that was not done in every trial, it was certainly not likely, but there must then be trials in the course of which they conceded the lawyer certain advantages in return for his services, since it must be in their interests, too, to maintain his professional reputation intact. But if that was really how things were, K. wondered how they would intervene in his own lawsuit which (as the lawyer explained) was a very difficult and, therefore, very important case which right from the very beginning had aroused a great deal of interest in the Courts. There could not be much doubt what they would do. The first indications had already been provided by the fact that the initial plea had still not been handed in, even though the case had already been going on for months, and by the fact that, according to the lawyer, everything was still in the preliminary stages. Of course, this was perfectly calculated to lull the defendant and keep him in a state of helplessness, in order then suddenly to surprise him with the verdict or at least with the news that the investigation had been concluded and had not come out in K's favour, and so the case was to be referred to higher authorities.

It was absolutely necessary for K. to take a hand himself. In states of extreme weariness, such as he was experiencing this winter morning, when thoughts ran quite haphazardly through his brain, he felt particularly incapable of dismissing this conviction. He no longer felt the contempt he had previously had for the case. If he had been alone in the world he could easily have ignored the case, even though in that event it was certain that the case would never have occurred at all. But now his uncle had already dragged him to this lawyer, and family considerations were also a factor. His own position was no longer completely independent of the course the case took, he himself had rather incautiously mentioned it, with a certain inexplicable satisfaction, when talking to acquaintances, while other people had learnt of it in some unknown fashion, and his relationship with Fräulein Bürstner seemed to fluctuate with the case. In short, he hardly had the choice now of accepting or rejecting the case, he was already in the middle of it and must protect himself. His being tired was a bad look-out for him.

Yet, for the time being, there was certainly no need for too much anxiety. In a comparatively short time he had managed to work himself up to the high position he held in the bank and to maintain himself in that position on his merits, which everybody acknowledged. Some of the ability which had made all this possible for him now simply had to be applied to the case, and there was no doubt that everything would turn out well. Above all, if he was to achieve anything, it was necessary that he should exclude from the very beginning any idea of possible guilt. There was no such guilt. The case was exactly like a big business transaction, such as he had often concluded to the advantage of the bank – a business transaction in which, as invariably happened, there lurked various dangers that had simply got to be averted. To ensure this, one certainly could not toy with thoughts of some guilt or other, but had to cling as firmly as possible to the thought of one's own advantage. Adopting this point of view, he would have no alternative but to take his affairs out of the hands of the lawyer very swiftly, ideally that very evening. By the man's own account, it's true, that was something unheard of and probably very insulting, but K. could not tolerate that his own efforts in the case should meet with obstacles which had perhaps been placed there by his own lawyer. Then, once the lawyer had been shaken off, the plea had got to be handed in immediately, and pressure must be exerted every day if possible to see that it was paid due regard. For this purpose it would naturally not be enough for K. to sit in the passage with the others and put his hat under the bench. He would have to go in person or send one of the women or somebody else, day after day, to besiege the officials and force them to sit down at their desks and study K's plea, instead of gazing through the lattice-work at the passage. There must be no slackening of these efforts, everything would have to be organized and properly supervised, so that for once the Court would be faced with a defendant who knew how to stand up for his rights.

But even though K. was confident he could do all this, the difficulty of drawing up the plea was overwhelming. Earlier on, about a week before this, he had had only a slight feeling of shame at the thought that it might be necessary some time for him to make this kind of plea himself: it had never occurred to him at all that it might also be difficult. He could remember how one morning, just when he was up to his ears in work, he had suddenly pushed everything aside and picked up his writing-pad and then tried to draft out the plan of just such a plea so that he might be able to put it at the disposal of the slow-witted lawyer. But then just at that moment the door of the Manager's office opened and the Deputy Manager came in, roaring with laughter. That had been very unpleasant for K., although, of course, the Deputy Manager was not laughing about the plea at all, of which he knew nothing – he was only laughing at a joke he had just heard at the Stock Exchange, a joke which, to be understood, needed illustrating, and so the Deputy Manager bent over K's desk and did the drawing with K's own pencil, which he took out of K's hand, on the very writing-pad K. had intended to use for the plea.

Today K. no longer felt any shame, the plea had got to be drawn up. If he had no time to do it at the office, which was very likely, he would simply have to compose it at night at home. If the nights were not enough either, he would have to take a holiday. Anything but stop halfway, that was the most senseless thing to do, not only in business but in anything else. It was true that the plea meant an almost endless amount of work. One did not have to be a very anxious kind of person to be easily persuaded into believing that it was going to be impossible ever to finish the plea. Not because of one's own laziness or other people's insidiousness, which could prevent only the lawyer from completing the plea, but because ignorance of the actual charges and of any possible extensions of them would make it necessary to survey and describe one's whole life from every conceivable angle, to recall to mind the very smallest actions and events. And, furthermore, what a depressing task this would be! Suitable, perhaps, as an occupation when one has retired and entered one's dotage or needs something to help while away the long days.

But at this moment, when K. needed to devote his mind entirely to his work, when every hour passed at such a hectic speed because he was still on the way up and already threatening to displace the Deputy Manager, and when he wanted to enjoy his short evenings and nights as a young man does, just at this of all moments he had got to start composing his plea. Once again his train of thought had issued into a rehearsal of his grievances. Almost involuntarily, simply to put an end to this, he fumbled for the button of the electric bell that rang in the outer office. As he pressed it, he looked up at the clock. It was eleven o'clock – he had been dreaming away for two whole hours, a long and valuable time, and he was naturally even more exhausted than before. But, even so, the time was not completely lost, for he had taken certain decisions which could be valuable. The clerks brought in various letters as well as the cards of two gentlemen who had already been waiting a considerable time for K. In fact they were very important clients of the bank, who really should not have been kept waiting under any circumstances. Why on earth did they come at such an inconvenient time, and why (he imagined the gentlemen for their part asking behind the closed door) was the industrious K. spending the best part of the working day on his own private affairs? Wearied by what had gone before and wearily awaiting what was to come, K. rose to his feet to receive the first of the clients.

This was a small, cheerful man, a manufacturer whom K. knew well. He regretted disturbing K. in the middle of important work, and K. for his part apologized for keeping the manufacturer waiting so long. But this very apology was spoken in such a mechanical way and was so falsely stressed that the manufacturer would have been bound to notice it, if he had not been taken up entirely with the business in hand. As it was, he hurriedly pulled calculations and tables out of every pocket, spread them out in front of K, explained different items, corrected a small arithmetical error which had caught his attention even during this cursory survey, and then reminded K. of a similar transaction that he had concluded with him about a year before. He mentioned in passing that, on this occasion, another bank was making great sacrifices to compete for the deal, and then finally fell silent in order to hear K's opinion. K. had in fact been following the beginning of the man's speech closely, for the thought of the important deal had at that stage seized his attention too, but unfortunately this didn't last, he had soon stopped listening and for a while had then only nodded at the manufacturer's more emphatic remarks. Finally, however, he had given up doing even that and confined himself to gazing at the man's bald head bent over his papers and to wondering when the manufacturer would eventually realize that his whole speech was useless. When the man stopped talking, K. actually believed at first that this was to give him an opportunity of confessing that he was not in a fit state to listen. But with some regret he noted, from the expectant look on the face of the manufacturer, who was obviously ready for all K's objections, that the business discussion had to be continued. So he bowed his head as if in obedience to an order and began to move his pencil slowly back and forth over the papers, stopping now and then to stare at a figure. The manufacturer presumed K. had objections, perhaps the figures in actual fact were not rigidly fixed, perhaps they were not the crucial thing, at any rate he covered the papers with his hand, and, moving up quite close to K, launched once again into a general account of the transaction.

'It's difficult,' K. said, pursing his lips, and since the papers, the only things he could grasp, were now covered, he sank back limply against the arm of his chair. He only looked up halfheartedly when the door of the Manager's office opened and the Deputy Manager appeared indistinctly, rather as if he were behind a gauze veil. K. thought no more about the Deputy Manager's entry, noticing only its immediate effect, which was very welcome to him. For at once the manufacturer leapt out of his chair and rushed over to the Deputy Manager, though K. would have liked him to have moved ten times as nimbly, since he was afraid the Deputy Manager might disappear again. He needn't have been afraid, for the two men met, shook hands and came over together to K's desk. The manufacturer complained that he had found the Senior Clerk to have little interest in the transaction, and he pointed at K. who, under the Deputy Manager's gaze, bent over the papers once more. Then, as the two leant against the desk and the manufacturer set about winning over the Deputy Manager to his proposals, it seemed to K. as if, above his head, two men, whose size he exaggerated to himself, were bargaining over him. He raised his eyes cautiously, and slowly tried to see what was happening above him, then, without looking at it, he took one of the papers from the desk, laid it on the palm of his hand and gradually lifted it, getting to his feet at the same time, up to the level of the two gentlemen. In doing this he was not thinking of anything in particular, but was merely acting in this way with a vague sense that this was what he would have to do once he had finished the great plea which was going to clear him completely. The Deputy Manager, who was completely engrossed in the conversation, only glanced cursorily at the paper without reading what was on it at all, for anything that was important to the Senior Clerk was quite unimportant to him; he took it out of K's hand saying, 'Thank you, I know all about it already,' and gently put it back on the table again.

K. cast a morose, sideways glance at him, but the Deputy Manager did not notice this at all, or, if he did, was only amused by it, he laughed loudly several times, and once he clearly embarrassed the manufacturer with a sharp retort, but then he immediately saved him from further embarrassment by finding a counter-argument himself and he ended by inviting him into his own office where they could complete the business.

'It is a very important matter,' he said to the manufacturer, 'I absolutely see that. And the Senior Clerk' – even when saying this he was really talking only to the manufacturer – 'will certainly be very glad if we relieve him of it. The thing needs to be thought out quietly. But today he seems to be overloaded with work, there are also some people in the outer office who have been waiting for him for hours.'

K. still had just enough composure to turn away from the Deputy Manager and address his friendly, but fixed smile only to the manufacturer. Otherwise he did not interfere, but simply stood there, supporting himself with both hands on the desk, bending forward slightly like some junior employee, and watched as the two men, without breaking off their conversation, picked up the papers from the desk and disappeared into the manager's office. In the doorway the manufacturer turned round and remarked that he would not say goodbye yet, as he would naturally see the Senior Clerk again to report on the outcome of the discussion, and, he said, he still had another little thing to tell him.

At last K. was alone. He had no intention of letting any more clients in, and dimly he began to realize how pleasant it was that the people outside thought he was still dealing with the manufacturer, so that there was no chance of anyone coming in, not even his assistant. He went to the window, sat on the sill holding the catch with one hand and gazed out at the square. The snow was still falling, and the sky had not yet cleared.

He sat like that for a long time without knowing what he was really worried about, only occasionally glancing in slight alarm over his shoulder towards the door of the outer office, mistakenly thinking he had heard a noise. But when nobody came, he grew calmer, went to the wash-basin, washed in cold water and came back to his seat by the window with a clearer head. The decision to take over his own defence himself now seemed to him more serious than he had originally presumed.

As long as he had palmed off the defence on to the lawyer, he had, in actual fact, been little affected by the case, he had observed it from a distance and had scarcely had any direct contact with it, he had been able to see, whenever he wanted, how matters stood, but he had also been able to withdraw whenever he wanted. Now, on the other hand, if he wanted to conduct his own defence himself, he would have – at least for the moment – to expose himself completely to the Court. The eventual consequence of this would be his absolute and final acquittal, but, in order to secure that acquittal, he had to place himself, temporarily at any rate, in much greater danger than before. If he had been in any doubt of this, today's meeting with the Deputy Manager and the manufacturer would have been enough to convince him completely. How could he have sat there, utterly bemused as he was by the mere decision to conduct his own defence? But how would it be later on? What days he had ahead of him! Would he ever find the path that would lead through all this to a happy ending? As for a careful defence – and any other kind of defence would be futile – did it not automatically mean abstaining as far as possible from doing anything else? Would he be able to do that successfully? And how would he be able to do all this from the bank? After all, it was not merely a question of the plea, some leave would perhaps have been enough for that, although it would certainly be very risky to ask for leave just at the moment. It was a question of a whole trial and there was no telling how long that would last. What a great obstacle was now suddenly menacing K's whole career!

And was he supposed to go on with his work for the bank now? (He looked down at his desk.) Was he supposed to let clients in to see him and do business with them now? And all the time his case was going ahead, all the time, up there in the attic, the Court officials were sitting poring over the documents of his trial, was he supposed to be attending to the affairs of the bank? Wasn't it rather like a form of torture, which, with the Court's backing, was connected with the lawsuit and was supposed to be an integral part of it? And when the people in the bank were judging his work, would they perhaps take account of the special situation he was placed in? No, none of them ever would. Of course, some people in the bank certainly did know about his trial, even though it was not quite clear yet who knew or how much they knew. But it was to be hoped that the rumour had not yet reached the Deputy Manager, otherwise there would have been no mistaking the way he would have used it against K. without any feelings of loyalty or humanity. And what about the Manager himself? There was no doubt that he was well disposed towards K. and, as soon as he heard about the trial, he would probably be willing to ease K's load in as much as it lay within his power to do so, but it was certain that he would not succeed, for, now that K's ability to counter-balance the Deputy Manager's power was beginning to decline, the Manager was falling more and more under the influence of the Deputy Manager, who, moreoever, was taking advantage of the Manager's ill health in order to increase his own authority. So what could K. hope for? Perhaps he was weakening his own powers of resistance by dwelling on these things, but it was, after all, necessary to be under no illusions and to view everything as clearly as was possible at the moment.

For no special reason, but simply to avoid going back to his desk yet, he opened the window. It was difficult to open, and he had to turn the catch with both hands. Then a mixture of fog and smoke billowed in through the whole area of the wide-open window and filled the room with a faint smell of burning. A few snowflakes were also blown in.

'What a horrible autumn,' K. heard the manufacturer say behind him; without being noticed, the manufacturer had come into the room from the Deputy Manager's office. K. nodded and gazed nervously at the briefcase, from which the manufacturer was sure now to take the papers, so that he could tell K. the result of his discussion with the Deputy Manager. But the manufacturer followed K's glance, slapped his briefcase and said without opening it:

'You'll want to hear what happened. I've almost got the contract here signed and sealed in my case. He's a charming man, your Deputy Manager, but a dangerous fellow to deal with.'

He laughed, shaking K. by the hand and trying to get him to laugh too. But K. now felt suspicious again, because the manufacturer did not seem to want to show him the papers, and he did not see anything to laugh at in the manufacturer's remark.

'My dear sir,' the manufacturer said, 'the weather must be getting you down . . . You look so depressed today.'

'Yes,' K. said and put his hand to his temple. 'Headaches, domestic worries . . .'

'Of course, of course,' said the manufacturer who was a hasty man and could never listen quietly to anyone. 'We all have our cross to bear.'

K. had involuntarily taken a step towards the door as if to show the manufacturer out, but the latter said:

'There's one other little thing I wanted to tell you. I'm afraid it's perhaps a bad time to be bothering you with it today of all days, but I've been to see you twice recently and I forgot about it both times. But if I put it off any longer, there probably won't be any point at all in telling you. And that would be a pity, for in actual fact what I have to say may not be without some value.'

Before K. could answer, the manufacturer stepped up close to him, tapped him on the chest with his knuckle and said softly:

'You've got a trial, haven't you?'

K. recoiled and cried out immediately:

'The Deputy Manager has told you!'

'No, no,' said the manufacturer. 'How would the Deputy Manager know about it?'

'And how did you know?' K. asked him with much greater composure.

'Now and then I hear a thing or two about the Court,' said the manufacturer. 'And that's just what I wanted to tell you.'

'So many people seem to be in touch with the Court,' K. said, his head bowed, as he led the manufacturer back to his desk. They sat down again, as before, and the manufacturer said:

'I'm afraid there's not very much I can tell you, but in situations like this one mustn't neglect the slightest thing. Besides, I feel I must help you somehow, however modest my support can be. We've always been good business friends, haven't we? Well, then . . .'

K. wanted to apologize for his behaviour during that morning's discussion, but the manufacturer would not allow any interruption. He just shoved his briefcase up high under his arm to show he was in a hurry to be gone, and continued:

'I know about your case from a man called Titorelli. He's a painter, Titorelli is only his professional name, I don't even know his real name. For years he has been coming to see me from time to time in my office, and he brings little paintings with him for which I always give him a sort of alms – he is almost a beggar. Besides, they're nice pictures, moorland scenes and that kind of thing. These sales – we had both got accustomed to them by now – were going quite smoothly. But I eventually found he was coming too often, I objected to this and we started talking. I was interested to know how he could support himself solely by painting, and then I discovered to my astonishment that most of his income came from portrait painting. He said he worked for the Court. "What court?" I asked him. And then he told me about the Court. You of all people can well imagine how amazed I was at what he told me. Ever since then, whenever he comes, he tells me something new about the Court, and so I've gradually gained a certain insight into how it works. Of course Titorelli can't stop talking and I often have to fend him off, not only because he's certainly a liar, but chiefly because a professional man like I am is almost collapsing under his own business worries and can't be bothered very much with other people's affairs. But that's by the way. Now perhaps – this is what I was thinking – Titorelli might be of some help to you, he knows many of the judges and, even though he may not have much influence himself, he may be able, after all, to give you some advice on how to get in touch with various influential people. And even if this advice may not be crucial in itself, it seems to me that you might be able to make very good use of it. For you're almost a lawyer yourself. I'm always saying: "The Senior Clerk is almost a lawyer." Oh, I'm not worried about your trial. Well, would you like to go and see Titorelli now? If I recommend you he'll certainly do everything he can. I really think you ought to go. Of course you don't have to go today, but some other time, whenever it suits you. And of course, I just want to say this, you're under no obligation at all to go to Titorelli just because I advise you to. If you think you can do without Titorelli, it is certainly better to leave him out of it altogether. Perhaps you already have a definite plan prepared and Titorelli would just spoil it. Then you certainly mustn't go and see him! It'd certainly cost a bit of an effort to take advice from a chap like him. Anyway, you do just as you like. Here's the letter of introduction and here's his address.'

K. felt disappointed as he took the letter and put it in his pocket. Even in the most favourable circumstances any advantage he might gain from this recommendation was completely out-weighed by the damage resulting from the fact that the manu-facturer knew about his trial and that the painter was spreading the news about it. He could hardly bring himself to say a few words of thanks to the manufacturer, who was already moving towards the door.

'I'll go and see him,' he said, as he took leave of the manufacturer at the door. 'Or, as I'm very busy just now, I may write and tell him to come and see me at the office one day.'

'I was sure,' the manufacturer said, 'you'd think of the best way of dealing with it. Only I should have thought you would prefer to avoid inviting people like this Titorelli to the bank to discuss your trial with him here. Besides, it's not always a good idea to let people like that get their hands on letters of yours. But I'm sure you've thought all that out and know what you should do.'

K. nodded and escorted the manufacturer through the outer office. But although K. seemed calm, he was absolutely horrified at himself. He had really only said that he would write to Titorelli in order to demonstrate somehow to the manufacturer that he valued the introduction and was giving immediate thought to the possibility of meeting up with Titorelli, but if he had thought Titorelli's assistance would be valuable, he would not have thought twice about actually writing to him. However, he did not see the dangers which that might entail until the manufacturer pointed them out. Could he really place such little reliance upon his own judgement? If he was capable of writing an unequivocal letter to such a dubious individual actually inviting him to the bank where, separated only by a door from the Deputy Manager, he could ask his advice about the trial, was it not then possible, or even very probable, that he was also overlooking other dangers or blundering into them? There wasn't always somebody near him who could warn him. And to think that, now of all times, when he ought to have built up his strength and be ready to act, he should be assailed by such doubts, hitherto alien to him, about his own alertness! Were the same difficulties which he was experiencing in carrying out his office work going to affect his trial now as well? He certainly had not the faintest idea how he could ever have dreamt of wanting to write to Titorelli and invite him to the bank.

He was still shaking his head over this when the clerk came up and reminded him that there were three gentlemen sitting on a bench in the outer office. They had already been waiting a long time to get in to see K. Now, when the clerk spoke to K, they all stood up and each of them sought to exploit the first chance of getting to K. before the others. If the people at the bank were so inconsiderate as to make them waste their time here in the waiting-room, they did not see why they should be any more considerate themselves.

'Sir,' one of them was already starting to say. But K. had already sent the clerk for his overcoat and while he was being helped on with it he said to all three:

'You must excuse me, gentlemen, I'm afraid I have no time to see you at the moment. I really do apologize, but I have some urgent business to see to and I must leave at once. You've seen for yourselves how long I've already been held up. Would you be so kind as to come back tomorrow or whenever you can manage it? Or perhaps we could discuss the business on the telephone? Or perhaps if you could now tell me briefly what it's about, I could then let you have a detailed answer in writing. But the best thing would certainly be if you came some other time.'

K's suggestions so astounded the three men, who now realized they had been waiting quite uselessly, that they gazed mutely at each other.

'So it's agreed, then?' K. asked, turning to the clerk, who had now brought him his hat as well. Through the open door of his room K. could see that it was snowing much harder outside now, so he put his coat collar up and buttoned it high around his neck.

Just at that moment the Deputy Manager came out of the next room, saw with a smile that K. was talking to the gentlemen with his overcoat on, and asked:

'So you're going out now, Herr K?'

'Yes,' K. said, drawing himself up, 'I have to go out on business.' But the Deputy Manager had already turned to the gentle-men.

'And what about these gentlemen?' he asked. 'I believe they've been waiting a long time already.'

'We've already agreed what to do,' K. said. But now the gentlemen refused to be restrained, they crowded round K. and explained that they would not have waited for hours if their affairs had not been important and needed to be discussed that very minute, in detail and in private. The Deputy Manager listened to them for a while and also looked at K, who stood holding his hat and dusting it here and there. He then said:

'Gentlemen, there's one very simple solution. If you're pre-pared to make do with me, I should be very glad to take over the negotiations in place of the Senior Clerk. Of course your affairs must be discussed straight away. We are businessmen like your-selves, and we know how valuable a businessman's time is. Would you please come in here?' And he opened the door which led to the anteroom of his own office. How adroitly the Deputy Manager usurped everything that K. was now having to sur-render! But was K. perhaps not giving up more than he ab-solutely had to? Whilst he went running off with vague and, as he had to admit to himself, very slender hopes to see some obscure painter, his prestige at the bank was suffering irreparable damage. It would probably be much better to take his overcoat off again and try to win back at least the two gentlemen who were still having to wait next door. And he might well have tried to do this if he had not just glimpsed the Deputy Manager in his room, looking for something in the files as if they were his own. As K. came to the door in a state of some agitation, the Deputy Man-ager shouted out:

'Ah, so you haven't gone yet!' He turned his face, on which the numerous taut lines seemed to betoken strength rather than age,

towards K. and then immediately resumed his search. 'I'm looking for a copy of an agreement,' he said, 'which the firm's representative says ought to be among your things. Won't you help
me look for it?' K. took a step forward, but the Deputy Manager
said:

'Thank you, I've got it already,' and went back into his room
with a huge bundle of papers, obviously containing not only the
copy of the agreement but a lot of other things as well.

'I'm no match for him just at the moment,' K. said to himself,
'but once my personal difficulties have been sorted out, he'll be
the first to know, that's for sure, and I'll really make him pay.'
The thought of this calmed him a little, so he told the clerk, who
had been holding the door to the corridor open for him for a long
time, to inform the Manager, when the opportunity arose, that
he had gone out on business, and then left the bank, almost elated
at the thought that now he could devote himself entirely to his
own affairs for a while.

He went straight to the painter, who lived in a suburb which
was in completely the opposite direction to where the Court
offices were. It was an even poorer district, the houses were even
gloomier, and the streets were full of filth which oozed slowly
about on the melted snow. At the house where the painter lived
only one wing of the big door was standing open, but there was a
hole in the brickwork under the other wing and, as K. approached, an obnoxious yellow steaming fluid poured out of this,
sending a few rats fleeing to the drain nearby. At the bottom of the
steps a small child lay on its belly on the ground and howled, but
it could scarcely be heard because of the deafening noise from a
tinsmith's workshop on the other side of the front door. The door
of the workshop was open, and three assistants were standing in a
semi-circle round some object and hitting it with their hammers.
A big sheet of tinplate hanging on the wall reflected a pale light
that passed between two of these assistants and lit up their faces

and aprons. K. glanced only briefly at all this. He wanted to get things settled here as quickly as possible; he proposed merely to sound the painter out with a few questions and then get back to the bank again immediately. If he had any success at all here, it would have a good effect on the work he was doing at the bank that day. When he got to the third floor, he had to slacken his pace; he was quite out of breath, for both the steps and the storeys were inordinately high, and the painter was supposed to live right at the top, in an attic. Moreover, the air was very stuffy as there was no well for these narrow stairs, which were shut in on both sides by walls, with only an occasional little window almost right at the top. Just as K. stopped for a moment, some young girls came running out of a flat and hurried on up the stairs laughing. K. followed them slowly, caught up with one of them who had stumbled and been left behind by the others, and as they climbed on together he asked her:

'Is there a painter called Titorelli living here?' The girl, slightly hunchbacked and barely thirteen years old, replied by poking him with her elbow and glancing up at him slyly. Neither her youth nor her physical deformity had prevented her from having already become completely debauched. She did not even smile, but stared earnestly at K. with a keen, provocative gaze. Pretending not to notice her behaviour, K. asked:

'Do you know the painter Titorelli?'

She nodded and in her turn asked:

'What d'you want him for?'

K. thought it would be useful to find out quickly a little more about Titorelli. So he said:

'I want him to paint my portrait.'

'Paint your portrait?' she asked, opening her mouth excessively wide, then she hit out at K. gently with her hand as if he had said something really surprising or tactless, lifted her already very short skirts with both hands and ran as fast as she could after the other girls, whose screaming was already fading somewhere up-stairs. But at the next bend in the stairs K. met them all again. Obviously the hunchback had told them what K. wanted, and they were waiting for him. They stood on either side of the stairs, squeezed up against the walls so that K. could easily pass between them, and smoothed their aprons with their hands. Their faces, and this lining up to make him run the gauntlet, all betrayed a blend of childishness and depravity. The girls who now closed in laughing behind K. were led by the hunchback, who took over the task of directing him. She was the one he had to thank for showing him the right way at once. He had been going to go straight on, but she showed him that he had to branch off up another stairway to get to Titorelli. This other stairway was extremely narrow and very long, without any bend in it, and visible over its whole length right to the top where it ended directly in front of Titorelli's door. This door, which in contrast to the rest of the stairway, was lit comparatively brightly by a small skylight set at an angle above it, was made of plain boards, on which the name Titorelli was painted in red in broad brush-strokes. K. was scarcely halfway up the stairs with his retinue when someone above, obviously disturbed by the noise of many footsteps, opened the door a little and appeared in the crack, apparently wearing nothing but a nightshirt. He cried out 'Oh!' when he saw them all coming, and disappeared. The little hunchback clapped her hands with joy, and the other girls pushed up behind K. to propel him forwards more quickly.

But they still had not even reached the very top when the painter flung the door wide open and, with a deep bow, invited K. to come in. The girls, on the other hand, he pushed away and wouldn't let one of them in, however much they begged and tried to push in against his will after he had refused them his permission. The hunchback was the only one who managed to slip through under his outstretched arm, but the painter chased her, grabbed her by the skirts, whirled her round him once and then deposited her outside the door with the other girls who, though the painter had deserted his post, had not dared to cross the threshold. K. did not know what to think of all this, for they all seemed to be on the friendliest terms. The girls at the door craned their necks one behind the other, yelling various jocular remarks at the painter which K. did not understand, and the painter himself was laughing as he almost threw the hunchback in the air. Then he closed the door, bowed to K. once again, shook him by the hand and introduced himself, saying:

'I am the painter Titorelli.'

K. pointed at the door, behind which the girls were whispering, and said:

'You seem to be very popular here.'

'Oh, those little brats!' the painter said and tried unsuccessfully to button up his nightshirt at the neck. He had no shoes on and his only other garment was a pair of wide yellowish linen trousers, fastened by a strap, the long end of which flapped loosely to and fro.

'Those little brats are a real nuisance to me,' he went on, giving up fiddling with his nightshirt as the top button had just come off. Then he fetched a chair and insisted that K. sat down.

'I once painted one of them – she's not there today – and since then they've all been pestering me. When I'm here myself, they can only get in if I let them in, but when I'm away one of them at least always gets in. They've had a key made to my door which they pass around among themselves. You can hardly imagine what a nuisance it is. For instance, I might come back with a lady whom I'm going to paint, I open the door with my key, and there I may find the hunchback over by the little table, painting her lips red with the brush, while all her little sisters she's supposed to look after are running around and making every corner of the room filthy. Or else, as happened only yesterday, I get home late in the evening – that's the reason for my present state and the mess in the room, you must excuse me – well, I come home late in the evening and start to get into bed and something tweaks my leg, so I look under the bed and drag out another of those little pests. I've no idea why they come bothering me so much, you must have just seen for yourself that I don't exactly go out of my way to entice them here. Naturally, all this disturbs my work as well. If it weren't that I have free use of this studio, I should have moved out long ago.' Just then, a little voice behind the door called out, nervously and tenderly:

'Titorelli, can't we come in now?'

'No!' the painter replied.

'Can't I come in by myself?' the voice asked again.

'No, you can't,' the painter said. He went to the door and locked it.

Meanwhile K. had been looking round the room. He himself would never have dreamt that this wretched little room could be called a studio. Two long strides would cover its area, lengthways and breadthways. Everything – floor, walls and ceiling – was made of wood, with little cracks in between the planks. Opposite K, against the wall, stood the bed, heaped high with different-coloured bedding. In the middle of the room was an easel with a painting on it covered by a shirt, the sleeves of which dangled down to the ground. Behind K. was the window, through which one was prevented by the fog from seeing anything but the snow-covered roof of the next house.

The turning of the key in the lock reminded K. that he had not meant to stay long. So he took the manufacturer's letter out of his pocket, handed it to the painter and said:

'I heard about you from this gentleman, an acquaintance of yours, and came here on his advice.' The painter hurriedly read the letter through and threw it on the bed. If the manufacturer had not most categorically described Titorelli as an acquaintance of his, as a poor man who was totally dependent on his charity, one might actually now have thought that Titorelli did not know the manufacturer or at least could not remember him. What was more, the painter now asked:

'D'you want to buy some paintings or have your portrait painted?' K. looked at him in astonishment. What on earth did the letter actually say? K. had taken for granted that in the letter the manufacturer told the painter K's reason for coming – to inquire about his trial, nothing but that. He had been in far too much of a hurry to come here! He hadn't thought about it long enough. But now he had to give the painter some sort of a reply, and with a glance at the easel he said:

'You're in the middle of working on something now?'

'Yes,' said the painter, and snatching the shirt from the easel, he threw it on the bed after the letter. 'It's a portrait. It's pretty good, but not quite finished yet.' K. was in luck, the opportunity to talk about the Court was literally being offered to him, since this was obviously the portrait of a judge. Moreover, it bore a striking resemblance to the painting in the lawyer's study. This was a completely different judge, however, a fat man with a bushy black beard that reached right up his cheeks on either side of his face – and also the other picture had been an oil-painting, whereas this one was done lightly and indistinctly in pastel. But everything else was similar, for here too the judge was poised to rise menacingly from his throne, fiercely gripping the arms of it. K. was about to say, 'That's a judge,' but he checked himself for the moment and went up to the painting, as if he wanted to study the details of it. Standing centrally behind the back of the chair was a tall figure which he could not explain, and he asked the painter about it. The painter replied that it needed to be filled in some more, he went and got a crayon from a small table and shaded in a little round the edges of the figure, without, however, making it much clearer for K.

'It's Justice,' the painter said at last.

'Yes, now I can recognize it,' K. said. 'There's the bandage over the eyes and here are the scales. But hasn't it got wings on its heels and isn't it flying through the air?'

'Yes,' said the painter, 'that's how I was commissioned to paint it. Actually it's Justice and the goddess of Victory in one.'

'That's not a good combination,' K. said with a smile. 'Justice ought to be quite still, or else the scales will fluctuate and a just verdict won't be possible.'

'I was just complying with my client's instructions,' said the painter.

'Yes, of course.' K. said, for he had not meant to hurt anyone's feelings with his remark, 'you've painted the figure exactly as it really is on the throne.'

'No,' said the painter, 'I haven't seen the figure or the throne, that's all pure invention, but I was told what to paint.'

'How d'you mean?' K. asked, deliberately pretending that he did not completely understand the painter. 'Surely that's a judge sitting on his official seat?'

'Yes,' said the painter, 'but he is not a very high-ranking judge, and he has never sat on a throne like that.'

'And yet he has himself painted in such a solemn attitude? He sits there looking like a President of the Court.'

'Yes, they're vain, these gentlemen,' said the painter, 'but they have official permission to have themselves painted like that. Each of them is told exactly how he can have his portrait painted. The only trouble is, this picture doesn't give you, unfortunately, a good idea of the details of the costume and the seat, pastel is not suitable for such pictures.'

'No,' K. said, 'it's strange that you did it in pastel.'

'That was what the judge wanted,' the painter said, 'he intends to give it to a lady.' The sight of the picture seemed to have given him a desire to work, for he rolled up his sleeves, picked up some crayons, and, as K. watched, a reddish shadow right next to the judge's head took shape beneath the tremulous tips of the crayons and faded away as it radiated out towards the edge of the picture. Little by little this play of shadow surrounded the head like a piece of finery or a sign of high distinction. But the figure of Justice was left bright, apart from an imperceptible tinge, and this brightness brought the figure into particular prominence so that it no longer recalled the goddess of Justice, nor the goddess of Victory, but now looked far more like the goddess of the Chase. Against K's will, the work painter's attracted him, but in the end he reproached himself for staying here so long without, as yet, having done anything about his own affairs.

'What's the name of this judge?' he asked suddenly.

'I'm not allowed to tell you that,' replied the painter, who had bent down low over the picture and was clearly taking no notice of his guest, whom at first he had welcomed so solicitously. K. thought it was just moodiness, and was annoyed that this was causing him to waste time.

'But you are trusted by the Court, aren't you?' he asked. The painter immediately put down his crayons, straightened himself, rubbed his hands together and looked at K. with a smile.

'Now come on, out with it,' he said. 'You want to find out something about the Court, just as it says in your letter of recommendation, but first you talked to me about my paintings, just to get me on your side. Not that I take any offence at that, for you couldn't know that that was the wrong way to approach me. Oh, please,' he said, sharply staving off K's attempted objections. Then he went on:

'Besides, you are absolutely right when you say that I am trusted by the Court.' Here he paused, as if to give K. time to take this in. Now the girls could be heard again behind the door. Probably they were crowding round the keyhole, and perhaps they could also see into the room through the cracks in the planks. K. gave up trying to make some sort of an apology, for he did not want to divert the painter from that particular topic of conversation, but neither did he want the painter to inflate his own importance and thus, in a way, put himself out of reach. So he asked:

'Is yours an officially recognized position?'

'No,' the painter said curtly, as if this question had snatched further words from his mouth. But K. did not want to stop him talking and said:

'Well, often these unofficial positions are more influential than the official ones.'

'That's just how it is with me,' the painter said, knitting his brow and nodding. 'I was talking to the manufacturer yesterday about your case, he asked me whether I would be willing to help you, and I told him you should come and see me some time, so now I'm glad to see you here so soon. You seem to be very affected by it, and that doesn't surprise me at all, of course. Perhaps first you'd like to take your coat off?' Although K. did not mean to stay there long, he was very glad to hear the painter suggest this. The air in the room had gradually begun to seem very stuffy, and several times already he had glanced in astonishment at a small, almost certainly unlit iron stove in the corner; he could not understand why the air in the room was so oppressive. As he took off his overcoat and even unbuttoned his jacket as well, the painter said apologetically:

'I have to have it warm. It's very cosy in here, isn't it? The room's very good from that point of view.'

K. made no reply, but it was not really the warmth which was making him feel uneasy, it was rather the stuffy air in which he could hardly breathe, for the room could not have been ventilated for a long time. What made things more unpleasant for K. was that the painter asked him to sit on the bed, while he himself sat in front of the easel on the only chair in the room. Moreover, the painter did not seem to understand why K. insisted on sitting on the edge of the bed; indeed he asked K. to make himself comfortable, and when K. hesitated, he came over and pushed K. deep into the bedclothes and pillows. Then Titorelli went back to his seat, and at last asked his first pertinent question, which put everything else out of K's head.

'Are you innocent?' he asked.

'Yes,' K. said. It really gave him a lot of pleasure to answer this question, especially as he was talking to a private individual and therefore had no need to worry about any consequences. So far, no one had asked him such a frank question. In order to savour this pleasure to the utmost he even added:

'I am completely innocent.'

'I see,' Titorelli said, then bowed his head and seemed to be thinking. Suddenly he raised his head again and said:

'If you're innocent, then the whole thing is very simple.'

A look of sadness spread over K's face, for this man, who was allegedly in the confidence of the Court, was talking like an ignorant child.

'My innocence doesn't simplify the matter,' said K. Nevertheless he could not help smiling and shook his head slowly. 'Everything depends on all the subtle devices in which the Court keeps on losing itself. And in the end, though there was nothing there at all in the first place, it produces a great load of guilt from somewhere.'

'Yes, yes, of course,' the painter said, as if K. was disturbing his train of thought for no reason. 'But you are innocent, you say?'

'Certainly I am,' said K.

'Well, that's the main thing,' said the painter. No counter-argument could move him, but in spite of his decisiveness it was not clear whether he was speaking like this from conviction or mere indifference. K. wanted to establish this first, and so he said:

'You certainly know the Court far better than I do, I know hardly any more than what I have heard from all sorts of different people. But they did all agree that frivolous charges are never made, and that once the Court has made an indictment, it is firmly convinced that the accused is guilty and it can be budged from that conviction only with difficulty.'

'With difficulty?' the painter asked, flinging one hand into the air. 'It's never possible to budge the Court. If I were to paint all the judges next to each other here on one canvas and you were to plead your case before that canvas, you would have more success than you would in front of the real Court.'

'Yes,' K. said to himself, quite forgetting that he had only wanted to sound the painter out.

Once more one of the girls behind the door began to ask:

'Titorelli, isn't he going to go soon then?'

'Shut up!' the painter shouted at the door. 'Can't you see that I'm having a discussion with this gentleman?' But the girl was not satisfied with that and asked:

'You're going to paint him?' And when the painter did not answer, she went on:

'Please don't paint him, he's so ugly!' Now the others voiced their agreement in a welter of incomprehensible shouts. The painter leapt to the door, opened it a fraction – through the crack the imploring, outstretched clasped hands of the girls could be seen – and said:

'If you don't keep quiet, I'll throw you all down the stairs. Sit down there on the steps and behave yourselves!' In all probability they did not do this at once, for he had to bellow out the order:

'Get down on the steps!' It was only then that silence fell.

'I must apologize,' Titorelli said when he came back to K. K. had hardly glanced at the door, he had left the question of whether and how he was to be protected entirely to the painter. Even now he scarcely moved, when Titorelli bent down to him and, so as not to be heard outside, whispered in his ear:

'These girls belong to the Court, too.'

'What's that?' K. asked, jerking his head to one side and looking at the painter, who now sat down again on his chair and said, half in jest and half by way of explanation:

'Everything, you see, belongs to the Court.'

'I didn't realize that,' K. said curtly. The generalized nature of Titorelli's remark robbed his reference to the girls of any disquieting purport. Nevertheless K. gazed for a while in the direction of the door, behind which the girls were now sitting quietly on the steps, except that one of them had pushed a straw through a crack between the boards and was working it slowly up and down.

'You don't seem to have any kind of general idea about the Court so far,' said Titorelli, stretching his legs out wide apart and tapping on the floor with his toes. 'But since you're innocent, you won't really need to. I can get you off by myself.'

'How are you going to do that?' asked K. 'You said yourself a moment ago that the Court is completely impervious to proof.'

'Only impervious to proof that is brought before the Court,' said the painter, raising his forefinger, as if there were a subtle distinction here which K had not noticed. 'But it's quite different with what one may attempt in this respect behind the scenes, that's to say in the consulting-rooms, in the corridors, or even here in this studio for example.'

What the painter was now saying did not seem quite so incredible to K. any more; in fact to a large extent it agreed with what K. had already heard from other people. Indeed it was even very hopeful. If the judges were really as easily influenced by personal relationships as the lawyer had portrayed them, then any links the painter might have with these vain judges were particularly important and, in any event, ought on no account to be underestimated. In that case the painter fitted very well into the circle of allies whom K. was gradually gathering about himself. His talent for organization had once been highly lauded at the bank, and now that he was left entirely to his own resources, it seemed a good opportunity to test that talent to the utmost. The painter observed the effect his explanation had had on K, and then remarked with a certain anxiety:

'Doesn't it strike you that I'm talking almost like a lawyer? It's being continuously with these gentlemen of the Court that affects me that way. Naturally I gain a lot from it, but it plays havoc with my artistic spontaneity.'

'How did you first come in contact with the judges?' K. asked him. He was anxious to win the painter's confidence first, before actually enlisting him into his service.

'That was very simple,' the painter said, 'I inherited the connection. My father was painter to the Court in his day. It's a position that is always handed on from father to son. You can't use new people for it. When it comes to painting the portraits of the various ranks of officials, there are so many different and intricate and, above all, secret regulations laid down that these are not known at all outside certain families. Over in that drawer, for instance, I keep all my father's sketches, and I never show them to anybody. And a man has to know these before he is capable of painting the judges. Yet even if I lost them I'd still be left with enough rules which I alone carry in my head to prevent anybody laying claim to my post. Every judge after all wants to be painted just as the grand old judges were, and there's no one who can do that except me.'

'I envy you,' K. said, thinking of his own position at the bank. 'So your position is unassailable?'

'Yes, unassailable,' Titorelli said, squaring his shoulders

proudly. 'And that's why I can take the risk now and then of helping some poor man who has a trial on.'

'And how do you do it?' K. asked, as if it were not himself whom the painter was referring to as a poor man. But the painter would not allow himself to be sidetracked; he said:

'In your case, for example, seeing that you're completely innocent, I should take the following course of action.' This repeated mention of his innocence was beginning to annoy K. It seemed to him at times as if, by slipping in such remarks, the painter were making the successful outcome of the case a condition for his help, and yet, if there were a successful outcome, that help would, of course, be valueless. In spite of these doubts, however, K. restrained himself and did not interrupt the painter. He did not want to do without Titorelli's help, he had already made up his mind about that, moreover, this help did not appear to be any more dubious than the lawyer's. In fact K. even preferred it, because it was offered more ingenuously and frankly.

Titorelli had pulled his chair up nearer the bed and went on in a subdued voice:

'I ought to have started by asking you what kind of acquittal you want. There are three possibilities, namely actual acquittal, apparent acquittal, and postponement. Actual acquittal is, naturally, the best, the only thing is I haven't the slightest influence on that kind of verdict. In my opinion there isn't a single person who could influence a verdict of actual acquittal. The deciding factor there is probably the innocence of the accused. As you're innocent, it really might be possible for you to rely solely on your innocence. But then you wouldn't need help either from me or anybody else.'

K. was nonplussed at first by this neat exposition, but then he said just as quietly as the painter:

'I think you're contradicting yourself.'

'How?' Titorelli asked patiently, leaning back with a smile.

This smile made K. feel that he was on the verge of uncovering contradictions not in what the painter said, but in the Court procedure itself. But he did not shrink from this and went on to say:

'Earlier you remarked that the Court was impervious to proof, and then you qualified this by saying it only applied to what happened in the public sessions of the Court, and yet now you're even saying that an innocent person needs no help before the Court. That in itself is one contradiction. What's more, you said earlier that the judges were open to personal persuasion, but now you deny this by saying that an actual acquittal, as you call it, can never be achieved by personal influence. There's your second contradiction.'

'These contradictions can easily be explained,' the painter said. 'We're talking about two different things here – there's what's laid down by the Law and there's what I've found to be the case in my own personal experience, and you mustn't confuse the two. The Law, which I must say I haven't read, naturally on the one hand states that innocent persons must be acquitted, but on the other hand it certainly doesn't state that the judges are subject to influence. Now, my experience tells me that exactly the opposite is true. I don't know of a single case of actual acquittal, but I do know of many instances of influence being used. Of course it's possible that in all the cases I'm acquainted with the accused man was not innocent. But isn't that unlikely? In so many cases not a single accused man innocent? Even as a child I listened carefully to my father when he talked at home about trials, and even the judges who came to his studio told stories about the Court – for in our circles no one ever talks about anything else. As soon as I got the chance to go to the Court myself, I took every opportunity to do so. I've listened to countless cases at their crucial stages and followed them up as far as they were open to the public, and I must confess I have never come across a single instance of actual acquittal.'

'Not a single actual acquittal then,' K. said, as if he were addressing himself and his own hopes. 'That confirms the opinion I've already got about the Court. From this point of view, too, it's a completely pointless institution. One single hangman could do the job of the whole Court.'

'You mustn't generalize,' the painter said irritably. 'I've only been talking about my own experience, you see.'

'That's sufficient,' K. said, 'or have you heard of acquittals in years gone by?'

'There are said to have been such acquittals,' the painter answered, 'only it's very hard to prove it. The Court's final verdicts are never published, they are not even available to the judges, and so only legends about old legal cases have come down to us. Certainly these legends do include instances of actual acquittal, such legends are indeed even in the majority, they can be believed but they can't be proved. Still, one mustn't ignore them altogether, there's almost certainly some truth in them, and they're very beautiful too. I myself have painted some pictures on the subject of legends like that.'

'It will take more than legends to alter my opinion,' K. said, 'and surely one can't cite these legends as evidence in one's defence before the Court, can one?'

The painter laughed. 'No,' he said, 'one can't do that.'

'Then it's no use talking about them,' K. said. For the time being he was ready to put up with any of Titorelli's opinions, even if he thought them far-fetched and even if they were contradicted by other reports. He did not now have the time to examine the truth of all the painter said, far less to argue with him. The most he could achieve would be to get the painter to help him in some way, even if the help should prove less than decisive. So he said:

'Let's leave actual acquittal out of it then, but you mentioned two other possibilities.'

'Apparent acquittal and postponement. It must be one of those,' said the painter. 'But don't you want to take your jacket off before we start talking about them? You must find it hot.'

'Yes,' K. said. Up to now, he had been thinking only about what the painter was explaining, but now that he had been reminded of the heat heavy perspiration appeared on his forehead. 'It's almost unbearable.'

The painter nodded, as if he perfectly understood K's discomfort.

'Couldn't we open the window?' K. asked.

'No,' said the painter, 'it won't open, it's only a pane of glass which has been firmly fixed in.' Now K. realized that all the time he had been hoping that either he or the painter would suddenly go to the window and wrench it open. He was prepared to inhale even gaping mouthfuls of fog. The sensation of being completely shut off here from the fresh air made him feel dizzy. He lightly patted the quilt beside him with his hand and said weakly:

'It's not very comfortable or very healthy.'

'Oh, no,' Titorelli said in defence of his window. 'Although it's only a single pane, the fact that it can't be opened keeps the warmth in here much better than double-glazing would. But if I want to air the room, which is not very necessary as air gets in through all the cracks, I can always open one of the doors or even both of them.' Slightly reassured by this explanation, K. looked around to find the other door. Titorelli noticed this and said:

'It's behind you, I had to put the bed in front of it.' Only now did K. spot the little door in the wall.

'Everything's simply much too small here for a studio,' said the painter, as if to forestall a criticism from K. 'I had to fit myself in as best I could. Of course that bed in front of the door is in a very bad place. For example, the judge I'm painting at the moment always comes through that door by the bed, and I've also given him a key to that door so that he can wait here in the studio for me when I'm not at home. Now, however, he usually comes early in the morning, when I'm still asleep. Of course when the door opens beside the bed I wake up with a start no matter how deeply asleep I am. You would lose any respect you have for the judges if you could hear the way I curse him when he climbs over my bed early in the morning. I could, it's true, take the key back from him, but that would only make things worse. In this place you could tear all the doors off their hinges with the minimum of effort.' Throughout this entire speech K. was wondering whether he should take off his jacket, but finally realizing that if he didn't he would be incapable of staying there any longer, he took it off and placed it on his knees so that, when their talk was over, he could put it on again at once. He had scarcely taken it off when one of the girls shouted:

'Now he's taken his jacket off!' and they could all be heard crowding round the cracks in the door to witness the spectacle for themselves.

'The girls, you see, think that I'm going to paint your portrait,' the painter said, 'and that's why you've taken your jacket off.'

'I see,' K. said, not very amused, since he hardly felt any better than he had before, although he was now sitting in his shirt-sleeves. Almost morosely he asked:

'What did you say the other two possibilities were?' He had already forgotten the terms.

'Apparent acquittal and postponement,' said the painter. 'It depends on you which one you choose. With my help you could get either of them, though of course not without some trouble, and when it comes to the trouble which one has to take, the chief difference is that apparent acquittal needs concentrated effort for a while, whereas postponement means there is much less effort expended, but it is expended continuously. Let's take apparent acquittal first. If this is what you want, then I write out a statement of your innocence on a sheet of paper. The text for this statement has been handed down to me by my father and is un-impeachable. Then with this statement I go the rounds of the judges I know. So I might begin by showing it to the judge I'm painting at the moment – perhaps I could show it to him this evening when he comes for his sitting. I put the statement before him, I explain that you're innocent and offer to guarantee it myself. And that's no merely formal guarantee, it's a real, binding one.' In the painter's eyes there was something amounting to a reproach that K. should want to burden him with a guarantee like that.

'That would indeed be very kind of you,' K. said. 'And the judge would be ready to believe you and yet not grant me an actual acquittal?'

'I've told you that already,' the painter answered. 'In any case it's not at all certain that every judge would believe me. For example, many of them would tell me to bring you along in person. Then you would have to come along too. Of course, in that case, the battle would be half won, especially as I would instruct you beforehand exactly how you ought to play it with any particular judge. It's worse with the judges who turn me away at the very start – and that'll happen. Although I would make sure that there would be no lack of endeavour, we would have to do without those, but we can do that all right since individual judges can't tip the balance. Then if I get a sufficient number of judges to countersign that statement, I take it to the judge who is actually conducting your trial. Just possibly, I may have already got his signature, and then the whole thing will move a little more quickly than otherwise. Generally speaking, there shouldn't be many difficulties at all after that, and it's then that the defendant can feel supremely confident. It's curious, and yet true, that people feel more confidence at this stage than they do after the acquittal. And now you don't have to do much more. In the statement the judge has the guarantees of a number of his colleagues, so he can order the acquittal with an easy mind and, naturally after going through various formalities, he will doubtless do this to please me and other acquaintances. But you can walk out of the Court a free man.'

'So then I'm free,' K. said with some hesitation.

'Yes,' the painter said. 'But only apparently free, or to put it a better way, provisionally free. You see, my acquaintances are the lowest grade of judges, and they don't have the right to give a final acquittal. Only the very highest Court, which is absolutely inaccessible to you, to me and to all of us, can do that. What the prospects are there, we don't know and, I may say in passing, we don't even want to know. So our judges don't have the prestigious right of setting the defendant free, but they do have the right to relieve him of the burden of the charge. That's to say, if you're acquitted in this manner, the charge is withdrawn from you for the moment, but it still continues to hang over you and, as soon as orders are sent down from above, it can at once come into effect again. As I'm so well in with the Court, I can also tell you how, in the regulations of the Court offices, the difference between actual and apparent acquittal is demonstrated in a purely external way. With an actual acquittal the documents of the case are said to be completely set aside, they vanish altogether from the proceedings; not only the charge, but the trial itself and even the acquittal are deleted, everything is deleted. With the apparent acquittal it's quite different. The documentary record undergoes no further alteration except that the statement of innocence is added, together with a note of the acquittal and of the grounds for it. But, in all other respects, as is required by the fixed routine of the Court offices, this documentary record remains in circulation, it is passed on to the higher Courts, then it comes back to the lower ones, and so it swings back and forth, with bigger or smaller oscillations, with longer and shorter delays. These movements are incalculable. Outwardly, it might sometimes look as if everything has long been forgotten, the record lost and the acquittal made absolute. No one familiar with the Court could believe this. No document ever gets lost, and there is no such thing as forgetting at this Court. One day – quite out of the blue – some judge or other looks through the record more carefully, realizes that in this case the charge is still valid and orders an immediate arrest. I've been assuming here that some considerable time elapses between the apparent acquittal and the new arrest, and that can happen, for I know of such instances, but it's just as possible for the acquitted man to go straight home from the Court and find agents waiting for him there who have been instructed to arrest him again. Then, of course, his freedom is at an end.'

'And the trial begins all over again?' K. asked, scarcely able to believe it.

'Certainly,' the painter said. 'The trial begins again. But once more there's a chance, just as there was before, of obtaining an apparent acquittal. Again one has to concentrate all one's energies and not give in.' The painter may have said this because he noticed that K. was looking a little deflated.

'But,' K. asked, as if to forestall any further revelations the painter might make, 'isn't a second acquittal more difficult to obtain than the first?'

'One can't say anything about that for certain,' answered the painter. 'I suppose you mean that the second arrest might influence the verdict of the judges against the defendant? That's not the case. Even when they were ordering the acquittal the judges have foreseen the possibility of a fresh arrest, so this fact of being arrested for a second time hardly affects it. But for count-less other reasons the judges' mood and their legal view of the case may have changed, and so efforts to obtain a second acquittal must be adapted to the changed circumstances and generally must be just as vigorous as for the first acquittal.'

'But even this second acquittal is not final,' K. said, turning his head away dismissively.

'Of course not,' said the painter. 'The second acquittal is followed by a third arrest, the third acquittal by a fourth arrest, and so on. That's inherent in the very concept of apparent acquittal.' K. said nothing. 'Apparent acquittal obviously doesn't strike you as particularly advantageous,' said the painter. 'Perhaps postponement would suit you better. Shall I explain the essence of postponement to you?'

K. nodded. The painter had leaned back comfortably in his chair, his nightshirt was wide open and he had slipped one hand under it and was stroking his chest and his ribs.

'Postponement . . .' Titorelli said, and gazed ahead for a moment as if trying to find an absolutely accurate explanation, 'postponement consists in preventing the trial from advancing beyond its earliest stages. To achieve this, the defendant and anyone helping him, particularly the latter, must keep in constant personal contact with the Court. I must stress again that this doesn't require anything like so much effort as the obtaining of an apparent acquittal, but it does require much greater vigilance. You mustn't lose sight of the case for a moment, you must visit the appropriate judge at regular intervals, and whenever anything out of the ordinary crops up, do everything possible to keep him on your side. If you don't know the judge personally, you must try to influence him through other judges you do know, but don't let that stop you trying to discuss things with him directly. If you omit to do none of these things, you can assume with a fair degree of certainty that the case will never get beyond its initial stages. Admittedly it's not quashed, but the defendant is almost as secure from conviction as if he were free. The advantage that postponement has over apparent acquittal is that the future of the defendant is less uncertain, he is spared the horror of sudden arrest and doesn't need to fear the prospect of having to burden himself – perhaps at precisely the times when his other affairs make it least convenient – with all the exertions and all the agitation inevitable in the achievement of apparent acquittal. Of course a postponement also has certain disadvantages for the defendant, and these mustn't be underestimated. In saying this I'm not thinking of the fact that with postponement the defendant is never free, for nor is he free in any real sense with an apparent acquittal. There is another disadvantage. The case cannot remain at a standstill without there being at least some plausible reasons for this. Something must at least appear to be happening in the case. From time to time, therefore, various instructions must be given, the defendant must be interrogated, there must be investigations and so on. The case must, you see, be kept revolving in the small circle to which it is artificially restricted. Of course this entails certain discomforts for the defendant, but again you mustn't imagine these to be too bad. It's all just show, the hearings for example are only quite short ones, and if you haven't got the time or the inclination to go one day, you can ask to be excused. With some judges you can even make the arrangements mutually a long time in advance. Basically it's just a question of reporting to your judge from time to time, because you are an accused person.'

Even while these last words were being spoken, K. had put his jacket over his arm and got to his feet.

'He's getting up now!' someone shouted outside the door.

'Are you going already?' asked the painter, who had risen too. 'It must be the air that's driving you away. I'm very sorry about it. There was lots more I wanted to say to you. I had to be quite brief. But I hope I've made myself understood.'

'Oh yes,' said K, whose head was aching with the effort of forcing himself to listen. In spite of this assurance, the painter went on to sum up everything once more, as if he wished to send K. home with a word of comfort:

'Both methods have this in common: they prevent the accused man from being sentenced.'

'But they also prevent any real acquittal,' K. said quietly, as if he were ashamed of having realized this.

'You've grasped the crux of the matter,' the painter said quickly. K. put his hand on his overcoat, but could not even decide to put on his jacket. What he would have liked to do most of all was to bundle them both together and run out with them into the fresh air. Even the girls could not induce him to put his garments on, although they were calling to each other, prematurely, that he was doing so. The painter was keen to interpret K's mood somehow, so he said:

'I don't suppose you'll have made your mind up yet about my suggestions. I'm sure you're right not to decide straight away. I would have even advised against it myself. The distinction between the advantages and disadvantages is hair-line. Everything has to be weighed up exactly. But of course you mustn't waste too much time either.'

'I'll be back soon,' K. said, putting on his jacket in a sudden access of resolution, throwing his coat across his shoulders and hurrying to the door, behind which the girls now began to shriek. K. felt he could see them through the door.

'But you must be sure to keep your word,' said the painter, who had not followed him to the door, 'or else I'll come to the bank myself and make inquiries.'

'Unlock the door, will you?' K. said, wrenching at the handle, which the girls, as he could tell from the resistance, were clinging on to from the other side.

'You don't want the girls to pester you, do you?' the painter asked. 'You'd better use this way out,' and he pointed to the door behind the bed. K. agreed with him and rushed back to the bed. But instead of opening that door the painter crawled under the bed and asked from underneath:

'Just one minute. Wouldn't you like to see a picture I might be able to sell you?' K. did not wish to be rude. The painter had really shown some interest in him and had promised to go on helping him. Besides, as a result of K's forgetfulness there had been no discussion at all of any reimbursement for the painter's assistance, so K. could not rebuff him now and agreed to see the picture even though he was trembling with impatience to get out of the studio. From under the bed the man pulled out a pile of unframed pictures which were so covered with dust that, when the painter blew it off the topmost picture, it swirled in front of K's eyes for some considerable time and left him choking.

'A landscape of a heath,' Titorelli said and handed K. the picture. It showed two stunted trees which stood far apart from each other in dark grass. The background was a sunset in a blaze of colour.

'Fine,' said K, 'I'll buy it.' He had not meant to be so curt, so he was pleased when the painter, instead of taking offence, picked up another picture from the floor.

'This is a companion piece,' the painter said. It might have been meant to be that, but it was impossible to detect the slightest difference between the two, there were the same trees, the same grass and the same sunset. But that did not matter much to K.

'They're fine landscapes,' he said. 'I'll buy the pair of them and hang them in my office.'

'You seem to like the subject,' Titorelli said, and produced another one. 'It's lucky I have another one like them here.' But it was not just like them, it was in fact exactly the same landscape. The painter was making good use of this opportunity to sell off his old paintings.

'I'll take that too,' K. said. 'How much for the three?'

'We'll talk about that next time,' said the painter. 'You're in a hurry now, and we'll be keeping in touch. I must say I'm glad you like the pictures, I'll throw in all the pictures I've got under here. They're all heath scenes, I've painted stacks of them. Quite a few people turn them down because they're too gloomy, but you're one of the people who prefer gloomy pictures.' Just at that moment K. had no interest in the professional experiences of this mendicant painter.

'Wrap them all up,' he interrupted him. 'Tomorrow I'll send my clerk to fetch them.'

'That's not necessary,' the painter said. 'I hope I can get you a porter to go with you straight away now.' And at long last he leaned over the bed and unlocked the door. 'Don't be afraid to climb on the bed,' the painter said. 'Everyone that comes here does it.' Even without being invited, K. would not have scrupled to do this, he had already put one foot right on the quilt, but when he looked out through the open door, he pulled his foot back again.

'What on earth's that?' he asked the painter.

'What are you surprised at?' asked the painter, surprised in his turn. 'Those are the Court offices. Didn't you know there were Court offices here? They're in practically all the attics, so why not here as well? Even my studio really belongs to the Court offices, but the Court has put it at my disposal.'

K. was shocked not so much at finding the Court offices even here, but principally at himself for being so ignorant about Court matters. He felt it should be a basic rule of a defendant's behaviour to be prepared for anything, never to let himself be taken by surprise and never to be caught looking unsuspectingly to the right when there was a judge standing near him on the left, and yet he was always breaking this of all rules again and again. In front of him stretched a long passage from which wafted a current of air; compared to this current, the air in the studio was refreshing. There were benches arranged on either side, just as in the waiting-room of the offices which had been authorized to deal with K's case. The furnishings of the Court offices seemed to be governed by precise regulations. At the moment there were not many clients present here. One man was half sitting, half lolling on the bench, with his face buried in his arms, and there was another standing in the semi-darkness at the end of the passage.

Now K. climbed across the bed, while the painter followed him with the pictures. Soon they met a Court usher – by now K. could recognize the servants of the Court by the gold button which they wore among the ordinary buttons on their civilian clothes – and the painter gave this man the job of accompanying K. with the pictures. K. was not so much walking as staggering along, holding his handkerchief pressed to his mouth. They had almost got to the exit when the girls came rushing to meet them, so K. had not even been spared them either. They had obviously seen the second door in the studio being opened and had made a detour to get in from this side.

'I can't come any farther with you!' Titorelli shouted, laughing as the girls thronged around him. 'Goodbye then! And don't be too long thinking it over!'

K. did not even look round. In the street he took the first cab that came his way. He was intent on getting rid of the usher, whose gold button kept impinging on his eye, though it probably did not strike anyone else. So zealous was the usher that he wanted to sit on the box with the driver, but K. made him get down. It was long after midday when K. arrived in front of the bank. He would have liked to leave the pictures in the cab, but he was afraid that at some future date they might be necessary to help him prove his identity to the painter. So he had them taken into his office and locked them up in the bottom drawer of his desk, where they would be safe, over the next few days at least, from the eyes of the Deputy Manager.

Chapter Eight

Block, the Businessman – Dismissal ot the Lawyer

K. had at long last decided to take his case out of the lawyer's hands. He had not, it is true, been able to eliminate all doubts about whether it was right to do this, but the conviction that it was necessary eventually triumphed. The decision had drained K. of a lot of energy on the day he planned to go to the lawyer; he worked unusually slowly, he had to stay very late at the office, and it was already past ten when he at last found himself standing in front of the lawyer's door. Before he rang he wondered whether it wouldn't have been better to dismiss the lawyer by letter or telephone, for a personal interview was bound to be very painful. Nevertheless, when all was said and done, K. did not want to reject the chance of a personal interview, any other kind of dismissal would be accepted in silence or with one or two formal words, and unless he could perhaps extract something from Leni, K. would never learn how the lawyer had taken the dismissal or what, in the not unimportant opinion of the lawyer, the consequences of the dismissal might be for K. But if K. confronted the lawyer and could surprise him with the dismissal, then K. would easily be able to deduce from the man's face and behaviour everything he wanted to know, even if the lawyer were very careful about what he allowed to be coaxed from him. It was just possible K. might be persuaded that, after all, it was best to leave the case for the defence in the lawyer's hands and, therefore, might change his mind about dismissing him.

As usual his first ring at the lawyer's door was fruitless.
Leni could get a move on, K. thought. But it was at least some-

thing that nobody else had interfered, as usually happened – the man in the dressing-gown, for example, or some other busybody. As K. pressed the button for the second time, he looked back at the other door, but this time it stayed shut, too. At last two eyes appeared at the peep-hole in the lawyer's door, but they were not Leni's eyes. Somebody unlocked the door but propped himself against it and held it shut for a moment, calling back into the flat:

'It's him!' and only then opened it wide. K. had been pushing against the door, for behind him he could already hear the key being hurriedly turned in the lock on the door of the other flat. So when the door in front of him eventually opened, he was almost hurled headlong into the hall and just glimpsed Leni, for whom the warning cry of the person opening the door had been intended, rushing off in her chemise down the passage which led between the rooms. He gazed after her a moment and then looked round to see who had opened the door. It was a skinny little man with a beard, holding a candle in his hand.

'Are you employed here?' K. asked him.

'No,' answered the man. 'I don't live here, I'm just a client. I'm here on legal business.'

'In your shirt-sleeves?' K. asked him, pointing with a gesture of his hand to the man's state of undress.

'Oh, I beg your pardon,' the man said, shining the candle on himself, as if it were only now that he realized his condition.

'Leni is your mistress, isn't she?' K. asked brusquely. He stood with his legs a little apart and his hands clasped behind him, holding his hat. The mere possession of a thick overcoat made him feel very superior to the emaciated little man.

'Good God, no!' the latter said, raising one hand in front of his face in horrified self-defence. 'No, no, what can you be thinking of?'

'I well believe you,' K. said with a smile. 'Anyway, come along.' He waved his hat for the man to go in front. 'What's your name, then?' K. asked, as they walked along.

'My name's Block, I'm a businessman,' the little man said, turning to introduce himself, but K. would not let him stop.

'Is that your real name?' K. asked.

'Of course it is,' was the answer. 'Why should you doubt it?'

'I thought you might have reason to conceal your name,' said K. He was feeling perfectly at ease, as one usually is only when speaking to one's inferiors in a foreign country, when one keeps one's own affairs to oneself and serenely discusses other people's interests, the importance of which is thereby inflated for one's own benefit yet can be summarily deflated at will. K. stopped at the door of the lawyer's study, opened it and shouted to Block, who had obediently gone on ahead:

'Not so fast! Bring the light here!' K. thought that Leni might have hidden in here, so he got Block to scour every corner, but the room was empty. In front of the picture of the judge K. grabbed the businessman from behind and held him back by his braces.

'D'you know that man?' he asked, pointing upwards. Block lifted the candle, blinking up at the picture, and said:

'It's a judge.'

'A senior judge?' K. asked and placed himself diagonally opposite the businessman to observe the effect the picture had on him. Block gazed up admiringly:

'He's a senior judge,' he said.

'You haven't got much insight,' K. said. 'He's the lowest Examining Magistrate of the lot.'

'Yes, I remember now,' Block said, lowering the candle, 'I've heard that before.'

'But of course,' K. shouted, 'I forgot, of course you must have heard it before.'

'But why? Why must I have heard it?' the businessman asked, moving towards the door as K. propelled him along. When they got out in the passage, K. said:

'You do know where Leni's hiding, don't you?'

'Hiding?' Block said. 'No, but she should be in the kitchen, making some soup for the lawyer.'

'Why didn't you tell me that straight away?' asked K.

'I was going to take you there, but you called me back again,' answered the businessman, as if he were confused by the contradictory instructions.

'No doubt you think you're being very crafty,' K. said. 'Well, take me there then!'

K. had never been in the kitchen before, it was surprisingly large and lavishly equipped. The stove alone was three times as big as an ordinary one. The other things could not be seen in detail, for the kitchen was now illuminated only by one small lamp which hung by the entrance. Leni was standing by the stove, in a white apron as usual, breaking eggs into a saucepan that stood on a spirit flame.

'Good evening, Josef,' she said, glancing sideways at him.

'Good evening,' said K, signing to Block to sit down on a chair which stood to one side, and Block complied. K. went up quite close behind Leni, leaned over her shoulder and asked:

'Who is this man?' Leni put one arm round K, whisked the soup with the other, and pulling him forwards to her and said:

'He's a pitiful creature, a poor businessman called Block. Just look at him.' They both looked back. Block was sitting on the chair to which K. had directed him, he had blown out the candle, which was no longer needed, and was pinching the wick with his fingers to stop it smoking.

'You were in your chemise,' K. said and with his hand turned her head back towards the stove. She said nothing. 'Is he your lover?' K. asked. She was about to reach for the saucepan, but K. took both her hands and said:

'Now answer me!'

She said: 'Come into the study and I'll explain everything to you.'

'No,' said K. 'I want you to explain here.' She clung to him and tried to kiss him. But K. pushed her away and said:

'I don't want you to kiss me now.'

'Josef,' Leni said, gazing into his eyes imploringly and yet frankly, 'you're not going to be jealous of Herr Block?' Then, turning to the businessman, she said:

'Rudi, come on, help me, you can see I'm under suspicion. Put the candle down.' One might have thought that he had not been paying any attention, but he knew perfectly well what was going on.

'It beats me too why you should be jealous,' he said rather lamely.

'It beats me as well,' K. said, smiling at him. Leni burst out laughing, taking advantage of K's inattention to link arms with him, and whispered to him:

'Leave him alone now, you can see what he's like. I took a bit of interest in him because he's one of the lawyer's best clients, and that's all there is to it. What about you? D'you want to talk to the lawyer again today? He's very ill, but if you want me to, I'll announce you. But you'll certainly be spending the night with me. It's been so long since you were here, even the lawyer's been asking after you. Don't neglect your case! I've also got various things to tell you that I've found out. But now take your coat off first!' She helped him out of his coat and took his hat from him, running out into the hall to hang the things up, and then she ran back again to look at the soup. 'Shall I announce you first or take him his soup first?'

'Oh, announce me first,' K. said. He was annoyed, for he had originally intended to discuss the whole thing fully with Leni first, especially the debatable idea of dismissing the lawyer, but the businessman's presence had put him off. However, he now felt his own affairs were too important for him to tolerate possibly decisive interference from this insignificant businessman, so he called Leni, who was already out in the passageway, back again.

'Take him his soup first,' he said, 'let him fortify himself for his interview with me, he'll need it.'

'So you're one of the lawyer's clients too,' Block said quietly from his corner, as if confirming a suspicion. But his remark was not well received.

'What's it got to do with you then?' K. said, to which Leni added:

'You be quiet. So I'll take his soup first then,' she said to K. and poured it into a dish. 'The only trouble is that he may soon fall asleep. He never takes long to fall asleep after he's been eating.'

'What I'm going to say to him will keep him awake,' K. said. All the time he wanted it to sound as if he intended to negotiate something important with the lawyer, he wanted Leni to ask him what it was and then, and only then, he would seek her advice. But all she did was carry out perfectly the instructions he had given her. As she was passing him with the soup-plate, she brushed against him on purpose and whispered:

'The moment he's had his soup, I'll tell him you're here, so that I can have you back as soon as possible.'

'Just get going,' K. said. 'Get going.'

'Do be nicer,' she said, turning right round once more in the doorway with the soup-plate.

K. gazed after her. Now it was definitely decided that he would dismiss the lawyer, and it was certainly better that he was not able to discuss it with Leni beforehand. Her view of the whole affair could hardly be adequate, she would certainly have tried to dissuade him, she might possibly have deterred K. from going through with the dismissal on this occasion, and then he would have been left in further doubt and anxiety until in the end, after a period of time, he did carry out his decision, for that decision was too compelling to be ignored. But the sooner it was carried out, the more damage would be averted. Perhaps, after all, the businessman was able to contribute something.

K. turned round, and as soon as the businessman saw this, he made to get up.

'Stay where you are,' K. said and drew up a chair. 'Are you an old client of the lawyer's?' K. asked.

'Yes,' said the businessman, 'a very old client.'

'How many years has he been representing you, then?' K. asked.

'I'm not quite sure what you mean,' said the businessman. 'I have a corn business and the lawyer has been acting for me in my commercial affairs ever since I took the business over, that's about twenty years. In my own personal case, which you're probably referring to, he's also been representing me since it began, and that's more than five years ago. Yes, much more than five years,' he then added, drawing out an old pocket-book. 'I've got it all written down here. I can give you the exact dates, if you like. It's difficult to keep it all in your head. My own case has probably been going on much longer than I said, it began just after my wife died, and that's more than five and a half years ago.'

K. moved closer to him. 'So the lawyer takes on ordinary legal cases too?' he asked. This alliance between Court and jurisprudence struck K. as profoundly reassuring.

'Of course he does,' Block said, and then whispered to K, 'It's even said that he's better in these ordinary legal cases than in the others.' But then, seeming to regret having said this, he put his hand on K's shoulder and said:

'I beg you, don't give me away.' K. patted him on the thigh reassuringly and said:

'No, I don't betray people.'

'You see, he's vindictive,' said the businessman.

'But he certainly wouldn't do anything to such a loyal client as you,' K. said.

'Oh, but he would,' the businessman said. 'Once he's roused, it doesn't make any difference. Besides, I'm not really as loyal to him as all that.'

'How d'you mean?' K. asked.

'I wonder if I should tell you,' Block asked doubtfully.

'I think you can,' K. said.

'Well,' said the businessman, 'I'll tell you a bit of it, but you'll have to tell me a secret too, so that we have some hold on each other with regard to the lawyer.'

'You're very cautious,' K. said, 'but I'll tell you a secret that will reassure you completely. How have you been disloyal to the lawyer?'

'Well,' the businessman said hesitatingly, as if he were confessing something dishonourable, 'I've got other lawyers besides him.'

'But that's not very serious,' K. said, rather disappointed.

'It is here,' said the businessman, who had been breathing heavily ever since his confession but gained in confidence as a result of K's remark. 'It's not allowed. And least of all is it allowed to have shady lawyers as well, when one already has an official one. And that's just what I've done. I have five shady lawyers as well as him.'

'Five!' exclaimed K, who was astonished only at the number, 'you've got five lawyers besides this one?' The businessman nodded.

'Yes, I'm in the middle of negotiating for a sixth.'

'But what d'you need so many lawyers for?' K. asked.

'I need them all,' the businessman said.

'But won't you tell me why?' K. asked.

'I'd be glad to,' said the businessman. 'Above all I don't want to lose my lawsuit, you can understand that. So I mustn't disregard anything that might be useful to me. I mustn't reject anything, even if the prospect of its being useful is only very slight. So I've spent everything I have on the case. For example, I've drawn all the capital out of my business. At one time my business offices almost took up a whole floor, but now one small room at the back is enough, where I can work with a single apprentice. Of course, not only the withdrawal of my money, but more than that, the withdrawal of my labour has caused this slump. If you want to do something about your case, you're not able to do much about anything else.'

'So you've even been working at the Court yourself, too?' K. asked. 'That's exactly what I'd like to hear something about.'

'I can't tell you much,' said the businessman. 'I did have a try, to begin with, but I soon had to give it up. It's too exhausting and doesn't achieve much. Working and negotiating there myself turned out to be far too much, for me, at any rate. Just sitting and waiting there was a great strain. You know yourself how stuffy the air is in the Court offices.'

'How did you know I'd been there?' K. asked.

'I just happened to be in the waiting-room when you came through.'

'What a coincidence!' exclaimed K, quite carried away and completely forgetting how ridiculous the businessman had seemed to him before. 'So you saw me! You were in the waiting-room when I went through. Yes, I did go through there once.'

'It's not such a great coincidence,' said the businessman. 'I'm there practically every day.'

'I shall probably have to go there fairly often now, too,' K. said. 'Only I'm hardly likely to be received with such honour as I was that time. Everyone stood up. They must have thought I was a judge.'

'No,' said the businessman. 'It was the usher we were standing up for then. We knew very well that you were an accused man. News like that spreads very quickly.'

'So you knew that already then, did you?' said K. 'But then perhaps my behaviour struck you as arrogant. Wasn't there any comment made about it?'

'No,' said the businessman. 'Quite the contrary. But all that's rubbish.'

'What do you mean, rubbish?' K. asked.

'What d'you want to know for?' the businessman said angrily. 'You don't seem to know the people there very well, and you might get the wrong idea. You must remember that in these proceedings lots of things continually get said that are beyond the grasp of reason, people are simply too tired and distracted to concentrate, and so instead they fall back on superstition. I'm talking about other people, but I'm as bad as any of them, myself. A typical superstition, for example, is that lots of people reckon they can tell from a defendant's face, and particularly the outline of his lips, what the outcome of his case is going to be. Well, these people maintained that, judging from your lips, you were certain to be convicted, and pretty soon at that. I repeat, it's a ridiculous superstition and, what's more, almost always completely contradicted by the facts, but if you live with those people, it's difficult to be impervious to their opinions. Just think what a powerful effect this superstition can have. You did speak to one of the men there, didn't you? And he was scarcely able to answer you? Of course there are plenty of reasons for being confused in that place, but one of the reasons he was confused was certainly the sight of your lips. He said afterwards that he thought he could also see on your lips the sign that he himself was going to be convicted.'

'On *my* lips?' K. said, taking out a pocket-mirror and looking at himself. 'I can't see anything special about my lips. Can you?'

'No, I can't either,' said the businessman, 'nothing at all.'

'How superstitious these people are!' cried K.

'Didn't I tell you?' the businessman asked.

'Do they see so much of each other then and exchange opinions?' K. asked. 'So far, I've kept away from them altogether.'

'Generally they don't see much of each other,' said the businessman. 'It wouldn't be possible, there are so many of them. And they have few common interests. If occasionally a few of them suddenly believe they have an interest in common, they soon turn out to be mistaken. And combined action against the Court can never achieve anything. Every case is investigated on its own merits, for the Court is extremely careful. And so combined action can achieve nothing, only an individual can occasionally achieve something by working in secret; the others only find out about it when the success has been achieved; nobody knows how it's been done. So there isn't any communal spirit, people meet up, it's true, every now and then in the waiting-rooms, but nothing much is discussed there. Superstitious beliefs have existed for ages and fairly multiply of their own accord.'

'I saw those people in the waiting-room,' K. said. 'It seemed to me pointless for them to wait.'

'It's not pointless,' said the businessman. 'The only thing that's pointless is to try acting on one's own. I already told you that I now have five other lawyers besides this one. You might have thought – I thought so myself at first – that now I could leave the whole thing entirely to them. But you'd be quite wrong. I have to concentrate on it more myself now than I would if I had only one lawyer. I imagine you find that difficult to understand?'

'No,' K. said, and, to restrain the businessman from talking too quickly, he patted him reassuringly on his hand. 'I only ask you to speak a bit more slowly, these things really are all very important to me and I can't follow you properly.'

'It's a good thing you reminded me,' the businessman said. 'Of course you're new to this game, you're an infant. Your case has been going for six months, hasn't it? Yes, I've heard about it. Such a young case! But I've had to think these things out countless times, they've become the most self-evident thing in the world to me.'

'You must be pleased that your case is so far advanced then?' K. inquired, not wanting to ask point-blank at what stage the businessman's affairs actually were. But he didn't get a clear answer.

'Yes, I've been keeping my case trundling along for five years,' the businessman said and let his head drop forward. 'That's no small achievement.' Then he fell silent for a moment.

K. listened to hear if Leni was coming back yet. On the one hand he did not want her to come now, for he still had a lot of questions he wanted to ask, and besides he did not want Leni to catch him deep in intimate conversation with the businessman. But on the other hand he was annoyed that, even though he was there, she was staying with the lawyer a lot longer than was necessary just to give him his soup.

'I can still remember very clearly,' Block resumed (and at once K. was listening intently), 'the time when my case had been going for about the same length of time that yours has. I only had this lawyer then, but I was not very satisfied with him.'

Ah, now I'm going to hear everything, K. thought to himself, and nodded his head excitedly, as if that would encourage the businessman to come out with everything worth knowing.

'My case wasn't making any progress,' Block went on. 'Of course there were investigations, and I attended every single one, I collected material and put all my accounts at the disposal of the Court, though I discovered subsequently that this wasn't even necessary, and I kept constantly running to see my lawyer. He produced various petitions—'

'Various petitions?' K. asked.

'Yes, certainly,' said the businessman.

'I find that very significant,' K. said. 'In my case he's still working on the first petition. He's not done anything yet. I can see now, he's neglecting me disgracefully.'

'There can be various legitimate reasons why he hasn't yet finished the petition,' the businessman said. 'Anyway, later on it turned out that my petitions were completely worthless. I even got to read one of them myself, thanks to the kindness of a Court official. Admittedly it was very scholarly, but there was actually no substance to it. First of all there was masses of Latin, which I can't understand, and then there were pages of general appeals to the Court, followed by flattery of various individual officials who were, it's true, unnamed, but certainly identifiable by anyone well informed of the Court's affairs, then self-applause on the part of the lawyer grovelling abjectly before the Court, and finally analyses of some very ancient cases that were supposed to resemble mine. As far as I could follow them, these analyses were certainly very carefully done. I'm not trying to criticize the lawyer's work by saying all that, and the petition I read was only one of several, but in any event, and this is what I want to talk about now, I couldn't at that time see that my case was getting anywhere.'

'Where did you expect it to get to then?' K. asked him.

'That's a very sensible question,' the man said with a smile. 'It's not very often that you see any progress in these proceedings. But I didn't know that then. After all, I'm a businessman, and I was much more of one then than I am now. I wanted to have some tangible results, either the whole thing should be coming to an end or at least it should be following a regular upward trend. Instead there were only hearings that were usually identical; I could reel off the answers like a litany. Several times a week Court messengers came to my business or my flat or wherever I could be found. Of course this was a nuisance (in that respect, at least, things are much better nowadays, for a telephone call is much less of a nuisance) and also rumours about my case began to circulate among my business friends, but especially among my relatives, so I was being hurt on all sides, though there wasn't the slightest indication that even the first hearing would take place in the near future. So I went to the lawyer and complained. He gave me lengthy explanations, but firmly refused to further my case. Nobody, he said, had any influence on when the day was fixed for the hearing, and to press for this in a petition (as I demanded) was simply unheard of and would be the ruin of me and him. I thought: if this lawyer won't or can't do it, another one will and can. So I looked around for other lawyers. I can tell you straight away that not one of them demanded, or managed to get a day fixed for the main hearing and – of course with one qualification, which I'll tell you about in a minute – it really is impossible, and so this lawyer wasn't deceiving me about it. Anyway there was never any reason for me to regret having turned to other lawyers. I expect Dr Huld may have told you quite a few things already about the shady lawyers, he has probably represented them to you as being very contemptible, and so they are. All the same, in speaking about them and comparing them with himself and his colleagues, he always lets one small mistake creep in, which I want to draw your attention to in passing. In order to make a distinction, he always refers to the lawyers in his circle as 'the great lawyers'. This is wrong, naturally anybody can describe himself as 'great' if he wants to, but in this instance only the usage of the Court can decide the matter. According to Court usage there are in fact small and great lawyers, in addition to the shady ones. This lawyer and his colleagues are, however, only the small lawyers, whereas I've never seen the great lawyers and only heard about them, for they are as far above the small lawyers as the latter are above the despised shady lawyers – in fact, incomparably further above.

'The great lawyers?' K. asked. 'Who are they then? How does one reach them?'

'So you've never heard about them,' said the businessman. 'Once he has heard about them, practically every accused man spends some time dreaming about them. But don't give in to the temptation. I don't know who the great lawyers actually are, and they certainly can't be reached at all. I don't know of a single case where you could say for certain that they'd intervened. They do defend some people, but you can't achieve that for yourself on your own initiative, they only defend the ones they want to defend. I imagine, however, that they only take on a case once it has passed through the lower Court. Generally speaking, it's better not to think about them at all, or else the discussions with other lawyers, their offers of help and advice, strike one as being so obnoxious and futile – I can tell you that myself – that one simply wants to chuck the whole thing up and go home to bed and never hear another word about it. Of course that again would be the stupidest thing in the world to do, and anyway one wouldn't be left in peace for long even in bed.'

'So you never thought of going to the great lawyers at the time?'

'Not for long,' the businessman said and smiled once more. 'Unfortunately you can't put them right out of your head, especially at night you find yourself thinking about them. But at that time I wanted immediate results, you see, so I went to the shady lawyers.'

'How close you are sitting to each other here!' cried Leni, who had come back with the soup-plate and stopped in the doorway. They were indeed sitting very close to each other, the slightest movement and they would have banged their heads together.

The businessman, who apart from being small also kept his back hunched up, had forced K. to bend down low too in order to hear everything that was said.

'Just a moment!' cried K, shooing Leni away and impatiently jerking the hand he still kept on the businessman's hand.

'He wanted me to tell him about my case,' the businessman said to Leni.

'Well, go on, tell him then,' she said. She spoke affectionately to the businessman, but also condescendingly, and K. did not like that. For he had now realized that the man did have a certain value, at least he had some experience which he knew how to communicate. Leni probably misjudged him. He watched with some irritation as Leni now took away the candle which the businessman had been holding on to all this time, then wiped his hand with her apron and knelt down beside him to scrape off some grease that had dripped from the candle on to his trousers.

'You were going to tell me about the shady lawyers,' K. said, pushing Leni's hand away without further comment.

'What are you doing?' Leni said, aiming a slap at K. and going on with what she was doing.

'Yes, the shady lawyers then,' the businessman said, running his hand over his forehead as if he were thinking.

K. tried to help him along and said:

'You wanted some immediate results and so you went to the shady lawyers?'

'That's right,' the businessman said, but he did not go on.

Perhaps he doesn't want to talk about it in front of Leni, K. thought to himself, but he mastered his impatience to hear the rest straight away and did not press him further for the moment.

'Did you say I was here?' he asked Leni.

'Of course,' she said. 'The lawyer is waiting for you. Leave Block alone now, you can always talk to Block later on, he's staying here.' But K. still did not move.

'You're staying here?' he asked the businessman. He wanted the fellow to answer for himself, he did not like Leni talking about Block as if he were not in the room, today he was filled with a kind of covert anger against Leni. But again it was Leni who answered for him:

'He often sleeps here.'

'*Sleeps* here?' K. exclaimed. He had imagined that Block would simply wait there for him while he swiftly got the interview with the lawyer over, and that they would then go off together and discuss the whole thing thoroughly without being disturbed.

'Yes,' Leni said. 'Not everyone's like you, Josef, allowed in to see the lawyer any time they like. You don't seem in the least surprised that in spite of his illness the lawyer is still prepared to see you at eleven o'clock at night. You take what your friends do for you far too much for granted. Well, your friends like doing things for you, or at least I do anyway. I don't want any thanks and I don't need any thanks: all I ask is that you should be fond of me.'

Fond of you? K. thought for a moment, and only then did it occur to him: but I *am* fond of her. Nevertheless, he ignored everything else and said:

'He's ready to see me because I'm his client. If even for that I needed someone else's help, I'd be simultaneously begging and saying thank you at every turn.'

'How awkward he's being today, isn't he?' Leni asked the businessman.

Now it's my turn not to be here, K. thought, almost losing his temper with the businessman too, when the latter, copying Leni's rudeness, said:

'The lawyer has other reasons for seeing him. His case, you see, is more interesting than mine. Besides it's only just begun, so it's probably not yet hopeless and the lawyer still likes handling it. That's bound to change later.'

'Yes, yes,' Leni said with a laugh and looked at the businessman.

'Doesn't he go on! You can't believe a word he says,' she added, turning to K. 'He's a nice chap, but he talks much too much. Perhaps that's the reason the lawyer can't stand him. In any event, he's never willing to see him unless he's in the mood. I've gone to a lot of trouble to alter that, but it can't be done. Just imagine, sometimes I announce Block and he doesn't get in to see the lawyer until three days later. And if Block isn't on the spot when he's called for, he loses his chance and has to be announced all over again. That's why I've let Block sleep here, for it has even happened that the lawyer's rung for him in the middle of the night. So now Block is ready even during the night. Of course it also happens that, if by any chance Block's here, the lawyer will sometimes countermand the order to let him in.' K. looked inquiringly over at the businessman, who nodded and replied as frankly as when he had spoken to K. before, or perhaps he was unsettled by a feeling of shame:

'Yes, as time goes by one gets very dependent on one's lawyer.'

'He's only pretending to complain,' Leni said. 'He's very glad to sleep here, as he's often confessed to me.' She went to a little door and pushed it open. 'D'you want to see his bedroom?' she asked. K. walked over and from the doorway gazed into the low, windowless room which was completely filled by a narrow bed. One had to climb over the bedposts to get into the bed. At the head of the bed there was a niche in the wall holding a candle, an ink-well and a pen, all meticulously arranged beside a pile of papers that were probably documents concerning his trial.

'So you sleep in the maid's room?' K. asked and turned back to Block.

'Leni vacated it for me,' the businessman answered. 'It's very convenient.' K. gazed at him; perhaps the first impression he had had of him was the right one after all. Block had some experience, for his case had gone on a long time, but he had paid dearly for it. Suddenly K. could not bear the sight of him any longer.

'Get him to bed!' he shouted to Leni, who did not seem to understand him at all. He himself wanted to go to the lawyer and, by dismissing him, free himself not only of the lawyer, but also of Leni and the businessman. But even before he had reached the door Block was saying to him in a low voice:

'Herr K.' K. turned round angrily. 'You've forgotten your promise,' the businessman said, leaning pleadingly towards K. from his chair. 'You were going to tell me a secret.'

'Yes, I was,' K. said, with a swift glance at Leni, who was watching him closely. 'Well, listen. It's hardly a secret any longer though. I'm on my way to the lawyer now to dismiss him.'

'He's dismissing him!' Block shouted, jumping from his chair and rushing round the kitchen with his arms in the air. Over and over again he shouted, 'He's dismissing the lawyer!' Leni was just about to make a dive at K. but the businessman got in her way, so in retaliation she struck him with her fists. Still clenching her fists, she ran after K, but he had a good start. He was already in the lawyer's room when Leni caught him up. He had almost closed the door behind him, but Leni got her foot in the door and held it open, grabbed him by the arm and tried to pull him back. But he squeezed her wrist so hard that with a moan she had to let him go. She did not dare come into the room now, however K. turned the key to make sure.

'I've been waiting for you for a very long time,' the lawyer said from his bed, placing on the little bedside table a document that he had been reading by the light of a candle and putting on his glasses through which he peered intently at K. Instead of apologizing, K. said:

'I'll be going in a moment.' Since this was not an apology the lawyer ignored K's remark and said:

'I shan't let you in another time as late as this.'

'That suits me,' K. said and the lawyer looked at him inquiringly.

'Sit down,' he said.

'If you wish me to,' K. said, pulling up a chair to the bedside table and sitting down.

'I thought I saw you lock the door,' the lawyer said.

'Yes,' said K, 'that was because of Leni.' K. did not intend to spare anybody. But the lawyer asked:

'Has she been pestering you again?'

'Pestering me?' asked K.

'Yes,' said the lawyer. He laughed as he said this, then he had a fit of coughing and, when that had abated, began laughing again. 'I imagine you must have noticed the way she pesters people?' he asked, patting K's hand which K. had abstractedly rested on the table and now hastily withdrew. 'You don't attach much importance to it then?' the lawyer said when K. did not reply. 'All the better, otherwise I might have had to apologize for her. It's a strange quirk of Leni's, which, incidentally, I've long ago forgiven her for and which I wouldn't even mention if you hadn't locked the door just now. This quirk of hers – you're certainly the last person I should be explaining this to, but since you're looking so nonplussed I'll tell you – this quirk of hers consists in the fact that she finds most accused men attractive. She runs after them all, falls in love with them all, and indeed they all seem to fall in love with her. When I let her, she sometimes tells me about them, in order to amuse me. I'm not as astonished about the whole thing as you seem to be. If one has the right eye for these things, accused men often really do seem attractive. It's certainly a remarkable, and in a way, a scientific phenomenon. Of course, it's not that being charged actually produces in a person's appearance an obvious change that can be precisely defined. After all, unlike defendants in other criminal cases, most people stick to their usual way of life, and if they have a good lawyer who looks after them, they're not handicapped by their case. Nevertheless, any person experienced in these matters can identify the accused men, one after the other, in the largest crowd. How? you may ask. My answer won't satisfy you. Precisely because they're the most attractive. It can't be the guilt that makes them attractive, for – here, at all events, I must speak as a lawyer – they're not all guilty after all, and it can't be the justice of the punishment they receive that makes them attractive, for they aren't all punished, so it must be the aura of the proceedings taken against them that somehow attaches itself to them. Of course, among the attractive ones, some are especially attractive. But they're all attractive – even that miserable worm Block.'

By the time the lawyer had finished talking, K. had regained his composure completely, and even nodded ostentatious approval of the lawyer's last words, seeing them as a confirmation of his old view that the lawyer always tried, and indeed was trying this time, to distract his attention with irrelevant general remarks and in this way divert him from the main question of what work he had actually done to promote K's case. The lawyer probably sensed that, on this occasion, K. was putting up more resistance to him than usual, for now he stopped talking to give K. a chance to speak himself, and, as K. said nothing, he asked:

'Did you come here today to see me for some particular reason?'

'Yes,' K. said, and shaded the light of the candle a little with his hand to see the lawyer better. 'I came to tell you that I'm taking my defence out of your hands, as from today.'

'Do I understand you correctly?' the lawyer asked, half raising himself in bed and propping himself up with one hand on the pillows.

'I think so,' K. said, sitting there as stiff as a ramrod, as if he were poised in ambush.

'Well, we can discuss this plan too,' the lawyer said after a pause.

'It isn't a plan any more,' K. said.

'Perhaps not,' said the lawyer. 'But don't let's rush things nevertheless.' He used the word 'us' as if he had no intention of letting K. go, and as if he were determined to continue advising K. at least, even if he could no longer act for him.

'There's no rush about it,' K. said, standing up slowly and stepping behind his chair. 'I've thought it over for a long time, perhaps too long even. My decision is final.'

'But just let me say a few more words then,' said the lawyer, pushing back the quilt and seating himself on the edge of the bed. His bare legs, covered with white hairs, were trembling with cold. He asked K. to hand him a blanket from the couch. K. did so and remarked:

'You're exposing yourself quite unnecessarily to a chill.'

'The occasion is grave enough,' the lawyer said, as he wrapped the quilt round the top part of his body and the rug round his legs. 'Your uncle is a friend of mine, and I've also got fond of you in the course of time. I admit that quite openly. I don't need to be ashamed of it.' The old man's sentimental remarks were most unwelcome to K, for they forced him to go into a more detailed explanation, which he would have liked to avoid, and unsettled him too, as he frankly admitted to himself, even if they in no way made him think of going back on his decision.

'I'm grateful for your friendly attitude,' he said, 'and I acknowledge, too, that you've shown as much interest in my case as you could and as you deemed would be to my advantage. Recently, however, I've become convinced that it isn't enough. Of course I shall never attempt to persuade you, who are much older and more experienced than I am, of the rightness of my conviction. If I have sometimes unintentionally tried to do this, please forgive me, but the matter is, as you yourself put it, grave enough, and I am certain it is necessary to take much more drastic measures in the case than have been taken hitherto.'

'I understand you,' the lawyer said. 'You are impatient.'

'I'm not impatient,' K. said, getting a little irritated and therefore not minding so much what he said. 'When I first came to see you with my uncle, you must have noticed that the case was of no great consequence to me, and I tended to forget about it altogether unless I was forcibly reminded of it, as it were. But my uncle insisted that I let you act for me and I did that to please him. One would have expected that the case would then weigh less heavily on me than before, for that is, after all, the reason one hands it over to a lawyer, namely to shift a little of the burden of the case from oneself. But exactly the reverse happened. Never before did I have so many worries about my case as I've had since you took it over. When I was alone, I did nothing about it, but I was hardly aware of it. But then, on the other hand, when I had someone acting for me, the scene was set for something to happen, with ever-growing and unabating eagerness I was waiting for you to intervene, but nothing was forthcoming. It's certainly true that you told me various things about the Court, which perhaps I couldn't have got from anyone else. But I need more than that, now that the case is closing in on me more and more, clandestinely as it were.' K. had now thrust the chair away and was standing upright, with his hands in his jacket pockets.

'After a certain time in one's practice,' the lawyer said quietly and calmly, 'nothing essentially new ever happens. How many of my clients have reached a similar stage in their cases and have stood, like you, in front of me saying exactly the same things!'

'Well then,' K. said, 'all these clients who were supposed to be like me were as much in the right as I am. That doesn't prove me wrong at all.'

'I wasn't trying to prove you wrong when I said that,' the lawyer said. 'But I wanted to add that I expected you to show more judgement than the others, especially as I gave you more of an insight into the nature of the Court and my work than I usually do with clients. And now it's obvious that in spite of all this you haven't enough confidence in me. You're not making things easy for me.' How the lawyer was demeaning himself in front of K! And not taking any notice of his professional dignity, which was surely most sensitive on precisely this point. Why did he do it? He appeared, after all, to be a very busy lawyer and a very rich man into the bargain, so the loss of K. as a client or the loss of his fee could not in themselves matter very much to him. Besides, his health was bad and he should have been anxious himself to have some of his work taken from him. And yet he was clinging on so hard to K! Why? Was it his personal feelings for K's uncle, or did he really regard the case as being so extraordinary that he was hoping to distinguish himself, either in front of K. or (and this possibility could never be excluded) in front of his friends at the Court? His expression revealed nothing, though K. submitted him to ruthless scrutiny. One might almost have thought the lawyer was deliberately keeping his face blank while he watched to see the effect of his words. But he was clearly putting too favourable an interpretation on K's silence when he went on:

'You will have noticed that, though I have a large office, I don't have any assistants. It wasn't always like that, there was a time when I used to have several law students working for me, but now I work on my own. That's partly due to the change in my practice, in that I've now confined myself more and more to legal cases like yours, and partly to the ever-growing knowledge I've acquired from these cases. I found that I couldn't delegate this work to anybody, unless I was going to wrong my clients and damage the case I'd taken on. But my decision to do all the work myself had certain natural results: I had to turn away almost everyone who asked me to represent them, giving in only to those I felt particularly touched by – well, there are plenty of wretches, even round here, ready to pounce on any scraps I throw away. And, what's more, I broke down through overwork. But still, I don't regret my decision, perhaps I should possibly have refused more applications for my services than I did, but the tactic of throwing myself wholeheartedly into those I did take on has turned out to be absolutely necessary and entirely justified by the results. I once saw beautifully expressed in a book the difference which obtains between legal representation in ordinary actions and legal representation in cases like this. This is what it said there: in one, the lawyer leads his client by a thread until the verdict is reached, and in the other he straight away lifts his client on to his shoulders and carries him, without putting him down, as far as the verdict and even beyond. And that's the way it is. But I wasn't quite right when I said that I never regret taking on this great task. When, as with you, I find my work so completely misunderstood, well, then I almost regret it.' This speech, instead of convincing K, only made him impatient. He thought he could detect in the lawyer's tone something that told him what to expect if he yielded. There would be the same empty promises, the same references to the progress of the petition, to the improved frame of mind of the Court officials, but also to the great difficulties confronting the lawyer's work – in short, everything he was sick and tired of hearing would be trotted out, either to delude him with vague hopes again or to torment him with shadowy threats. That must be prevented once and for all, so he said:

'What steps would you propose to take in my case if you continue to represent me?' The lawyer showed no resentment even at this insulting question and replied:

'Go on with those steps I'd already taken on your behalf.'

'That's what I thought,' K. said. 'There's no use saying any more.'

'I'll make one more attempt,' the lawyer said, as if what was provoking K. were happening not to K, but to him, the lawyer. 'I get the impression, you see, that what's misled you not only into misjudging my legal assistance but also into behaving the way you have up till now is that, even though you're an accused man, you've been treated too well, or, to be more correct, you've been treated remissly, at least that's what it looks like. Of course there's a reason for this; it's often better to be in chains than to be free. But I'd like to show you how other accused men are treated, and perhaps you'll manage to learn something from it. What I'm going to do is send for Block now, so unlock the door and sit down here next to the bedside table!'

'With pleasure,' K. said and did what the lawyer had demanded. He was always ready to learn. But in order to safeguard himself against any eventuality, he asked once more:

'It has sunk in on you that I'm taking the case away from you, hasn't it?'

'Yes,' said the lawyer, 'but you may yet change your mind about it today.' He lay back in bed again, pulled the quilt up to his chin and turned to the wall. Then he rang.

Leni appeared almost at once, glancing swiftly around to find out what had happened. The fact that K. was sitting quietly by the lawyer's bedside seemed to reassure her. She nodded and smiled at K, who just glared back at her. The lawyer said:

'Bring Block here.' But instead of going to fetch him, she simply stepped outside the door and shouted:

'Block! The lawyer wants you!' And then, probably because the lawyer was still facing the wall, apparently unconcerned about anything, she slid behind K's chair. From then on she proceeded to irritate him by leaning over the back of his chair and running her hands, admittedly very tenderly and cautiously, through his hair and over his cheeks. In the end K. tried to stop her doing this by grasping one of her hands, which she surrendered after a brief struggle.

Block had answered the summons immediately, but stopped outside the door, apparently wondering if he should come in. He raised his eyebrows and cocked his head, as if listening for a repetition of the order that he should come to the lawyer.

K. could have encouraged the man to come in, but he had made up his mind to break for good and all not only with the lawyer but with everyone in the flat, so he made no move. Leni was silent too. Block realized that at least no one was going to drive him away, so he came in on tiptoe, his face taut, his hands clenched tight behind him. He had left the door open in case he needed to retreat. He did not look at K. at all but gazed only at the heaped-up quilt, beneath which the lawyer, having pushed himself up quite close to the wall, was not even visible. Then the lawyer's voice was heard, asking:

'Is Block there?' Block, who had come forward quite a bit, staggered as if the question had literally struck him twice – once in the chest and once in the back. Bent low, he stopped and said:

'At your service.'

'What do you want?' asked the lawyer. 'You've come at an inopportune moment.'

'Wasn't I called for?' Block asked, speaking more to himself than to the lawyer, putting up his hands as if to protect himself and all ready to run away.

'Yes, you were called for,' said the lawyer, 'and yet you've come at an inopportune moment.' And then after a pause he added, 'You always do.' Since the lawyer had been speaking Block had stopped looking at the bed and gazed blankly away into a corner, merely listening, as if the sight of the speaker were too dazzling for him to endure. But even listening was difficult, for the lawyer was speaking quickly and softly right up against the wall.

'D'you want me to go away?' Block asked.

'Well stay, now you're here!' said the lawyer. One might have thought that, instead of granting Block's wish, the lawyer had threatened him, with a beating perhaps, for now Block actually began to tremble.

'Yesterday,' the lawyer said, 'I was with the Third Judge, who is a friend of mine, and I gradually got the conversation on to you. D'you want to know what he said?'

'Oh, please,' said Block. Because the lawyer did not reply at once, Block repeated his plea, and then bowed as if he were going down on his knees. At that point, however, K. snapped at him:

'What are you doing?' As Leni had tried to prevent him shouting out, he seized her other hand as well. It was not a loving grip in which he held her tight, and she gave frequent sighs, trying to wrench her hands free. But Block was punished for K's outburst, for the lawyer asked him:

'Who is your lawyer?'

'You are,' said Block.

'And who else?' the lawyer asked.

'No one except you,' said Block.

'Then don't listen to anyone else!' the lawyer said. Block acknowledged the full implications of that remark, he glared at K. and shook his head at him violently. Translated into words, the gestures would have made a torrent of crude insults. And K. had wanted to discuss his own case amicably with this man!

'I won't interrupt you again,' K. said, leaning back in his chair. 'Kneel down or crawl on all fours, do what you want. It won't bother me.' But Block still had some sense of honour, at least in front of K, for he went up to him, beating the air with his fists, and shouted as loudly as he dared in the lawyer's presence:

'You can't talk to me like that, it's not allowed! Why are you insulting me? And here, of all places, in front of the lawyer, where we're both, you and me, suffered out of the kindness of his heart. You're no better than I am, for you're an accused man too and have a trial too. But if you are nevertheless still a gentleman, then I'm a gentleman too, just as great as you, and perhaps even greater. And I want to be addressed as one, especially by you, of all people. But if you think yourself privileged because you're allowed to sit there and just listen, while I have to crawl around on all fours (as you put it), then let me remind you of the old legal adage: it's better for a suspected man to keep on the move than be stationary, for the man who is stationary may, without knowing it, be in the scales and be weighed with his sins.'

K. said nothing, but merely stared in astonishment and with unwavering eyes at this confused man. What changes had been wrought in Block even during the last hour alone! Was it his lawsuit that tossed him first this way, then that way, so that he no longer knew who were his friends and who his enemies? Did he not see, then, that the lawyer was deliberately humiliating him and on this occasion had no other aim but to vaunt his power before K. and thus perhaps force K. to bow before him too? If, however, Block was incapable of realizing this, or if he was so frightened of the lawyer that the realization was of no use to him, how did it come about that he was cunning or bold enough to deceive the lawyer and to conceal that he had other lawyers working for him? And how could he dare to attack K, knowing that the latter might straight away reveal his secret? But he risked even more, he stepped over to the lawyer's bedside and began to complain about K.

'Dr Huld,' he said, 'did you hear how this man spoke to me? You could count up the number of hours his case has lasted, and yet he's trying to tell me what to do, when I've been involved in my case for five years already. He even insults me. Doesn't know a thing and yet insults me, when I, to the best of my feeble ability, have made a careful study of what decency, duty and the usage of the Court demand.'

'Don't worry about anyone else,' the lawyer said. 'Just do as you think right.'

'Of course,' Block said, as if to encourage himself, and with a quick sideways glance knelt down close to the bed. 'I'm kneeling, Dr Huld,' he said. But the lawyer made no reply. Block cautiously stroked the quilt with one hand. In the silence that now reigned, Leni said, freeing herself from K's grasp:

'You're hurting me. Let me go. I'm going to Block.' She went and sat on the edge of the bed. Block was delighted that she had come, and with silent, lively gestures he immediately begged her to intercede for him with the lawyer. It was obvious that he very urgently needed to hear what the lawyer had to say, but perhaps only so that his other lawyers could make full use of it. Leni apparently knew exactly how to get round the lawyer, for she pointed to his hand and pouted her lips in a kiss. Block immediately kissed the lawyer's hand, then did it again a second time at a sign from Leni. But the lawyer still said nothing. Then Leni bent over him, showing off the beautiful shape of her taut body as she stretched out, and, bending down low to his face, stroked his long white hair. That did indeed force an answer from him.

'I hesitate to tell him,' the lawyer said, and one could see him shaking his head a little, perhaps just to derive more pleasure from the pressure of Leni's hand. Block listened with his head bent, as if, by listening, he were infringing a law.

'Why do you hesitate?' Leni asked. K. had the feeling he was listening to a carefully rehearsed conversation that had often been repeated and would be time and again, and which only for Block would never lose its novelty. Instead of replying the lawyer asked:

'How has he behaved today?' Before giving her opinion on that, Leni looked down at Block and watched him for a moment holding out his hands towards her and rubbing them together imploringly. Finally she nodded solemnly, turned to the lawyer and said:

'He's been quiet and industrious.' Here was an old businessman with a long beard beseeching a young girl to put in a good word for him! Whatever ulterior motives Block might have in acting like this, nothing could justify him in the eyes of a fellow human being. K. did not understand how the lawyer could have dreamed of winning him over with this demonstration. If the lawyer hadn't already driven him away, this little scene would have done the trick. It was almost degrading just to witness it. So the lawyer's method, which luckily K. had not been exposed to for long enough, in the end caused the client to forget the whole world and have no hope but to drag himself along this illusory path until the very end of the case. The client ended up, therefore, not as a client but as the lawyer's dog. If the lawyer had ordered this man to crawl under the bed as if into a kennel, and bark there, he would have enjoyed doing it. K. listened to everything with censorious superiority, as if he had been entrusted with the task of carefully absorbing everything that was said here, to report on it to a higher authority and to furnish a written account.

'What's he been doing all day?' asked the lawyer.

'So that he wouldn't disturb my work,' Leni said, 'I locked him in the maid's room, where he generally stays anyway. I could look through the gap in the door from time to time to check what he was doing. He was always kneeling on the bed reading, with the papers you lent him laid out on the window-sill. That made a good impression on me because, you know, the window only looks out on an air-shaft and gives hardly any light. The fact that Block was reading just the same showed me how obedient he is.'

'I'm glad to hear it,' the lawyer said, 'but did he understand what he was reading?' Throughout this conversation Block was continually moving his lips, obviously framing the answers that he hoped Leni would give.

'Naturally I can't answer that with absolute certainty,' Leni said. 'But at any rate I did see that he was reading properly. He was on the same page the whole day and, as he was reading, he was following the words along the lines with his finger. Whenever I looked in at him he was always sighing as if the reading was a terrible effort. Probably the papers you lent him are very difficult to understand.'

'Yes,' said the lawyer, 'they certainly are, and I don't believe either that he understood any of them. They are supposed to give him just an idea of what a terrible struggle I have to conduct his defence. And for whom do I carry on this hard struggle? It's almost absurd to say it – but I'm doing it for Block. He must learn to understand what that means too. Was he reading continuously?'

'Almost,' Leni replied. 'He did ask me for a drink of water once, so I gave it to him through the hatch. At eight o'clock I let him out and gave him something to eat.' Block glanced briefly sideways at K, as if really praiseworthy things were being said about him which must be impressing K. He seemed to be full of high hopes now, was moving more relaxedly and kept shifting to and fro on his knees. So it was all the more obvious when he stiffened at the lawyer's next words.

'You are praising him,' said the lawyer, 'but that just makes it difficult for me to say what I have to. For what the judge had to say was not favourable, either to Block himself or to his case.'

'Not favourable?' Leni asked. 'How can that be so?' Block was gazing intently at Leni, as if he thought she was capable even now of re-interpreting in his favour the words which the judge had spoken so long ago.

'Not favourable,' the lawyer said. 'He didn't even like it when I started to talk about Block. "Don't speak about Block," the judge said. "He's my client," I said. "You're wasting your time," he said. "I don't consider his case hopeless," I said. "You're wasting your time," he repeated. "I don't think so," I said, "Block is very active in his case and is always pursuing it. He almost lives at my flat, so as to be up to date with what is happening. Such enthusiasm is most unusual. Of course personally he's not very nice, his manners are horrible and he's dirty, but as far as organizing a legal case is concerned he's irreproachable." I said "irreproachable", I was exaggerating on purpose. But he retorted,

"Block is merely cunning. He's amassed a lot of experience and knows how to drag the case out. But his ignorance is much greater even than his cunning. What would he say, do you think, if he found out that his case had not even begun yet, or if he were told that the signal to begin it had not even been given?" Quiet now, Block,' the lawyer said, for Block was just starting to raise himself on his shaky legs and obviously meant to ask for an explanation. This was the first time the lawyer actually addressed himself directly to Block at some length. With a weary glance he looked down, half of his attention focused on nothing at all, half on Block, who slowly subsided on to his knees again beneath that gaze.

'The judge's remark has no significance for you at all,' the lawyer said. 'Don't take fright at every word! If that happens again, I won't tell you anything more at all. I can't start talking without your looking at me as if the final judgement were about to be passed on you. You ought to be ashamed of yourself acting like that before another client of mine! And you're shaking the confidence he has in me! What are you trying to do, then? You're still alive, you're still under my protection. There's no point in being afraid! You've read somewhere that the final verdict frequently comes without warning, delivered at random by some chance person at some unexpected time. Of course that's true, with many reservations, but it's also equally true that your fear nauseates me because I can see in it your lack of trust in me. What have I said, except to report what a judge told me? You know perfectly well that various opinions accumulate around a case until a state of impenetrability is reached. For example, this judge and I differ about the moment when the proceedings begin. A difference of opinion, nothing more. It's an old custom that a bell is rung at a certain stage in the proceedings. This judge takes the view that this signals the beginning of the case. I can't now go into all the counter-arguments, you wouldn't understand them either. You'll just have to accept the fact that there are a lot of counter-arguments.'

In his embarrassment Block was running his fingers through the fur of the bedside rug, the fear aroused in him by what the judge had said made him even forget for the time being his subjection to the lawyer, he was thinking at that moment only of himself, turning the judge's words over and over and looking at them from all sides.

'Block!' Leni said in a warning tone, jerking him up a little by the collar. 'Leave that rug alone and listen to the lawyer!'

[This chapter was left unfinished]

Chapter Nine

In the Cathedral

K. was given the task of showing a few of the town's art monuments to an Italian business associate who was a very important client of the bank and was staying in the town for the first time. It was an assignment he would have been very honoured to receive at any other time, but which he accepted reluctantly now, because at the moment it was only with great effort that he was able to maintain his reputation at the bank. Every hour that took him away from the office was a cause of distress to him; it's true that he was not nearly as capable of making good use of his time at the office as he had once been, he spent many hours pathetically pretending to be doing real work, yet that only increased his anxiety when he was not actually in the office. He thought he saw the Deputy Manager, who anyway had always been waiting to trap him, coming into his office every now and then, sitting down at his desk, leafing through his papers, receiving clients with whom, over the years, K. had almost made friends and whom he now lured away from K, and perhaps even discovering mistakes, by which K. now found his work threatened from a thousand different directions and which he was no longer able to avoid. So if now he was charged with a business errand, whether it was one that brought him a certain distinction or amounted only to making a short journey – and assignments like that had recently multiplied quite by chance – it was natural that he should suppose he was being removed from the office for a while so that his work could be investigated, or at the very least that his presence in the office was considered to be far from indispensable.

He could easily have refused most of these assignments, but he did not dare do that, for, if there were even the slightest grounds for his suspicions, the refusal of an assignment would have been tantamount to admitting his fear. For this reason he accepted each assignment with apparent equanimity and once, when he was supposed to go away on an exhausting two-day business trip, he even said nothing about a serious chill he had so that he would not run the risk of having someone use the prevailing rainy autumn weather as an excuse for preventing him from going on the journey. When he got back from this trip, with a raging head-ache, he learnt that he had been selected to accompany the Italian business associate the very next day. The temptation to refuse just this once was considerable, particularly as what he had been asked to do was not directly connected with bank business. However, the discharge of this social duty towards a business associate was doubtless important enough, though not to K, who knew very well that he could save himself only by success at work and that, without this, it would be quite useless to him even if he should unexpectedly captivate the Italian with his charm. He did not want to be pushed outside the range of his work even for a single day, for the fear of not being allowed back was too great, a fear which he well knew was exaggerated, but one which nevertheless oppressed him. On this occasion anyway it was almost impossible to find a plausible excuse, for his knowledge of Italian, though not very great, was certainly adequate. The crucial factor, however, was that K. did have some knowledge of art history, acquired some time before, and this had become known – and grossly exaggerated – at the bank on account of the fact that K. had been for a time, incidentally merely for business purposes, a member of the Society for Preserving Municipal Art Treasures. Rumour had it that the Italian, however, was a connoisseur of art, and so the choice of K. as his escort followed as a matter of course.

It was a very wet and stormy morning when, at seven o'clock,

K. arrived in the office. exasperated at the thought of the day ahead of him and anxious to get at least some work done before being snatched away from it by his visitor. He was very tired, as he had spent half the night poring over an Italian grammar in an attempt to prepare himself a little. The window, at which he had adopted the habit of sitting much too often recently, looked more attractive than his desk, but he resisted the temptation and sat down to work. Unfortunately the clerk came in at once and said that the Manager had sent him to see whether the Chief Clerk was there yet, and if so, to ask him to be kind enough to come over to the reception-room, as the gentleman from Italy had already arrived.

'I'm just coming,' K. said. He put a small dictionary in his pocket, picked up an album of the town's sights which he had got ready for the foreigner, put it under his arm and went through the Deputy Manager's office into the Manager's room. He was glad to have come to the office so early and to be available immediately, which in all probability no one had seriously expected him to do. The Deputy Manager's office was, of course, still as empty as if it had been the middle of the night; the clerk had probably been told to summon him to the reception-room as well, but had not been able to. When K. went into the reception-room the two men rose from deep armchairs. The Manager smiled in a friendly way, obviously very pleased to see K, and went on at once to introduce them. The Italian shook K. firmly by the hand and with a smile said that someone seemed to be an early riser. K. did not quite understand whom he meant, for it was an odd phrase, the sense of which it took K. a little while to guess. He replied with a few polished sentences which the Italian received with another laugh, nervously and repeatedly stroking his bushy greyish-blue moustache. This moustache was obviously scented, and one was almost tempted to go up and sniff it. When they all sat down again and a little introductory conversation began, K. was greatly disconcerted to find that he could only understand fragments of what the Italian said. When the man spoke calmly K. could understand almost everything, but such occasions were rare exceptions, mostly the words gushed out of the Italian's mouth and he shook his head as if enjoying it all. But when he spoke like that he regularly broke into some dialect or other, which no longer sounded remotely like Italian to K. but which the Manager could not only speak but could also understand, something which K. should certainly have foreseen, since the Italian came from Southern Italy where the Manager had also spent some years. Anyway, K. realized that the possibility of communicating with the Italian had virtually disappeared, for the man's French was just as hard to grasp, and his lip movements, which might have helped K. to understand him, were concealed by the moustache. K. began to foresee a good deal of trouble, and for the moment he gave up trying to understand the Italian – while the Manager, who understood him so easily, was there it would have been wasted effort. He confined himself to watching sulkily the way in which the Italian reclined so low and yet so lightly in the armchair, frequently plucking at his short, tightly fitting jacket and once raising his arms and gesturing with his loose-jointed hands in an attempt to demonstrate something that K. failed to understand, though he leaned forward studying the hands intently. Finally, as K. was doing nothing but mechanically following with his eyes the to-ing and fro-ing of the conversation, his earlier tiredness made itself felt again, and to his horror, but luckily just in time, he caught himself on the point of absent-mindedly standing up to turn round and go away. At last the Italian looked at his watch and jumped up. Having said goodbye to the Manager, he pressed up close to K, so close, in fact, that K. had to push his chair back to give himself room to move. The Manager, obviously having seen from K's eyes that this peculiar version of the Italian language was causing him some distress, now took a hand in the discussion, but so skilfully and tactfully that it looked as if he were only appending little fragments of advice, whilst in fact he was conveying most succinctly to K. the meaning of everything that the Italian said in his tireless interruptions of the Manager. K. gathered that the Italian had a few things to attend to in the immediate future, that he was afraid he didn't have much time anyway, nor did he have any intention at all of trying to race round all the sights, on the contrary, he had resolved – though of course only if K. agreed, it was K's decision alone – just to have a look round the cathedral, a good look round, however. He was exceedingly glad to have a chance of doing so in the company of such a learned and charming man – he meant K, who was concentrating solely on bypassing the Italian and swiftly grasping what the Manager was saying. If it was convenient, he asked if K. would come to the cathedral in two hours' time, which would be at about ten o'clock. He himself hoped that he could be there for certain by about that time. K. said something appropriate in reply, the Italian clasped first the Manager's hand, then K's, and then the Manager's again and went off to the door, followed by both of them, and though he was only half turning towards them he still kept up the flow of words. K. stayed for a while with the Manager, who was looking particularly ill that day. He seemed to feel he ought to apologize to K. somehow and said (they were standing intimately close to each other) that he had first been meaning to go with the Italian himself, but then decided (he gave no explicit reason) to send K. instead. He said that if K. did not understand the Italian at the very beginning, he must not allow that to disconcert him, he would very soon catch on, and even if there was a lot he did not understand at all, that wasn't the end of the world either, for it wasn't so very important to the Italian to be understood. Besides, K's Italian was surprisingly good and he was sure to cope extremely well. With that K. was dismissed. He spent the time he still had left copying out from the dictionary various unusual words which he would need for showing someone round the cathedral.

It was an extremely tedious task, clerks brought in the post, officials came with various queries, stopping at the door when they saw K. was busy but not moving till he had given them a hearing, and the Deputy Manager did not miss the opportunity of annoying K. He came in a number of times, took the dictionary out of K's hands and made no secret of leafing through it quite haphazardly. Whenever the door opened, clients could even be glimpsed in the half-light of the outer office where they bowed tentatively – they wanted to attract attention to themselves but could not be sure if they had been seen. All this activity was going on around K. as if he were its focus, while he himself was making up a list of the words he needed, then looking them up in the dictionary and writing them down, practising their pronunciation and eventually trying to learn them off by heart. His memory, once so reliable, seemed, however, to have deserted him completely, and sometimes he got so infuriated with the Italian who was causing him all this trouble that he buried the dictionary under his papers, firmly resolved to suspend his preparations, but then he realized that he could not walk the Italian up and down in front of the cathedral's art treasures in complete silence, and with even greater fury he would pull the dictionary out again.

At exactly half past nine, just as he was going to leave, he got a telephone call. Leni wished him good morning and asked how he was. K. thanked her hurriedly and said he couldn't possibly embark on a conversation then as he had to go to the cathedral.

'The cathedral?' Leni asked.

'Yes, the cathedral.'

'But why the cathedral?' Leni said. K. tried to explain to her briefly, but he had hardly started when Leni suddenly said:

'They're hounding you.'

K. could not stand this pity, which he had neither invited nor expected, he said two words by way of goodbye, but as he was replacing the receiver he said, half to himself and half to the girl now far distant and no long able to hear him:

'Yes, they're hounding me.'

It was getting late by now and there was already a danger that he would not arrive in time. He went in a taxi; at the last moment he had remembered the album, which he had not had a chance to hand over yet, so he took it with him now. He had it on his knees and restlessly drummed on it with his fingers during the whole of the journey. The rain had eased off, but it was damp and cold and dark, they wouldn't be able to see much in the cathedral, and standing for any length of time on the cold flag-stones would doubtless be very bad for K's chill. The cathedral square was completely empty, and K. remembered how it had struck him, even as a small child, that almost all the houses in this narrow square always had their blinds drawn. With the weather as it was today, though, that was more understandable than usual. The cathedral seemed to be empty too, for naturally no one thought of coming there now. K. hastened through both the side-aisles without meeting anybody except one old woman, wrapped in a warm shawl, kneeling before a Madonna and looking at it. Then in the distance he saw a hobbling verger disappearing through a door in the wall.

K. had arrived punctually, it had just been striking ten as he came in, but the Italian was not there yet. K. went back to the main entrance, where he stood undecidedly for a time, then circled the cathedral in the rain to make sure the Italian was not perhaps waiting at some side entrance. He was nowhere to be found. Perhaps the Manager had been wrong about the time? How could anyone understand this man properly? Be that as it may, K. would in any event have to wait at least half an hour for him. Feeling tired, he went back into the cathedral to sit down, and there he found, on a step, a small tatter of carpet which he edged with his toe towards a nearby pew, wrapped his coat more tightly round him, turned up his collar and sat down. To while away the time he opened the album and turned a few pages, but he soon had to stop, for it got so dark that, when he looked up, he could scarcely make out a single detail in the nearby aisle.

On the high altar in the distance, a great triangle of candle flames was sparkling, K. could not have said for sure whether he had seen them earlier. Perhaps they had only just been lit. Vergers are by profession furtive movers, one never notices them. Turning round by chance, K. noticed there was another candle burning not far behind him, a tall, fat one fixed to a pillar. Beautiful as it was, it was utterly inadequate for lighting up the altar-pieces, which were hanging mostly in the dark side-chapels. In fact, it increased the gloom. It was a sensible, as well as an impolite action on the Italian's part not to come, for it would have been impossible to see anything; they would have had to content themselves with examining a picture or two inch by inch by the light of K's electric torch. To try to find out what kind of result might be expected from using such a method, K. went to a nearby side-chapel, climbed a few steps to a low marble balustrade and, leaning over this, flashed his torch on the altar-piece. The perpetual light of the sanctuary-lamp hanging in front got in the way. The first thing he saw, partly by guesswork, was a tall armoured knight on the extreme edge of the picture. He was leaning on his sword, which he had thrust into bare ground in front of him – only a few blades of grass poked out here and there. He seemed to be watching intently some event being enacted in front of him. It was astonishing that he stood still like that, without going any nearer. Perhaps he was meant to be standing guard. K, who had not seen any pictures for a long time, studied the knight for a good while, although he could not stand the green light of the oil-lamp without continually blinking. Then when he shone the torch on the rest of the picture, he found it was a conventional interpretation of Christ being laid in the tomb, it was incidentally quite a modern painting. He put the torch in his pocket and went back to his seat.

It was probably no longer necessary now to wait for the Italian, but no doubt it was pouring with rain outside and as it was not so cold inside as he had expected, K. decided to stay there for the time being. Not far away was the great pulpit, and fixed at a slant on its little round canopy were two empty golden crosses, the extreme tips of which touched each other. The outside of the balustrade and the connection with the supporting pillar were composed of green foliage into which little angels, now animated, now reclining, stretched clutching hands. K. went up to the pulpit and examined it from all sides; the stonework was extremely carefully wrought, the deep patches of darkness within and behind the foliage seemed to be caught and trapped there. K. put his hand into one such patch and cautiously felt the stone, he had never known that this pulpit existed. Then he happened to spot a verger behind the nearest row of pews, standing there in a loose-hanging, creased black coat and watching him, with a snuff-box in his left hand. What does that man want then? K. thought. Do I look suspicious to him? Is he after a tip? But when the man saw that K. had noticed him, he pointed in some vague direction with his right hand, still holding a pinch of snuff in his fingers. It was difficult to work out what his gestures meant, so K. waited a little longer, but the verger went on indicating something and reinforced the signal by nodding his head.

'What on earth does the fellow want?' K. asked quietly, not daring to speak loudly in the cathedral. Then he pulled out his purse and pushed along the next pew to get closer to the man. The verger, however, immediately waved K. away, shrugged his shoulders and limped off. With a gait similar to this rapid hobbling, K. had tried as a child to imitate a man riding a horse. What a childish old man, K. thought, with just about enough brains to be a verger. Just look how he stops when I stop, and hovers there to see whether I go on. Smiling to himself, K. followed the old man the whole length of the aisle almost as far as the high altar. The old man never stopped indicating something, but K. deliberately did not turn round, for the verger's only purpose in pointing was to shake K. off. However, eventually he let the man alone, not wanting to frighten him too much or to scare this apparition away entirely, in case the Italian might still come.

When he went back to the nave to look for the seat on which he had left the album, he noticed a small side pulpit by a pillar almost adjoining the chancel, quite a simple pulpit made of smooth, pale stone. It was so small that from a distance it looked like an empty niche meant to house a statue. The preacher could certainly not have taken a good step back from the balustrade. Moreover, the stone vaulting of the pulpit's canopy began unusually low and curved forward and upward, though it was quite unadorned, in such a way that an average-sized man would not be able to stand upright there but would have to lean over the balustrade all the time. It was as if the whole thing were intended to torture the preacher; it was impossible to see the point of having it when the other large pulpit, so beautifully decorated, too, was already available.

Indeed K. would certainly not have noticed this small pulpit if there had not been a lamp fastened above it, the sort that is usually put there ready just before a sermon. Surely there wasn't going to be a sermon now? In the empty church? K. looked down the steps, which curled round the pillar up to the pulpit and seemed so narrow that it looked as if they were not meant to serve as a staircase for human beings but rather as an ornament for the pillar. But K. smiled with astonishment to see that the priest really was standing at the foot of the pulpit, putting his hand on the rail to climb up and staring at K. He gave a little nod of his head, K. crossed himself and bowed, as he should have done before. The priest swung himself lightly on to the bottom step and climbed into the pulpit with quick, short paces. Was there really going to be a sermon starting now? Perhaps the verger had not been so completely out of his mind after all, and had just been trying to propel K. towards the preacher, something which was certainly necessary in the empty church. But somewhere in front of a Madonna there was an old woman who ought to have come too. And if there was going to be a sermon, why was it not introduced by the organ? But the organ was quite silent, its soaring pipes shining only feebly out of the darkness.

K. wondered if he ought not now to get away quickly, for if he did not go now he would have no chance to do so during the sermon, and then he would have to stay till the end. He was losing so much time at the office and he was no longer duty-bound to wait for the Italian. He looked at his watch, it was eleven o'clock. But was it possible that there really was going to be a sermon? Could K. represent the congregation just by himself? What if he had been a stranger who only wanted to visit the church? That was basically all he was. It was absurd to think there was going to be a sermon at eleven o'clock on a weekday, and in such terrible weather. Obviously the priest – for he was without doubt a priest, a young man with a smooth, dark face – was only climbing up to put out the lamp, which had been lit by mistake.

But that was not the case, on the contrary the priest tested the lamp and screwed it a little tighter, then he turned slowly towards the balustrade and grasped the front angular edge with both hands. He stood like that for a while and looked round without moving his head. K. had gone back quite a distance and was leaning his elbows on the front pew. Without being able to pinpoint the spot exactly, he was still vaguely conscious of the verger crouching somewhere, with bent back, quiet and relaxed,

233

as if his task had been successfully completed. How silent it was now in the cathedral! However, K. had to break this silence, he had no intention of staying here. If it were the priest's duty to preach a sermon at a particular time, irrespective of the circumstances, let him do it, he could do it successfully without K's assistance, just as K's presence would certainly not increase the effect. So K. started off slowly; tiptoeing and feeling his way along the pew, he reached the broad centre aisle, and there he walked quite undisturbed, except that even his lightest footstep made the stone floor ring, and the vaulted roof echoed weakly, but continuously, in repeated, regular progression. K. felt a little forlorn as he went on alone between the empty pews, perhaps with the priest watching, and the vastness of the cathedral seemed to him to lie on the very limits of what a man could bear. When he got to his old seat, he did not stop, but literally snatched the album he had left lying there and took it with him. He had almost got clear of the pews, and was nearing the empty space between them and the door, when for the first time he heard the priest's voice. A powerful, well-trained voice. How it rang through the expectant cathedral! But the priest was not addressing the congregation, what he said was quite unambiguous and there was no escaping his call of:

'Josef K!'

K. came to a halt and stared at the ground in front of him. For the moment he was still free, he could go on and make his escape through one of the three little dark wooden doors just in front of him. This would simply mean that he had not understood, or that he had understood but did not care about it. But once he turned round, he would be caught, for that would be tantamount to admitting that he had understood very well, that he really was the person who had been summoned and that he was also ready to obey. If the priest had called again, K. would certainly have gone on, but as everything remained quiet although he continued to wait, K. turned his head slightly to try to see what the priest was now doing. He was standing calmly in the pulpit as before, though it was clear he had seen K. turning his head. It would have been a childish game of hide-and-seek if K. had not turned round completely now. When he did so, the priest beckoned him nearer. Now that there was no need to prevaricate, K. ran – because he was curious and because he wanted to get the whole affair over – with long, flying strides towards the pulpit. He stopped at the first pews, but the priest seemed to think he was still too far away and stretched out his hand, pointing his forefinger steeply down at a spot right in front of the pulpit. K. went there, but once at that spot he had to bend his head a long way back so that he could still see the priest.

'You are Josef K?' the priest said, raising his hand from the balustrade in a vague movement.

'Yes,' K. said, and reflected how freely he always used to give his name and how for some time it had been a burden to him. Now it was known even to people he was meeting for the first time, how nice it had been not to be known until one introduced oneself.

'You are an accused man,' the priest said very quietly.

'Yes,' said K, 'so I've been informed.'

'Then you are the man I'm looking for,' said the priest. 'I am the prison chaplain.'

'Oh, are you?' K. said.

'I had you summoned here,' said the priest, 'to have a talk with you.'

'I didn't know that,' said K. 'I came here to show an Italian round the cathedral.'

'Keep to the point,' the priest said. 'What's that you have in your hand? Is it a prayer book?'

'No,' K. answered, 'it's an album of things worth seeing in the city.'

'Put it down,' said the priest. K. hurled it away so violently that it flew open and slid some way across the floor with the pages crumpled.

'Do you know that your case is going badly?' the priest asked.

'That's the impression I have too,' said K. 'I've taken as much trouble as I could, but so far without any success; though my petition isn't ready yet.'

'How do you think it's going to end?' asked the priest.

'I used to think it was bound to end all right,' said K, 'but now I sometimes doubt it myself. I have no idea how it will end. Do you know?'

'No,' the priest said, 'but I'm afraid it will end badly. You are considered to be guilty. Your case may not get beyond a lower Court at all. For the moment at least, your guilt is taken as proven.'

'But I'm not guilty,' said K. 'It's a mistake. How can a person be guilty at all? Surely we are all human beings here, one like the other.'

'That is right,' said the priest, 'but that is the way the guilty are wont to talk.'

'Are even you prejudiced against me?' K. asked.

'No, I'm not prejudiced against you,' said the priest.

'I'm grateful to you,' K. said. 'But everybody else who is concerned in these proceedings is prejudiced against me. They make even those who aren't involved prejudiced against me. My position is getting more difficult all the time.'

'You are failing to understand the facts of the case,' the priest said. 'The verdict does not come all at once, the proceedings gradually merge into the verdict.'

'So that's how it is,' K. said and let his head drop.

'What do you plan to do next in your case?' the priest asked.

'I'm going to get some more help,' K. said, raising his head to see what the priest thought of this. 'There are still certain possibilities I haven't made the most of.'

'You ask for too much help from other people,' the priest said disapprovingly, 'especially women. Don't you see that that is not the kind of help you need?'

'Sometimes, even frequently, I would admit you're right,' said K. 'But not always. Women have great power. If I could get some of the women I know to join together in working for me, I would be bound to win through. Especially with this Court, where they're practically all women-chasers. You only have to show the Examining Magistrate a woman in the distance and he will knock over the table and the defendant to get to her before she disappears.' The priest leant his head over the balustrade as if the canopy of the pulpit were oppressing him now for the first time. What sort of bad weather might there be outside? It wasn't dull daylight any more, it was already pitch-dark. Even the faintest glimmer from the stained glass in the big windows could not pierce the dark wall. And the verger chose this of all moments to start putting out the candles on the high altar, one by one.

'Are you angry with me?' K. asked the priest. 'Perhaps you don't realize the kind of Court you're serving?' He got no answer. 'I'm only telling you what I've experienced,' K. said. There was still no answer from up above. 'I didn't mean to offend you,' said K. Then the priest shrieked down at K:

'Can't you see what is just in front of your nose!' It was a howl of anger, but at the same time it sounded like the cry of someone who sees another person fall and, because he is frightened himself, screams unwarily, involuntarily.

Neither said anything for a long time. It was so dark beneath the pulpit that now the priest certainly could not make K. out distinctly, whereas K. could see him clearly by the light of the little lamp. Why did the priest not come down? He had not given a sermon, of course, but had only told K. a few things that would probably do him more harm than good if he paid close heed to them. Yet it seemed to K. that the priest undoubtedly meant well; it was not outside the bounds of possibility that, if he came down, they might come to some agreement, it was not impossible that K. might get crucial and acceptable advice from him which might, for example, show him not just how to influence the course of the case, but how to break away from it, how to avoid it altogether and live beyond the reach of the Court. There must be a possibility of this, recently K. had often thought about it. And if the priest knew of such a possibility, perhaps, if one begged him, he might reveal it, though he belonged to the Court himself and though he had suppressed his gentle nature and had shouted at K. as soon as K. had attacked the Court.

'Won't you come down?' said K. 'You don't have to preach a sermon. Join me down here.'

'Now I can come down,' the priest said, perhaps regretting that he had shouted. As he detached the lamp from its hook, he said:

'First of all I had to speak to you from a distance. Otherwise I am too easily influenced and then I forget what I ought to be doing.'

K. waited for him at the bottom of the steps. While he was still coming down, the priest stretched out his hand towards K. from one of the topmost steps.

'Can you spare me a little time?' K. asked.

'As much as you need,' the priest said and handed him the little lamp to carry. Even now that he was close, he did not lose a certain air of solemnity.

'You're being very kind to me,' K. said as they walked side by side up and down the dark aisle. 'You're an exception amongst those who belong to the Court. I trust you more than any of them, though I've got to know a lot of them. I can speak freely to you.'

'Don't delude yourself,' said the priest.

'How am I supposed to be deluding myself?' K. asked.

'You're deluding yourself about the Court,' the priest said. 'In the writings which preface the Law it says about this delusion: before the Law stands a door-keeper. A man from the country comes up to this door-keeper and begs for admission to the Law. But the door-keeper tells him that he cannot grant him admission now. The man ponders this and then asks if he will be allowed to enter later. "Possibly," the door-keeper says, "but not now." Since the door leading to the Law is standing open as always and the door-keeper steps aside, the man bends down to look inside through the door. Seeing this, the door-keeper laughs and says: "If it attracts you so much, go on and try to get in without my permission. But you must realize that I am powerful. And I'm only the lowest door-keeper. At every hall there is another door-keeper, each one more powerful than the last. Even I cannot bear to look at the third one." The man from the country had not expected difficulties like this, for, he thinks, the Law is surely supposed to be accessible to everyone always, but when he looks more closely at the door-keeper in his fur coat, with his great sharp nose and his long, thin black Tartar beard, he decides it is better to wait until he receives permission to enter. The door-keeper gives him a stool and allows him to sit down to one side of the door. There he sits, day after day, and year after year. Many times he tries to get in and wears the door-keeper out with his appeals. At times the door-keeper conducts little cross-examinations, asking him about his home and many other things, but they are impersonal questions, the sort great men ask, and the door-keeper always ends up by saying that he cannot let him in yet. The man from the country, who has equipped himself with many things for his journey, makes use of everything he has, however valuable, to bribe the door-keeper, who, it's true, accepts it all, saying as he takes each thing: "I am only accepting this so that you won't believe you have left something untried."

'During all these long years, the man watches the door-keeper almost continuously. He forgets the other door-keepers, this first one seems to be the only obstacle between him and admission to the Law. In the first years he curses this piece of ill-luck aloud, and later when he gets old, he only grumbles to himself. He becomes childish and, since he has been scrutinizing the door-keeper so closely for years that he can identify even the fleas in the door-keeper's fur collar, he begs these fleas to help him to change the door-keeper's mind. In the end his eyes grow dim and he cannot tell whether it is really getting darker around him or whether it is just his eyes deceiving him. But now he glimpses in the darkness a radiance glowing inextinguishably from the door of the Law. He is not going to live much longer now. Before he dies all his experiences during the whole period of waiting merge in his head into one single question, which he has not yet asked the door-keeper. As he can no longer raise his stiffening body, he beckons the man over. The door-keeper has to bend down low to him, for the difference in size between them has changed very much to the man's disadvantage.

' "What is it you want to know now then?" asks the door-keeper. "You're insatiable." "All men are intent on the Law," says the man, "but why is it that in all these many years no one other than myself has asked to enter?" The door-keeper realizes that the man is nearing his end and that his hearing is fading, and in order to make himself heard he bellows at him: "No one else could gain admission here, because this door was intended only for you. I shall now go and close it." '

'Then the door-keeper deceived the man,' said K. immediately, very strongly attracted by the story.

'Don't be too hasty,' said the priest. 'Don't accept someone else's opinion without testing it. I've told you the story exactly as it's written. It doesn't say anything about deception.'

'But it's obvious,' K. said, 'and your first interpretation was quite correct. The door-keeper did not give the message of salvation till it could no longer help the man.'

'He wasn't asked until then,' said the priest. 'And remember, he was only a door-keeper and as such fulfilled his duty.'

'Why do you think that he fulfilled his duty?' K. asked. 'He didn't fulfil it. It might have been his duty to turn away all strangers, but the entrance was intended for this man and he should have let him in.'

'You don't show enough respect for what is written, and you're changing the story,' the priest said. 'The story contains two important statements by the door-keeper about admission to the Law – one at the beginning and one at the end. In one place it says that he cannot grant the man admission now, and in the other it says that this entrance was intended only for the man. If there were any contradiction between these two statements you would be right and the door-keeper would have deceived the man. But there isn't any contradiction. On the contrary, the first statement actually implies the second. One might almost say that the door-keeper exceeded his duty in holding out to the man the prospect of perhaps being admitted some time in the future. The door-keeper's duty seems to have consisted at that time solely in turning the man away, and in fact many commentators have been surprised that the door-keeper gave any hint at all of such a prospect, since he seems to be a stickler for precision and very jealous of his office. During all those years he never leaves his post and does not shut the door completely until the very last moment, he is very conscious of the importance of his work, for he says, "I am powerful," and he has respect for his superiors, for he says, "I am only the lowest door-keeper." He is not over-talkative, for the story says that, throughout the many years, he asks only "impersonal questions". Nor can he be bribed, for when he takes a gift he says, "I am only accepting this so that you won't believe you have left something untried." Where it is a question of fulfilling his duty, he can be moved neither to resentment nor pity, for the story says that the man "wears the door-keeper out with his appeals". And finally even his external appearance hints at a pedantic nature, the big pointed nose and the long, thin black Tartar beard. Could you have a more conscientious door-keeper? But the door-keeper's character is compounded of other elements which tend to favour considerably someone seeking admission and which nevertheless make it understandable enough that he might exceed his duty somewhat by suggesting the possibility of admission in the future. For it's undeniable that he's a little simple-minded and therefore a little conceited as well. Even if his remarks about his power and the power of the other door-keepers and about how even he can't bear to behold them – I maintain that even if they are essentially true, the way he comes out with these remarks shows that his interpretation is clouded by both simple-mindedness and arrogance. Commentators say: "The correct interpretation of a certain subject and misunderstanding of the same subject do not wholly exclude each other." At any rate it must be assumed that that simple-mindedness and arrogance, in whatever trivial way they may manifest themselves, are defects in the door-keeper's character and do indeed weaken his guardianship of the entrance. One must also add that the door-keeper seems by nature to be friendly, and by no means always does he play the official. In the very first moments we notice that he jokingly invites the man to enter, despite the rigorously maintained prohibition on entry, and then he doesn't, for example, send him away but gives him, we are told, a stool and lets him sit to one side of the door. The patience with which he puts up with the man's appeals over all those years, the little cross-examinations, the acceptance of gifts, the gracious way he allows the man to curse aloud right near him the unlucky chance that has posted the door-keeper before this door – all this implies that he feels sympathy. Not every door-keeper would have acted like that. And in the end, when the man beckons to him, he bends down low to give him a chance to ask that one last question. And in his words "You're insatiable" there is merely a slight hint of impatience, for the door-keeper knows that the end is near. Many people go even further in this kind of exegesis and hold that the words "You're insatiable" imply a sort of friendly admiration tinged, though, with condescension. At any rate the door-keeper's character emerges differently from the way you see it.'

'You know the story in more detail than I do, and you've known it longer,' K. said. They were both silent for a while. Then K. said:

'So you don't believe the man was deceived?'

'Don't misunderstand me,' the priest said, 'I'm only telling you the different opinions there are about it. You mustn't pay too much attention to them. The scripture is unalterable, and the opinions are often merely an expression of despair on the part of the commentators. In this case one opinion even has it that it is the door-keeper himself who is deceived.'

'That's going a bit far, isn't it?' K. said. 'What's the evidence for that?'

'The evidence for that,' answered the priest, 'is based on the premise of the door-keeper's simple-mindedness. It's argued that he doesn't know the inner world of the Law. He only knows the path to it, and the entrance to that path which he has constantly to patrol. The ideas he has of that inner world are felt to be childish, and it's thought that he himself fears what he tries to make the man afraid of. Yes, he fears it even more than the man, for the man wants nothing else except to enter, even when he has heard about the terrible door-keepers inside, whereas the door-keeper doesn't want to enter – at least we don't hear that he does. Other people, it's true, say that he must have already been inside, since, after all, once upon a time he was recruited to the service of the Law and that, they say, can only have happened inside. The answer to that is that he might well have been appointed to the post of door-keeper by someone calling from inside, and that he could not have been right inside anyway, since he could not bear the sight of even the third door-keeper. Moreover, there is no report that in all those years he ever said anything about the inside, except for his remark about the door-keepers. He might have been forbidden to do so, but there is no mention of that either. All this implies that he doesn't know anything about the appearance or the significance of the inside, and so he is deluding himself. He is even misled, some people argue, about the man from the country, for he is subordinate to this man and does not know it. You should still be able to remember many things that show he treats the man from the country as his subordinate. But, according to this version of the story, it is perfectly clear that it is, in fact, he who is subordinate. First and foremost, a free man is superior to one who is bound. Now the man from the country is actually free, he can go wherever he wants, it is only entry to the Law that is forbidden him, and then only by one individual, the door-keeper. If he sits on a stool beside the door and stays there for the rest of his life, this is a voluntary action, the story says nothing about compulsion. The door-keeper, on the other hand, is duty-bound to stay at his post, he may not go out into the country, nor apparently is he allowed to go into the interior of the Law, even if he wanted to. What is more, he is, it's true, in the service of the Law, yet he serves only this entrance, and therefore only this man, for whom alone this entrance is intended. For this reason, too, he is subordinate to the man. It must be assumed that, for many years, for the length of time it takes a man to reach maturity, his duty was in a way an empty one, for it is said that a man comes, that is a fully grown man, and that therefore the door-keeper had to wait a long time before the purpose of his service was fulfilled, and indeed he even had to wait till it pleased the man to come, for the man came of his own free will. But there is also the fact that his service ends only when the man is dead, and so the door-keeper remains subject to him until the very end. And it is stressed all the time that the door-keeper seems to be unaware of all this. But there's nothing remarkable about that, for according to this interpretation the door-keeper is labouring under a much more serious delusion – concerning his own duties.

'At the end, talking about the door, he says, "I shall now go and shut it," but at the beginning we are told that the door to the Law is standing open as always, but if it's *always* open, that is to say independently of the life-span of the man for whom it is intended, then it must be impossible for the door-keeper to close it. Opinions differ about whether the door-keeper, in announcing that he is going to shut the door, is merely giving an answer, or is seeking to underline his official duty, or simply wants to cause the man sadness and remorse in his last moments. But many people are agreed that it will not be possible for him to close the door. They even believe that, at least at the very end, he is also subordinate to the man in the matter of knowledge, for the man from the country sees the radiance coming from the entrance to the Law, while the door-keeper, in his official capacity, presumably has to stand with his back to the entrance and, moreover, gives no indication that he has noticed any change.'

'That is soundly argued,' said K, who had repeated to himself in a low voice individual parts of the priest's explanation. 'It is soundly argued, and I now believe too that the door-keeper is under a delusion, but that doesn't mean that I've abandoned my earlier opinion, for to some extent the two opinions overlap. It makes no difference whether the door-keeper can see clearly or is under an illusion. I said the man was deceived. If the door-keeper sees things clearly, there might be some doubts about that, but if the door-keeper is under an illusion, his illusion must necessarily be communicated to the man. In that case the door-keeper is not, it is true, a deceiver, but he is so simple-minded that he ought to be dismissed from his office immediately. You must remember that the delusion under which the door-keeper labours doesn't hurt him, but it does infinite damage to the man.'

'There's a contrary opinion to be mentioned there,' the priest said. 'Many people say, you see, that the story gives no one the right to pass judgement on the door-keeper. Whatever we may think of him, he is a servant of the Law, and therefore belongs to the Law, and that places him beyond human judgement. Nor should one, therefore, believe that the door-keeper is subordinate to the man. To be bound by one's office, even if that only means guarding the entrance to the Law, is incomparably more important than to live at liberty out in the world. The man is only coming to the Law, the door-keeper is already there. He has been appointed by the Law, and to doubt his worthiness would be to doubt the Law.'

'I don't agree with that point of view,' K. said, shaking his head, 'for if one does subscribe to it, one has to accept everything the door-keeper says as true. Yet that isn't possible, as you've shown very clearly yourself.'

'No,' the priest replied, 'one doesn't have to accept everything as true, one only has to accept it as necessary.'

'What a gloomy point of view,' K. said. 'The lie has become the order of the world.'

K. said this definitively, but it was not his final judgement. He was too weary to be able to grasp all the implications of the story, and he was unaccustomed to the trains of thought into which it led him; they seemed unreal things which could be more appropriately discussed by a clique of Court officials than by him. The basic story had become shapeless and he wanted to cast it from his mind. The priest, who now showed great tactfulness, tolerated this and accepted K's remark in silence, though K's opinion certainly did not agree with his own.

They walked on for a time in silence, K. kept close to the priest without knowing where they were. The torch he was holding had long since gone out. Once the silver statue of a saint shone directly in front of him, but only with the gleam of its own silver, and then immediately vanished into the darkness. In order not to be completely dependent on the priest, K. asked him:

'Aren't we near the main entrance now?'

'No,' said the priest, 'we're a long way away. Do you want to go now?' Although at that particular moment he had not been thinking of leaving, K. said at once:

'Yes, of course I have to go. I'm Senior Clerk at a bank and they're expecting me there. I only came to show a business friend from abroad round the cathedral.'

'Well,' the priest said, and held out his hand to K, 'then go.'

'I don't think I can find my way alone in the dark,' K. said.

'Go to the wall on your left,' said the priest. 'Then keep along that wall, don't leave it, and you'll find a door.' The priest had only taken a step or two away from him, but K. shouted very loudly:

'Wait, please, just a moment!'

'I'm waiting,' said the priest.

'Don't you want anything more from me?' K. asked.

'No,' said the priest.

'You were being so kind to me earlier,' K. said, 'and you were explaining everything to me, but now you're sending me off as if you weren't interested in me.'

'But you have to go,' said the priest.

'Well yes,' K. said, 'you must understand that.'

'But you must first understand who I am,' said the priest.

'You're the prison chaplain,' K. said, moving closer to the priest. His immediate return to the bank was not as necessary as he had made out, he could perfectly well stay here a little longer.

'Therefore I belong to the Court,' the priest said. 'So why should I want anything from you? The Court doesn't want anything from you. It receives you when you come, and it dismisses you when you go.'

Chapter Ten

The End

On the evening before K's thirty-first birthday – it was about nine o'clock, the time when the streets grow quiet – two men came to his flat, pale and fat men in frock-coats and apparently immovable top-hats. There was a little show of formality at the door of the flat about who was to go in first, and this was repeated more elaborately in front of K's door. Although he had been given no notice of their visit, K, who was also wearing black, was sitting in a chair near the door, slowly pulling on a pair of new gloves that stretched tightly over his fingers, in the attitude of someone expecting guests. He stood up at once and looked at the men with curiosity.

'So you're assigned to me?' he asked. The men nodded, each pointing to the other with the top-hat he was holding. K. admitted to himself that he had been expecting somebody different. He went to the window and looked down once more at the dark street. Nearly all the windows on the other side of the street were also dark, and in many of them the curtains were drawn. At one lighted window on the floor small children were playing behind a grille, reaching out their little hands towards each other but unable to move from where they were.

'So they send old ham actors for me,' K. said to himself, looking round again to make sure. 'They're trying to get rid of me on the cheap.' He turned suddenly towards the men and asked:

'What theatre are you playing at?'

'Theatre?' one of the men asked, the corners of his mouth

twitching as he glanced at his companion for advice. The other man behaved like a mute struggling with the most recalcitrant disability.

'They're not prepared to answer questions,' K. said to himself and went to get his hat.

No sooner had they got to the stairs than the men tried to link arms with K, but he said:

'Wait till we get down in the street, I'm not ill.' But right outside the street door they clung on to his arms in a way that K. himself had never used when walking with someone. They kept their shoulders tucked in close behind his and, without bending their elbows, wound their arms around the full length of K's arms, clasping his hands in a systematic, well-drilled and irresistible grip. K. walked rigidly between them, and all three were now locked together into a single unit in such a way that, if one had been knocked down, they would all have fallen. It was the kind of unity that can usually only be formed by lifeless matter.

By the light of the street lamps, K. tried several times, difficult though this was when they were linked so closely, to have a better look at his companions than had been possible in the half-light of his room.

Perhaps they are tenors, he thought when he saw their heavy double chins. He was disgusted by the cleanliness of their faces. One could still literally see how a cleansing hand had been thrust into the corners of their eyes, had rubbed the top lip and scrubbed out the folds in their chins.

When K. noticed this he stopped, thus making the others stop too. They were on the edge of an open and deserted square, decorated with flowerbeds.

'Why did they have to send you of all people!' he said, it was more of a shout than a question. The men seemed to have no answer to this, they continued to wait, each with one arm hanging free, like male nurses pausing while their patient takes a rest.

'I shan't walk any farther,' K. said tentatively. They didn't have to reply to that, it was sufficient that they did not loosen their grip and tried to hoist K. from the spot, but he resisted. I shan't need my strength much more, I may as well use it all now, he thought. He was reminded of flies, tearing their little legs off trying to escape from fly-paper. These gentlemen are going to have a hard job of it.

Just then Fräulein Bürstner came into sight in front of them, climbing up a small flight of steps that led into the square from a street situated at a lower level than theirs. He was not absolutely certain it was Fräulein Bürstner, though the resemblance was strong. Anyway it was of no importance to him whether it really was Fräulein Bürstner; what was important was that he suddenly realized how useless it was to resist. There was nothing heroic about resisting, or making things difficult for these men now, or seeking to enjoy the last glimmer of life by putting up a struggle. He moved off again, and some of the pleasure this gave to the men was communicated to K. himself. They let him decide which way to go and he followed the direction taken by the young woman, not, as one might have expected, in order to catch up with her, or indeed to keep her in sight for as long as possible, but just so that he would not forget the warning she implied.

'The only thing I can do now,' he said to himself, and the exact correspondence between his steps and those of the other two confirmed his thoughts, 'the only thing I can do now is to keep my mind calm and orderly up to the very end. I always wanted to snatch at the world with twenty hands, and, what's more, for no particularly praiseworthy motive. That was wrong of me. Am I now going to demonstrate that not even this trial, which has gone on for a year, has taught me anything? Am I going to depart this life a dim-witted man? Are people going to be able to say about me that at the beginning of the case I wanted to end it, and that now, when it's coming to an end, I want to start it all over again? I don't want people to say that. I am grateful that these two half-dumb imbecilic men have been sent to escort me on this journey and that it's been left to me to tell myself all that needs to be said.'

In the meantime the young woman had turned into a side-street, but K. did not need her any more and he surrendered himself to his companions. In total accord all three now passed over a bridge in the moonlight, the men were quite willing to submit to any slight movement K. made, and when he turned slightly towards the railings they turned that way too, in unison. The water, gleaming and shivering in the moonlight, parted around a small island, on which the foliage of trees and shrubs rose in dark masses as if thrust together. Beneath the trees, invisible now, were gravel paths with convenient benches, where K. had lain stretched out many a time in summer.

'I didn't want to stop at all,' he said to his companions, put to shame by their readiness to indulge him. Behind his back one of them seemed to reproach the other gently for stopping by mistake, and they all moved on again. They went through several steeply sloping streets where there were policemen standing or walking about, some in the distance and some very near at hand. One with a bushy moustache, holding his hand on the hilt of his sabre, came up as if with intent and approached the not wholly unsuspicious-looking group. The two men stopped and the policeman seemed about to open his mouth when K. drew the men forcibly onwards. He kept turning round cautiously to see if the policeman was following, but as soon as they had put a corner between themselves and the policeman, K. began to run, so that the two men had to run as well although they were very short of breath.

They were soon out of the town, which on this side led, almost without transition, into the fields. A small quarry, deserted and bare, lay quite near what was still very much a town house. The two men stopped here, either because this was the place they had been making for from the very beginning, or because they were too exhausted to go any farther. They let go of K. now, he stood waiting in silence while they took off their top-hats and wiped the perspiration from their foreheads with handkerchiefs, looking round the quarry at the same time. The moonlight shone on everything with that particular naturalness and peace which no other light has.

After exchanging a few polite formalities about which one of them was to carry out the next task – the men seemed to have received no separate instructions – one of them went up to K. and took off K's coat, his waistcoat and finally his shirt. K. could not help shivering, whereupon the man gave him a light, reassuring pat on the back. Then the man folded the clothes carefully together as if they were going to be used again, though perhaps not straight away. In order not to leave K. standing still, at the mercy of the cold night air, he took him by the arm and walked him up and down a little, while the other man was scouring the quarry for some suitable place. When he found one, he signalled, and the other man led K. there. It was near the wall of the quarry, where a loose piece of rock was lying on the ground. The two men laid K. down, leant him against the rock and pillowed his head on it. In spite of all their efforts and all K's readiness to help, the position of his body remained very forced and unlikely. So one man asked the other to let him arrange K's body by himself for a moment, but that did not improve matters either. In the end they left K. in a position that was not even as good as some of the others they had already contrived. Then one of the men opened his frock-coat and from a sheath that hung on a belt tied tight around his waistcoat drew a long, thin, two-edged butcher's knife, held it up and examined the edges in the moonlight. Once again the odious courtesies began, as one of them handed the knife across K. to the other, who then handed it back across K. K. now knew perfectly well that it was his duty to grasp the knife himself as it passed from hand to hand above him, and to plunge it into himself. However, he did not do so, instead he turned his neck, which was still free, and looked about him. He could not completely prove his worth, he could not relieve the authorities of all their work; the responsibility for this last failure lay with whoever had denied him the remnant of strength necessary for the deed. His eyes fell on the top storey of the house adjoining the quarry. Just like a light flashing on, the casements of a window flew open there, and a human figure, indistinct and tenuous at that distance and height, suddenly leaned a long way out and stretched both arms out farther still. Who was it? A friend? A good man? Someone who cared? Someone who wanted to help? Was it only one person? Was it the whole of mankind? Was help still possible? Were there objections which had been overlooked? Surely there were. Logic may indeed be unshakeable, but it cannot withstand a man who is determined to live. Where was the judge he had never seen? Where was the High Court he had never reached? He raised his hands and spread out all his fingers.

But the hands of one of the men closed round his throat, just as the other drove the knife deep into his heart and turned it twice. As his eyes grew dim, K. could still see the two men right in front of his face, their cheeks touching as they watched the decisive moments.

'Like a dog!' he said.

It was as if the shame of it should outlive him.

Picador

☐	**The Beckett Trilogy**	Samuel Beckett	£2.50p
☐	**Williard and His Bowling Trophies**	Richard Brautigan	£1.25p
☐	**Bury My Heart at Wounded Knee**	Dee Brown	£2.75p
☐	**Our Ancestors**	Italo Calvino	£3.50p
☐	**Auto Da Fé**	Elias Canetti	£1.75p
☐	**Hidden Faces**	Salvador Dali	£1.95p
☐	**Nothing, Doting, Blindness**	Henry Green	£2.95p
☐	**Household Tales**	Brothers Grimm	£1.50p
☐	**Meetings with Remarkable Men**	Gurdjieff	£1.50p
☐	**Roots**	Alex Haley	£2.95p
☐	**Growth of the Soil**	Knut Hamsun	£2.95p
☐	**Meanwhile**	Max Handley	£1.50p
☐	**When the Tree Sings**	Stratis Haviaras	£1.95p
☐	**Dispatches**	Michael Herr	£1.75p
☐	**The Greenpeace Chronicle**	Robert Hunter	£2.50p
☐	**Three Trapped Tigers**	G. Cabrera Infante	£2.95p
☐	**Man and His Symbols**	Carl Jung	£2.50p
☐	**China Men**	Maxine Hong Kingston	£1.50p
☐	**The Woman Warrior**		£1.50p
☐	**The Other Persuasion**	edited by Seymour Kleinberg	£1.75p
☐	**The Case of the Midwife Toad**	Arthur Koestler	£1.25p
☐	**The Ghost in the Machine**		£2.50p
☐	**The Roots of Coincidence**		£1.00p
☐	**The Thirteenth Tribe**		£1.50p
☐	**The Memoirs of a Survivor**	Doris Lessing	£1.95p
☐	**Albert Camus**	Herbert Lottman	£3.95p
☐	**The Road to Xanadu**	John Livingston Lowes	£1.95p
☐	**McCarthy's List**	Mary Mackey	£1.95p
☐	**Short Lives**	Katinka Matson	£2.50p
☐	**The Snow Leopard**	Peter Matthiessen	£2.25p
☐	**The Man Without Qualities, Vol. 1**	Robert Musil	£1.95p
☐	**The Man Without Qualities, Vol. 2**		£2.25p
☐	**Great Works of Jewish Fantasy**	Joachim Neugroschel	£1.95p
☐	**Wagner Nights**	Ernest Newman	£2.50p

☐	**The Best of Myles**	⎫	£2.25p
☐	**The Dalkey Archive**	⎬ Flann O'Brien	£1.50p
☐	**The Hard Life**		£1.25p
☐	**The Poor Mouth**	⎭	£1.25p
☐	**After My Fashion**	⎫	£2.95p
☐	**A Glastonbury Romance**	⎬ John Cowper Powys	£2.95p
☐	**Owen Glendower**		£2.50p
☐	**Weymouth Sands**	⎭	£3.50p
☐	**Hadrian the Seventh**	Fr. Rolfe (Baron Corvo)	£1.25p
☐	**On Broadway**	Damon Runyon	£1.95p
☐	**Snowblind**	Robert Sabbag	£1.50p
☐	**The Best of Saki**	Saki	£1.50p
☐	**Sanatorium under the Sign of the Hourglass**	Bruno Schultz	£1.50p
☐	**Miss Silver's Past**	Josef Skvorecky	£2.50p
☐	**Visitants**	Randolph Stow	£1.95p
☐	**The Bad Sister**	⎫ Emma Tennant	£1.50p
☐	**Wild Nights**	⎭	£1.95p
☐	**The Great Shark Hunt**	Hunter S. Thompson	£3.25p
☐	**The Forest People**	Colin Turnbull	£1.50p
☐	**The New Tolkien Companion**	J. E. A. Tyler	£2.95p
☐	**From A to B and Back Again**	Andy Warhol	£1.50p
☐	**Female Friends**	Fay Weldon	£1.95p
☐	**The Outsider**	Colin Wilson	£1.75p
☐	**The Kandy-Kolored Tangerine-Flake Streamline Baby**	Tom Wolfe	£2.25p

All these books are available at your local bookshop or newsagent, or
can be ordered direct from the publisher Indicate the number of copies
required and fill in the form below   3

Name_____
(block letters please)
Address_____

_____

Send to Pan Books (CS Department), Cavaye Place, London SW10 9PG
Please enclose remittance to the value of the cover price plus:

25p for the first book plus 10p per copy for each additional book ordered
to a maximum charge of £1.05 to cover postage and packing
Applicable only in the UK

While every effort is made to keep prices low, it is sometimes
necessary to increase prices at short notice. Pan Books reserve
the right to show on covers and charge new retail prices which
may differ from those advertised in the text or elsewhere